## ALSO BY ABDULRAZAK GURNAH

# Theft

*Abdulrazak Gurnah*

RIVERHEAD BOOKS   NEW YORK   2025

RIVERHEAD BOOKS
An imprint of Penguin Random House LLC
1745 Broadway, New York, NY 10019
penguinrandomhouse.com

*Book design by Alexis Farabaugh*

Library of Congress Cataloging-in-Publication Data

Names: Gurnah, Abdulrazak, 1948– author.
Title: Theft / Abdulrazak Gurnah.
Description: New York : Riverhead Books, 2025.
Identifiers: LCCN 2024042627 (print) | LCCN 2024042628 (ebook) |
ISBN 9780593852606 (hardcover) | ISBN 9780593852613 (ebook)
Subjects: LCGFT: Bildungsromans. | Novels.
Classification: LCC PR9399.9.G87 T47 2025  (print) |
LCC PR9399.9.G87 (ebook) | DDC 823/.914—dc23/eng/20241214
LC record available at https://lccn.loc.gov/2024042627
LC ebook record available at https://lccn.loc.gov/2024042628

Simultaneously published in hardcover in Great Britain by
Bloomsbury Publishing Plc, London, in 2025
First United States edition published by Riverhead, 2025

Printed in the United States of America
1st Printing

The authorized representative in the EU for product safety and compliance is
Penguin Random House Ireland, Morrison Chambers, 32 Nassau Street,
Dublin D02 YH68, Ireland, https://eu-contact.penguin.ie.

In a general way it's very
difficult for one to become remarkable.

JOSEPH CONRAD, *CHANCE*

# Part One

*1.*

Raya's marriage happened in a panic. Her father found out that a young man was paying unmistakable attention to her, at first with long looks and a knowing smile as he walked by, then he saw with his own eyes how the young man stopped her in the street and held her in conversation for several minutes, probably making impossible promises and arranging an assignation. This all happened in front of him. It was improper and ill-mannered behavior, and disrespectful to him, the father. He knew who the young man was, which was why the attentions to Raya alarmed him. It would have been even worse if he was a stranger, of course, but this was calamity enough. His name was Rafik, and he had grown up a boy familiar and ordinary, the son of neighbors with whom scarcities had been shared over the years, who ran up and down the streets with other boys and played football with them on the beach. Then, in the upheavals and confusions of the struggle to rid themselves of the British, he joined the comrades, as they called themselves, and became a member of the Umma Party. Along with other comrades, he was sent for military training to Cuba, under the noses of the British colonial authorities who either could not see the meaning of this excursion or could not care less. They were ready to go home.

Rafik returned more handsome than ever, transformed into a heroic, slender warrior in a solid-green khaki uniform, and wearing a hard round cap unlike any they had seen before. He and the other comrades were back just in time to participate in the revolution and its aftermath. The warriors of that time, of whom Rafik was then one, knew only how to terrify people since there really was no enemy in sight, just scared, browbeaten citizens. Even that word, *citizen*, was in dispute, and was one that the heroes liked to play with. So you think you are a citizen. Let's see your birth certificate. What do you mean you don't have one? Many people of a certain age had not bothered to get one, so the paper was demanded only if the desire was to humiliate or to intimidate, or very often both. What kind of bloodsucker are you, pretending to be a citizen? It was all part of the joy of power, to chasten, to terrify, or to expel at will.

In any case, Rafik came back from Cuba, resplendent in his uniform and the cap that Fidel Castro loved to wear—or as a variation he wore a black beret like Che Guevara—greeting his comrades with salutations that were new to everyone but would soon become familiar: venceremos, la luta continúa, vamos. He also started casting glances at Raya and talking with her in the street while he wore a playful smile. Anyone could see what he was up to. She was seventeen years old and beautiful, and he was now notorious for messing up young women.

I don't like the way he was talking to you. You know what these people are like, her father said angrily. Don't try to fool me. Usin-danganye. I saw you smiling at him as if you liked his talk. He is after you. Couldn't you see that? He will disgrace you. He will shame all of us.

Raya started to protest. What was she to do? She could not pre-tend not to know him. She did not want to offend him. Her father swiped his arm through the air, signifying that he required her to be silent, and then he waved her away out of his sight. He consulted with his elder brother, Hafidh, who was just as fearful of shame as he was, and would understand his panic about Rafik's interest in Raya. They kill our sons and then look to dishonor our daughters, Hafidh said. They both understood what he was talking about. The brothers looked desperately around for who could save her, and save everyone from humiliation and disgrace. Her father usually sought out his brother's sagacity when it suited him, or when he needed to borrow money, or both, as on this occasion. For any ar-rangement they were to come up with was certain to require money to pay for celebrations and gifts and food. Raya's father was not blessed with a skill for making money, as his elder brother was, and he was generous with it.

The person they found for her was Bakari Abbas, an amiable man in his forties who lived in Pemba, previously divorced and of respectable means. He was a building contractor, and acquaintances who were contacted spoke well of him, and so Raya's parents ar-ranged her life with him. When her father told her, in that sad-dened, self-pitying way he adopted when he wanted to persuade her or her mother to agree with him, she did not think there was any real choice, either accept the arrangement that would preserve the respectability and honor of her parents and herself or choose the hooligan soldier. It did not occur to anyone but her to ask if she might have chosen to take her chances with the hero. She suppressed that thought and did not mention it to anyone. Everything had gone too far for that and maybe it would all turn out well.

So it was that her father, who was physically frail but domineering by temperament, made Raya agree to a marriage that she feared she would hate. That was how she had been brought up and how everyone she knew lived their lives. She endured the sudden, intense preparations, and the advice of aunties and other people she hardly knew, who washed her and stroked her and fed her the lore of obedience to male lust, who whispered how being cherished would ripen and inflame her, how the affectionate attentions of a husband would fulfill her world, and how God would bless the outcome. Then, on the night of her capture, she lay in the bed of Bakari Abbas and knew for the first time the shock of eager, overbearing flesh upon her unresisting body. She could not resist, not that night nor the nights that followed, because she had been instructed not to. It was his right, and her duty required submission.

Bakari Abbas was a man of personable and even pleasing appearance, wiry and strong and of middle height, well over five feet. He was amiable to the world, a man of business, with the effortless courtesy and flourishes of someone of his profession. But to Raya he was sometimes curt, and he was relentless in his demand for her body, every day, sometimes two or three times in a day. What at first was strange and frightening grew increasingly crushing and somehow humiliating, but she submitted because she did not know what else to do. She told herself that this was how it was for every woman, to endure the energetic invasions that were necessary to satisfy her husband's need, and to find what pleasure she could for herself. She could have been more artful, could have feigned enjoyment to temper his desire for her surrender, but she was too young and too repelled. She could not help cringing while he took his pleasure, her face puckered and her eyes closed tight. He laughed to see her quailing so and tried to cajole her with soft whispers and little kisses, and when that did not work, he became adamant for her to respond more joyfully to his exertions. Her reluctance and mute resistance made him determined to awaken her, as he put it. She came to know his smile at such moments. Come, my bulbul, give me one small groan of pleasure, he murmured to her as he pounded his bony pelvis on the soft flesh of her widespread thighs.

She learned to make it easier for herself, to evade pain by preparing her body to receive him. She learned to acquire some control so she was not always at his mercy, to delay and postpone, and to feign enjoyment. She said no when she could, and fought back when he rebuked her, returning vicious abuse to his hectoring threats. It was a nightmare she could not tell anyone about. There were times when she wondered if she might have done better with handsome Rafik, but she already knew how badly that would have ended. Rafik had been shot dead in a bloodletting orgy that happened a year after her wedding.

The bickering with Bakari went on for what seemed like forever to Raya, and seemed to get worse after the birth of her son, Karim. Bakari grew increasingly impatient with her reluctance to let him lie with her so soon after giving birth, and his rages when he was thwarted were out of control. The reports of his amiability were not exaggerated. He was charming with other people from what she could observe, but he reserved his cruelty for her and took pleasure in it, and she feared that one day his viciousness would become violent. She did not know whether it was best to cower and tremble in front of him as a sign of her capitulation, which she knew he desired, or to be obstinate and abusive in return. She was learning to live with his contempt and her own self-disgust, but she was frantic for her child's safety. She wondered, at times, if this was what life was like for most women, if they lived this way, in terror of their men. Why did they not speak? She did not know who she could speak to.

When Karim was a child of three, after silent planning and stubborn cunning, she took him and moved back to Unguja, leaving her husband. She went to Unguja to visit her parents and refused to return. Her life with Bakari Abbas had shown her the futility of the obedience she had been raised to observe and that had finally enraged her enough to resist. She ignored the messages he sent summoning her back, and ignored his threat to divorce her and leave her without a cent. She ignored his citation of the law, both civil and religious, for the return of his son. So, in short, they parted in acrimony, on her part with disgust for his violence, his promiscuous lusts, and the coercion that had forced her into marriage with him, on his with outrage that he expressed by refusing to offer her any financial support, ever. He could have been compelled by the law or even by customary practice, but Raya was too dismayed and too bitter to bother, despite her father's and her uncle's urgings. She could not be frank with them about his cruelties. She was too ashamed. All she could say was that they were bickering all the time and she did not want to live like that. Then, she forbade them from asking for a single shilling of his money.

Raya and Karim moved back into the family home. Her parents rented two gloomy rooms on the first floor of a house and shared a kitchen and a bathroom with the tenants upstairs. To Raya the rooms felt closed in and the whole house smelled sour. There was a narrow lane between their house and the one next door, and men passing by sometimes used the alley as a urinal. Karim slept on the floor in his grandparents' room, and Raya rolled out her bedding in the other room when it was time to sleep. She had moved in reluctantly, not eager to return to the airless cells in which she had grown up, even though she felt relief that her mother took over some of the care of her child. Nor was her father happy to have her back, muttering about duties and a poor man left alone with no one to look after him. She dreaded her father's overbearing ways, his passive bullying. Didn't anybody hear me calling? This coffee is cold, is bitter, is thin. Are we so poor that we can't afford decent coffee? Why is nobody listening to me? Where is my bathing water? My back is hurting. I can't sleep with all the noise from upstairs. Can't you women stop talking?

His one redeeming quality for Raya was his ability to tell stories. Those stories had charmed her childhood. She had believed they were true, and even once she knew they were not, she could not shake off their reality. He did not make up the stories, she understood that later. He had been told those same stories as a child, as had her mother, but her mother did not have his gift for telling and often forgot important details, smiling apologetically as the punch line evaded her. He told the stories really well, of talking animals when she was younger and later, fantasies and adventures in the great world, narrating the different parts with a canny judgment of tone and voice. But then the stories dried up. She knew why. A bitterness entered her father's mind after the revolution, and a recitation of injustices and grievances replaced the stories that had charmed her childhood.

The story drought was also to do with what happened to her cousin Suleman, the son of Hafidh, her father's elder brother. Suleman had joined the new security force that was formed as independence approached. At the same time as Fidel Castro was training the comrades to come back and make a revolution, the new government about to take over from the British was creating a paramilitary police force to provide security. The existing police force was an imperial creation, intended to control its colonial subjects, the incoming government told them. The new security unit would be a fresh start, a force to protect its citizens rather than intimidate them. That was what they were told. Most of the recruits were recent school-leavers, the majority in their late teens. Still, the unit commander was British because why not use their expertise while they were still in place. One night, there were rumors of a planned disturbance, and the commander did not want to risk some riffraff breaking into the armory while he was at a party arranged long before. So he kept the keys to the armory in his pocket or maybe at home in his briefcase or maybe somewhere else. In any case, he left the teenagers unarmed in their barracks, and the youngsters, who had received only minimal training, who had no idea what to do, and no means to defend themselves, were cut to pieces. That was the opening act of the revolution. Hafidh's son, Suleman, was one of those boys. He had joined up just after the end of school in December and was only a fortnight into his training.

They could not find him, not among the wounded nor the mutilated nor the perished, and in the aftermath of the events and the stories that followed, and in the boasts of the victors, they could only assume he was among the disappeared. The brothers never spoke about the boy between them except to mention him in their prayers. His mother mourned him and wept for him, and in her bereavement thought herself worthless and unfit to live. It broke Baba, even though he was not the father. Something went out of him, and that's when the tales dried up or turned into bitter laments. As time passed, the memory of the stories grew fainter, but she could still remember that some of them were funny and tender. The one about the beggar who was charged with stealing the aroma of the sultan's banquet, and how Abunuwas helped him pay for doing so by throwing coins on the palace floor and requesting the sultan to accept the jingling of the money in payment. Or there was one about an ostrich that came to a bad end that she could no longer recall the details of. There was also an ominous one about a castle on top of a black magnetic mountain that could not be taken because as the enemy approached, their swords and lances flew out of their hands and onto the mountainside. Or the refined sisters who ate rice with a needle, one grain at a time. The memory of the stories could not make up for his endless groans and grumbles, which grew longer and deeper as he aged. It was not as if he could help himself, she knew that, but it was still difficult to witness and bear his aches and pains.

Her mother had to give him a full-body massage first thing

every morning and last thing every night, and any time in between if he desired it. She crouched on her knees and moved from his neck and shoulders all the way down to his toes, while he groaned with masochistic contentment. After the morning massage, he dressed and waited for the day's first cup of tea to arrive, accompanied by a freshly fried mandazi bun. Often the tea would not be right in some way or the mandazi would be too sweet, or there was something else that was not to his liking. When Raya returned with Karim, he tried to recruit her into the labor force that served his needs, calling her to administer a massage when her mother was busy, but she resisted. She had learned enough in her time with Bakari Abbas to ignore his grumbles.

At twenty-one, Raya was a beauty, although she did not fully know that about herself. In any case, she did not care for the attention of men. She thought she had had enough of that kind of hunger, and just wanted to be left to herself, to find some ordinariness and small content. Despite herself, she found it some relief to be back with her mother and father, a lightening of the burden of responsibility she had felt for her son, and a kind of safety for both of them. It surprised her, the alacrity with which she allowed her mother to take over caring for Karim, but as her guilt about that shift diminished, she began to look at the child with more detachment and could not help associating him with troubled times.

In her father's eyes she was young enough to be a source of shame and dishonor, attracting the attention of men of disrepute. Think of your child, he said.

I am thinking of my child, she said.

He will grow up without a father, he persisted. It is your husband's right to demand the child's return. Go back to him. You have a duty, your son needs his father. Or let us find you another husband. Divorce is not the end of the world, it's nothing.

Raya shrugged and did not reply. To herself she said, You did a fine job the first time round. Nothing that you say will persuade me to return to Bakari Abbas.

## 2

Karim had an elder brother, Ali, who was the son of a different mother. Ali's mother, Mamkuu, had divorced Bakari Abbas when her son was a child of eight, and had moved them both from Pemba back to Unguja. Three years later, Bakari Abbas had married Raya, so the boys were twelve years apart in age.

Ali was still at school when Karim and his mother came to live in Unguja. The brothers did not look at all alike. At sixteen Ali had already assumed the shape and outline of his adult self. His face was sharp-featured like his father's, but he was shorter than him, an inch under five feet, and his body was muscular and promised to be stocky in later years, whereas his father was trim and bony. Yet unlike his father's face, Ali's glowed with youthful mischief and easily burst into smiles. He loved the sea and the company of fishermen, many of whom were also boys just a little older than him who lived in the neighborhood and had been his playmates since childhood. Sometimes he missed school and went fishing with his friends, and although he tried to hide his truancy from his mother, she always found him out.

I can smell the sea on you. You have been missing school again, she would say, and he would drop his head in such exaggerated contrition that his mother would slap him lightly instead of giving him the thrashing she told him he deserved.

His mother, Mamkuu, worried about the company of the fishermen because they had a reputation for rowdiness and smoking hashish, or rather, the other way round, they smoked hashish and became rowdy and insolent. She worried about Ali missing school, about his streetwise swagger, and she hectored him repeatedly to no effect. He promised to be good but just became a little more stealthy about his mischief. He loved his mother and did not want her to worry, but he also loved going out to sea. He was a strong boy who knew how to take care of himself, and there really was nothing for his ma to worry about.

It was not as if he hated school. He had friends there, and they often had fun at the teachers' expense. Ali was a champion clown at school, somehow able to make the other boys laugh without any effort. One of his tricks was to parody the way the teachers walked and talked. He could do most of them, striding, slouching, hectoring, while the other pupils laughed and sometimes joined in. His best impression was of the mathematics teacher, a man who terrified them with his violence and his grim silences. During every lesson someone was certain to be slapped or hauled to his feet and lashed across the backside with a cane. Ali struggled with the subject to begin with, and the menace this man generated in the classroom made it impossible for him to concentrate on anything but survival until the end of the period. On one occasion, Ali was sauntering in front of the class imitating the peculiar gait of this teacher, glaring at the boys while they tittered at his performance, when the man himself walked in behind him. Ali's buttocks began to tingle and his stomach churned with terror, but he put on a brave face, smiled at the teacher, and walked back toward his seat. Before he had taken a couple of steps, the teacher was on him and knuckled him on the back of the head with such force that Ali almost swooned into his seat. He was a hero that day because he kept the smile on his face, but he never mimicked that teacher again.

Much of what was expected of him at school was tedious, it seemed to him, but he exerted himself to the extent necessary to maintain self-respect and not to be thought stupid. There was also sports. He was athletic in a dogged way, a quality that made him a competitor, not a winner, and that got him on to the school football team, where he was rated a tough, disciplined defender.

Karim, too, had his father's sharp-featured face, and he was slim like his father as well, but he had his mother's melting eyes. When he was very young, those eyes often looked as if they were likely to dissolve into tears. Unlike his spirited elder brother, Karim was prone to silence when addressed, and to grim sulks when he was thwarted. The brothers did not have much to do with each other because their mothers did not get on, or could not take the trouble to get to know each other. Mamkuu was almost forty, nearly twenty years older than Raya. The age difference between them was too big for friendship, Raya thought, and perhaps, too, she felt a stab of shame that she had allowed herself to be browbeaten into accepting the condition that the elder woman had already known and rejected. She suspected that Mamkuu despised her for having yielded so submissively, although Mamkuu had put up with Bakari Abbas for far longer than Raya had.

The age difference between the brothers also felt big at the time when they met. Sixteen- and four-year-olds cannot be expected to have a great deal to share, especially when one is a cheeky rascal and the other is a little boy disconcerted by the events that have overtaken his life. In addition, they lived in different parts of town, and Karim was too young to be wandering the streets, where Ali was most likely to be found, and so they almost never bumped into each other by chance. Yet as the years passed, they nevertheless came to know more of each other. During Idd, each went to pay his respects to the other's mother, and there were times when they came across each other at an event or game.

By the time Karim started school, Ali had finished and joined the customs police, which to Mamkuu was preferable to the fishermen because it was on the right side of the law. But Karim went to the same school that Ali had gone to, and the teachers were mostly the same. They spoke about them as brothers and compared their behavior and their achievements, as teachers do with brothers. As Karim progressed through the years, he came out very well in these comparisons, the teachers praising him for his abilities and his obedient ways, so unlike the provocative and annoying ways of his brother. Your kaka was a little devil when he was here, they told him. The headmaster, who lived two streets away from Karim, visited their house and told Karim's mother, Your boy is a little gem. This news inevitably reached Ali, who chuckled with pleasure and remembered all the mischief of his school days. When he saw Karim in the streets, he always asked him first about school, How are you getting on there? Are you shining? He cajoled him to boast about his latest triumphs, which Karim was never reluctant to do. At times Karim even volunteered news of an achievement. Ali would ask after Auntie, which was his way of referring to Raya. If anyone else was around, he introduced Karim as his smart little brother and patted him on the shoulder in a protective manner. Karim loved these encounters, and his heart swelled whenever Ali put his arm around him or gave him a friendly tap. It made him feel proud to be acknowledged in this way.

Karim's mother treated him like a possession she was fond of but the details of whose welfare she was happy to leave to her parents. It was not so unusual for that to happen, for an aunt or a grandmother to become the mother figure, or for a child to grow up with a sense of having more than one such figure. It might happen as a result of the real mother's youth, or her inability to cope with too many off-spring, or her ambition. In the case of Raya, she had discovered a new life of her own and had found work in a large clothing store, which allowed her to learn about fashion and to indulge her love of it. She relished advising customers about styles and outfits, and dis-playing the latest arrivals for them. She made some new women friends in this way and began making up for those miserable years forced on her by her father. In the busyness of her new life, she grew a little detached from her child, and was perhaps a little tetchy with him. At times, in the guilty aftermath of her impatience, she had to remind herself to show him tenderness.

It was Karim's grandmother who fussed over him, shook him

awake in the morning, and gave him his cup of tea before hurrying him off to school. It was to her that he repeated his most amazing discoveries of the day, the unsettling claim that the core of the world was molten, and the stories he read in his book of Greek myths: the beheading of Medusa, the man who stole fire from the Greek gods, the labors of Hercules. From his schoolbook he read to her of the journeys of Sindbad. Sometimes she was skeptical, as with the story of the Trojan horse. They must have been simple, those Trojans, to fall for a trick like that. It was she who dabbed stinging iodine when he stumbled and grazed his knee, who rubbed pungent embrocation on his ankle or wrist when he came home howling after a fall. He loved the smell of the embrocation and loved the name. Embrocation. When no one was around, he uncorked the bottle, sniffed its contents, and winced at its stinging aroma.

Karim grew up fast, and in a few short years was taller than his elder brother. Every few months, Ali stood him against the wall and marked his height. Yallah, you're like a coconut tree, all stick and no muscle, he said. Karim grew into a lanky, soft-spoken, self-possessed boy whose unwavering gaze sometimes disconcerted grown-ups. Ali was now even more proud of his little brother, and he often came to the house to take him swimming or to see a football match or just to take a walk with him.

Their father passed away when Karim was in secondary school. Bakari Abbas's last years had been plagued by diabetes and a troublesome enlarged prostate, but he had decided not to have it surgically reduced after the doctor warned that his diabetes might interfere with the anesthetic or cause other complications. He did not understand everything he was told, but surgery sounded dangerous, so he chose to live with the pain. Only he did not live much longer, because his heart suddenly gave way. He was fifty-eight years old when he died.

Karim had not had anything to do with his father after his mother took him away from Pemba, because she forbade it, though she did not explain why. Her face and dismissive gesture at the mention of his name made clear that she had no time for him. Karim did not know what his father had done that could not be spoken of, but he knew it must have been something bad. So Bakari Abbas's passing did not provoke grief so much as some regret that the rancor between his parents had left him without something that other people took for granted. It was an exception that embarrassed him when he was younger, and there had been times when he spoke of his father in Pemba as if he knew him and was intimate with him, when really he had last seen him eleven years before, at the age of three.

Karim at times wondered why parents like his, who were neglectful and unloving, bothered to have children. He had only a hazy memory of his father, and his mother often rebuked him for what she called his antics and often seemed to find him irritating and hardly ever sat to talk with him in the way his grandmother did. Sometimes his mother surprised him with that lazy smile he so loved and even gave him a hug and a caress, but often her address to him was a grumble or an impatient command. Stop that running around and making so much noise, kisirani we. Why don't you go outside and play with the other children? He did not know when he began to think like this, and perhaps he did not think about it as fluently and succinctly as this at first, but he had known the frustration of it from a very early age. He would do things differently when he became a father, that was certain. He would make sure his child knew it was desired, that it was loved. If he ever bothered to have a child, that is. He did not speak these thoughts to anyone until much later, as it seemed to him ungrateful and even sinful to do so, and by then it did not matter as much as it once did.

Ali had been a more dutiful son to his father and had regularly visited him in Pemba before his death. That was how Karim knew what little he knew about his father, including his medical travails. Raya said the visits to Pemba were a deliberate ploy by Ali's mother, Mamkuu. That woman's a plotter. She sends her son visiting to make sure he will inherit what his father leaves behind.

That was how it turned out. Bakari Abbas had married again after Raya, so he was not on his own in his last days. His wife inherited the house they lived in and its effects, furniture, mats, and pots and pans, and Ali inherited what was left of the business. Neither Ali's mother nor Karim's mother nor Karim was mentioned in Bakari Abbas's will, and although Raya could have challenged the will under religious law, to argue for Karim's share, she chose instead to scorn Bakari Abbas's malice. Mamkuu was content with Ali's inheritance, as was he. Ali sold the business, married Jalila, to whom he had long been betrothed, and bought a house in Unguja. Mamkuu had no wish to move out of her house, which she had inherited many years before from her mother. Ali was by then a fully fledged customs officer in the port, his uniform always crisp and his step jaunty and purposeful. Newly wed, he was a man with a place in the world.

At the time of his father's passing away, Karim's mother was no longer living with her parents, or not permanently. She made her escape gradually. She rented a room in an apartment where one of her women friends lived with her mother, and every few days she would come to stay in the rooms with her parents and son. The days between visits increased as the months passed, until in the end she called in for only an hour or two now and then before returning to her rented room. There was no space for a teenage boy in the new accommodation, Raya said, so he had to stay behind with his grandparents. Of course, he could come and visit whenever he wanted, but she had to move. She needed more air. It is stifling in these rooms, she told her son, speaking softly so her mother would not hear. I'm suffocating, I can't stay here. Everything smells stale and bad. It's the dirt of years. The bathroom is filthy, and that alleyway stinks of urine. And you . . . you are getting too big to be sleeping in the same room as your grandparents.

What else am I supposed to do? When you are not here, I sleep in this room. You don't like me to sleep in the same room as you, he grumbled, wounded by her criticism.

Well, you can have it, his mother said, smiling at the sulky childishness in his voice. You are welcome to it.

A few months after Karim's father passed away, Karim's grandmother also suddenly collapsed. She had always been a tireless woman, up first, warming water, making tea, doing the washing, cooking, cleaning, from dawn until the closing of the day, and then the last one up at night. One morning she could not rise from her bed but lay there with eyes wide open, softly panting. Her collapse created consternation in the household. She had enough strength to send Karim to fetch Raya so that she could take over the cooking and the fussing over her father and his needs. On the night of her second bedridden day, she passed away with a minimum of fuss, going as quietly as she had lived her life. In the days following, their lives were taken over by the formalities of death, the washing of the body, the preparation for burial, the prayers, the funeral that only her husband and Karim could attend, the readings at the mosque and at home. To Karim it seemed as if everything suddenly came to a head in this way. His distant, unknown father passed away, then his mother no longer lived with them, then his grandmother went suddenly, from one day to the next.

You had better stay and look after your grandfather, his mother said. He'll need you here. We'll have to think how to organize ourselves. I can't come back to live here. I'll arrange for the people upstairs to prepare your lunch, and I'll come by every day, don't worry. It'll be all right.

I hope so, he said sulkily, but she took no notice, preoccupied with her own thoughts.

What Karim did not know but was soon to understand in full was that his mother had been preparing for departure for some time. For nearly a year, Raya had been in an affair with a man from Dar es Salaam whose name was Haji Othman. They met when she went visiting a friend in Dar. Nothing much came of that encounter except that she liked his looks and his cheerful manner and spent ten minutes or so in conversation with him among other people. Then a few days after her return, he telephoned her at the clothing store where she worked. I'll be coming to Zanzibar next week, and I wondered if we could meet for lunch? Later, she found out that he had asked the friend in Dar about her and whether she was attached. When he found out she was not, he asked the friend for her work telephone number, and she had given it unhesitatingly because she liked Haji and she liked Raya and she was intrigued about how it would work out. That was how it began. He came to Zanzibar, they had lunch, and after that he rang her every few days, and everything else followed discreetly. She visited his hotel when he was in Zanzibar, and sometimes she went to Dar. A few months afterward, they began talking of marriage. By then she was living permanently in her own rented room. Her mother's passing had hastened her decision. She had no intention of taking her mother's place as her father's skivvy.

Karim was nearly fifteen when his mother married again and followed her new husband to Dar es Salaam, where he owned a pharmacy in Fire Station Road. Karim was not completely surprised by her departure. When he learned of her forthcoming marriage, he suspected that she did not intend for him to follow her. By then he was not uncomfortable in the home his mother so bitterly despised, even though he had been irked by her casual assumption that he would look after his grumbling grandfather. The neighbors upstairs cooked their food, which he collected when he came home from school and served to his grandfather and himself. He was doing extremely well at school, was acknowledged by the teachers and by his fellow students to be highly talented, and he had no desire to move to Dar es Salaam, which he had never even visited. He knew that his grandfather, who was used to having his daily needs seen to in detail, understood that he could not demand the same care from him, a teenage boy who could not cook, nor knew how to prepare his tea as it should be done every morning nor had the patience to give him his daily massages morning and night nor could do his laundry properly, and who spent his spare time playing football or wandering the streets with his friends, or buried in his books. So it was that soon after Raya's departure for Dar es Salaam, his grandfather gave up the rented rooms and went to live with his elder brother's family. Karim was sent to live with Ali and Jalila, and they took him in without hesitation. It seemed to Karim that he had lost his mother with little more than a shrug.

This is our house. I bought it with the money our father left to me, so it is yours too, Ali said after the first meal Karim enjoyed in his new home. Jalila gave an emphatic nod, which Karim came to know as her no-nonsense affirmation. No further discussion was required.

Of course, Ali continued with a mischievous smile, there will be children running up and down the stairs one day, but that won't be for a while yet, hey habibi. For now it is right that my younger brother should come and live with his family.

It was a small, narrow house near Mnazi Mmoja, behind the old madrassa that was now used as offices by a travel business. The house had two stories, with a bedroom and kitchen upstairs and a wide landing that served as their dining area and was where they sometimes sat and talked. The bathroom was downstairs, as was another large room by the front door, which became Karim's. The room was furnished with an iron-frame bed, a small desk, and a mkeka, a rough straw mat. A large window overlooked the street, with bars and solid shutters that were to be kept closed when Karim was out. He had to keep the lower shutters closed even when he was in the room to have any privacy from passersby, who had no inhibition about having a good look as they walked by, or even stopping for a moment or two to carry out a proper inspection. The sun came round in the afternoon and planted a slowly moving square of light on the side wall, revealing the grainy texture of the lime whitewash.

It's a scholar's room, perfect for you, Ali said in his teasing way. It is so good to have you here with us. But listen, you have to be serious about this. Both Jalila and I were unlucky with our schooling. I just made too much mischief for my own good. To be honest, I could not wait to leave school. The school Jalila went to taught her nothing much. There were never enough teachers, sometimes one teacher for over a hundred pupils. There was no order, there was constant bullying and chaos, there were few books and hardly any desks or chairs. Everything was broken and dirty. For us and our years, noise and indiscipline was what school had to offer. Are you listening to me? You are luckier than us, and you deserve it too. You have a good head, big brains. The school you are in now is one of only two schools which work well, and you know why, don't you? It's because that's where the government bastards who have not yet stolen enough from the state to pay for overseas boarding schools send their children. You got in because you're clever and passed the entrance examination so brilliantly. You must make the most of your good luck.

Jalila never tired of reminding Karim of his luck, and fussed over him to do his assignments and boasted of his talents and achievements to anyone who cared to listen. She was only seven years older than Karim, but from the day he moved in she treated him like a much younger brother, one who needed direction and encouragement. Karim did not complain, but at times he smiled at her mothering and condescension. She smiled too. You think I'm too bossy, don't you? It's for your own good, she said. Ali sometimes came to Karim's room and browsed through his books while he did his homework, or chatted with him about sports or whatever came up. If he was in the mood, he recounted highlights from his days as a school scamp or relived some of his sporting feats for Karim, once demonstrating in detail the tackle that saved an almost certain goal.

Two years after his mother's departure for Dar es Salaam, Karim was invited to visit her. The invitation was a surprise, as he had not had much to do with her since she'd left. He knew it was meant as a kind of reward for completing his secondary school studies so successfully, and a holiday before he started senior secondary school. It would be his first journey since his arrival from Pemba, and he could not remember anything about that. As the day of the trip approached, Ali gave him copious advice, as if he was a seasoned traveler himself. Don't leave your bag unattended. Don't get stuck in a crowd. There's bound to be a pickpocket among them. Sit in the middle of the ferry, not at the back. You'll get sick if you sit at the back. He bought the ferry ticket for Karim, and used his customs police uniform to shepherd him through the terminal as if Karim was a VIP. Karim was anxious about his arrival because he knew no one was meeting him. When you get to the ferry terminal, just get a taxi and head for Auntie's house, Ali told him. There's nothing to worry about. Karim nodded politely although he knew very well that Ali had never been to Dar es Salaam either.

Not only had Karim not seen his mother in those two years, but he had not received a letter or even a postcard from her, although sometimes he had news of her from people who had met with her in Dar. It had taken her all that time to make this little gesture of affection, but he was resigned to her lack of interest in him and would do his best to be dutiful. He was not frightened at the prospect of meeting her again, just not sure how it would go. In addition to that anxiety, he wanted to make sure he did not get lost or look stupid. He took a taxi as instructed and arrived at the house without mishap, feeling that he had done something difficult and impressive.

It's lovely to see you, his mother said, holding him by the shoulders and smiling at him. Come and have something to eat, then you can tell me everything that has been happening to you. Look how tall you are, so handsome and so clever!

He grinned at the flattery and relished her pleasure. Somewhere in the depths of his modesty, he did not think it was misplaced. His mother was not the first to describe him as handsome, and he knew very well that he was clever. He was sixteen years old and beginning to fill out in the chest and shoulders. His hair was turning bushy and wiry and he liked to let it grow, oblivious to Jalila's repeated instruction that he should have it cut. You look like a lunatic, Jalila said, but he thought he looked fine.

Her husband, Haji, was a slim, active man with a dark complexion and tightly curled hair cut short. Karim guessed that he was nearly the same age as his mother. It was their first meeting apart from a brief encounter during the wedding, but Karim was quickly at ease with Haji and his endless bantering, joining in the laughter even when it was at his expense. Raya and Haji sat and talked with him while he had a late lunch, before Haji returned to his pharmacy.

Karim's mother showed him to his room, and afterward he went to her in the upstairs sitting room. She asked him questions about Ali, about his schooling, and she was rapt in smiling attention as he recounted his performance in the recent examinations. He was surprised how easy he found it to be with her now.

They lived upstairs in a spacious house they shared with Haji's father, who had his rooms downstairs. The reception room at the front of the house was for his use exclusively, along with his radio and a couple of friends who came to share the radio with him in the evenings. Karim did not go in there, and met the gloomy, silent man only at mealtimes. He hardly ever spoke. His face was weary and down-drawn, his head was shaved, and his eyes were bloodshot. Karim's first sight of him almost drew a gasp of surprise at his appearance, which he just managed to suppress. He seemed like a person grieving. One afternoon, Karim saw him smile. He could not remember what drew that out of him, but the smile was brief and radiant, like a sudden burst of sunlight on a cloudy day. It made Karim wonder if perhaps the weary look was not grief but a matter of health, if he was just unwell. When he asked his mother, she shrugged noncommittally. It was something he was not supposed to be curious about. He left matters there and took care to stay clear of the old man.

Karim could see how much pleasure his mother and Haji took in each other. She called her husband Mganga, the Herbalist, even though there was something dubious and witchcrafty about that line of work, and her husband dealt in respectable pharmaceutical products. He called her habibi, beloved, and they spoke to each other in this open, loving fashion without display or intensity, as if this was how they addressed each other when they were on their own. They were prosperous enough to employ a gardener, old Juma as Haji called him, who came once a week, and Farida, a woman who came to do the laundry and clean the house twice a week. Karim met her on the second day of his stay. She was elderly, soft-spoken, and unsmiling in her greeting. After that she went about her tasks and spoke to him only once, to ask him if Raya was his mother. He thought she looked exhausted.

Raya had her doubts about Farida.

I know she needs the work, what with all the children her daughter keeps producing. She ends up raising those children, I know that. But I don't like servants in the house, rummaging around and pilfering from you, she said to Haji.

She glanced at Karim as she said that about Farida raising her daughter's children, and he wondered if she heard an echo of her neglect of him.

You are not looking at this in the right way, habibi. Yes, she needs the work, but she is also helping you with the unpleasant jobs, so you need only to do the cooking, which you like to do. She takes food from us, and that helps her out. We don't pay her such a lot. Think of this as an opportunity to do good and to have time for a little gentle exercise, Haji said, trying to make light. You don't have to go out to work, and if you don't exercise, you'll get fat.

You can get fat yourself, she said, which seemed unlikely, as they were both so slim. I come to help out at the pharmacy when you need me. I hate cleaning and dusting, but I still don't like having a servant around.

Who will do the washing if she doesn't? Haji asked in a tone that suggested this was his trump card.

There is such a thing as a washing machine, she said, to which he only made a face and looked away.

Karim stayed for a month that first time he went to visit them. He would wake up late and spend the day wandering the streets of Dar es Salaam. At first he walked only the length of Independence Avenue and then along Ocean Road. Later he turned corners at random and trusted his luck. It was exhilarating to walk around and meet no one he knew. Haji gave him some money when he first arrived—a large sum of money, it seemed to Karim—and at some stage in his wanderings he would stop at a café and buy himself a snack and a cup of tea, a paratha, a slice of fish, a plate of sambusa, or a dish of fried plantain. As he became more familiar with the city, he headed in a different direction every day but he always tried to get to the sea. If he found a shady and comfortable spot on a beach, he sat and read one of the detective novels he was then obsessed with. He had a feeling of risk as he wandered and got lost a few times, but sooner or later he found somewhere he recognized, the port, the bus station, or a familiar street from which he could find his way home. He would get back in the late afternoon, just as the city was preparing for its workers' homebound rush. Then after supper Haji went to sit and listen to the radio with his father in the reception room, from where Karim could hear him holding forth while he spent time with his mother in the upstairs sitting room. They had plenty to say to each other, catching up on the silences of his childhood. He ached to ask about his father, but each time he approached the subject it was as if she sensed it and headed him off.

Do you know, I have never visited Pemba, he might begin, and she would quickly say, Oh you will one day, it's nothing special. Do you visit your grandfather? How is he? I don't expect he ever visited Pemba either.

When Karim's time with them came to an end, they made him promise to come again, and Haji pressed more money on him. Karim thought his mother looked happier and more beautiful than he remembered her. He also felt that something had changed between them, and that she was more affectionate with him than she used to be. It was to do with her happiness, he suspected, or perhaps now that her desperate escape was complete, she could recognize her abandonment of him and make up for it.

Karim spent the remaining two years of his school life with Ali and Jalila, content with his routine and untroubled beyond the unease and fretfulness and stupidity that are unavoidable in those youthful years. If Karim was in his room, Ali always stopped when he came in from work, to talk for a few minutes, or if he was in a boisterous mood, to shove and punch and tussle with him, before he made his way upstairs to his wife. Jalila gave birth to their first child toward the end of those two years, a boy they called Ibrahim. He was born just as Karim received notification that he had been awarded a scholarship to study at the University of Dar es Salaam. He would have been surprised if he had not got it. It is a sign, Ali pronounced, first hugging his brother and then kissing his baby son. Little Ibrahim is going to be a scholar just like his clever uncle.

The degree program Karim was selected for was specified for him without consultation, geography and environmental studies. He would have preferred something more grand, medicine or economics, but he did not complain and resolved to make the most of what he was offered. The scholarship also provided for his university accommodation.

He's going on holiday, Ali said. They pay him money to go on holiday.

If you had used your head when you were at school instead of cheeking the teachers and going fishing, you might have been going to university too, Jalila scolded.

Did I say I wanted that kind of holiday? It would only give me a headache, Ali said. It will suit him, our brainy scholar. One in the family like that is enough.

And so, two years after his first visit, Karim returned to Dar es Salaam to start at the university, no longer anxious about finding his way, on the threshold of exciting times and a new freedom. After fulfilling his registration requirements, he checked into his accommodation and settled into his shared room. Then he made his way to Haji's pharmacy. Haji knew he was coming, and together they drove home for lunch, leaving an assistant to look after the shop for a while. That was how it continued that first year in Dar es Salaam: every few weeks he called on them, they gave him lunch or dinner and regaled him with news and asked for his, and then he went back to his studies and his friends at the university. Every time he visited Haji told him, There is a room ready for you upstairs. Why don't you move in with us instead of living in a cramped hostel and eating bad canteen food? Come and enjoy your mother's food.

Cooking was something Raya had come to love since marrying Haji. Karim could not remember her doing much of that when she lived with her parents. But despite the lure of his mother's food, which was indeed good, Karim resisted Haji's beckoning. He loved the feeling of freedom and the company of his friends, so he laughed off the invitation and said the accommodation was already paid for, but perhaps next year.

He found it easy to study. He had always done so. He had the ability to lose himself in his work, to be absorbed by it so completely that nothing else intruded for a while, neither hunger, nor noise, nor people. He had wondered, when he was first told about the accommodation arrangements, what sharing a room with three strangers would be like. It turned out to be less uncomfortable than he had expected. There was no space to study in the room, when they were all in there, they were like puppies in a den, but their gaiety and laughter made it easy for everyone to get along, at least until the novelty wore off and irritating eccentricities made themselves evident. Karim made other friends too, with whom he played table tennis and badminton and volleyball, and sometimes a small group of them went to see a movie on campus or to watch a football match. They spent hours talking, sometimes late into the night, about their studies, their teachers, and other students. Often their talk wandered into more intimate reflections about their memories and feelings, or at times to larger matters that loomed over their world. He found that the others listened to him when he spoke. They had to learn to trust one another before they could free themselves to talk openly, for rumors existed of informers among the students who reported conversations to the authorities. No one knew for certain what was reported or what the outcome might be, but the rumors existed. These were days they would always remember, they told themselves, the best years of their lives.

One morning during class, Karim found a note tucked into a folder he had left on a laboratory bench while he went to check rainfall readings in the seedling nursery. The note was sealed with a lipstick impression of puckered lips. It read: *My darling Karim. I know you will be surprised to receive this loving tribute. I adore you. I cannot keep this to myself anymore. My nights are sleepless, my body is aching with desire. You are so handsome. I want to be yours. Do not spurn me. It will destroy me. Please wait for me on the library steps this evening at 6:00. I will be carrying a green bag and wearing a white scarf. I cannot wait to be in your arms.*

He read the note and put it on the bench beside him while he recorded his results. His heart pounded with surprise and some excitement. Who was it? He guessed that whoever put the note in his folder was in the room, watching him. They were a mixed class of twenty, five of them women, and without looking round he did a mental tour of the room to see if he could identify the sender of the note. Saada with the thick black-framed glasses was far too stern and truculent for such a frivolous note. Rahma had a benign friendly face and a mischievous smile, but seemed to him more like someone's younger sister than a woman capable of writing *my body is aching with desire.* You could never tell, though. Tasnim was a seriously pious young woman, or else just carried herself with serious dignity, her head covered in a shawl, her garment buttoned down to the wrists and calves. Yet he had made brief eye contact with her and had seen a spark. Could it be her? She had a faint dark down over her upper lip, the beginnings of a mustache. Still, there could be a way of getting rid of that. Fortuna was older than the others and already a mother, not likely. She was always rushing away after class and was not likely to be hanging around the library steps at six in the evening. The one he thought most attractive was Jamila. She was elegantly proportioned, precise in her movements, and withdrawn in a way he found seductive. He liked that her eyes glinted with amusement when their glances crossed. At first he had thought it was disdain because she had sensed his interest, a signal for him to keep his distance, as if it was likely that he would do anything more—the possibility of his making a move was so far-fetched as to be absurd. She was always with the other women students, who mostly stayed together, protecting one another from unwanted approaches.

He had found his feet in many ways at university, but he was an innocent in matters of sex, which irked him. He was rarely at ease with people the way Haji was, although at other times he felt comfortable and thought himself suave in his manner. He was certainly not at ease with women. He had never had a girlfriend, although he and his friends talked about women often. He glanced at the note now and then, entertaining the fantasy that it could be from Jamila, while trying to maintain a casual air. He did not want to seem eager and foolish, so he continued with his note-making and calculations until he felt sufficient time had passed, then he looked up and around for the sender. Catching a pair of eyes roving across him, pretending not to look, he was immediately struck by a new thought. It was Seif, another student from Unguja, whose talk was so often about seductions that everyone guessed these stories were vainglorious fantasies. With sudden certainty, Karim knew that the note was from him. He smiled to think what a fool he could have made of himself and put the note away in his folder.

The next day there was another note: *Oh Karim, you did not come! You are breaking my heart. I could not sleep all night from disappointment and sorrow. I had looked forward with such joy to holding you in my arms, but you did not come. I asked a friend to deliver this note for me in case you thought I was teasing. Don't abandon me. I will wait for you this evening at the same place.* He shook his head at the obvious fakery and put the note away, not even bothering to glance at Seif. The following day there was another note: *Have mercy on me!* He laughed out loud when he read that and so did several other students, so they must all have been in on it, including some of the women. Seif laughed the loudest, announcing himself as the mastermind.

Karim suspected that many of them were tormented to different degrees by fantasies about sex, but most of them did not know what to do about it. That was not true of all the students, some of whom went on secretive trips to the city and returned with superior airs. It was true of those from the islands, who were brought up to think of the consequences and perils of casual sex, and it was also true of Muslim students from the coast, and especially of the women. What young woman would allow herself to be groped in a gloomy corner of campus by an audacious cavalier high on testosterone who would then boast of his daring? Word would go round within hours, and a reputation would be earned for all time. So the young men looked and they talked, but it was only the more brazen among them who found willing partners in the city. Karim found more cautious, solitary ways of managing his fantasies and feelings of inadequacy, as he imagined most of his fellow students did.

He returned home to Unguja at the end of that first year, having not only survived but utterly prevailed over the anxiety that he might find himself beyond his depth. Quite the opposite, he had succeeded in all his courses. His room in Ali and Jalila's house was as he had left it, the window closed to keep the dust and the bugs out, and his few items, the detective novels and the tattered notebooks, neatly piled on his desk. It's your room, Ali said when Karim expressed surprise that they had left the room untouched while he was away. So long as you live here, it's yours. Tell me about the big school, is it as grand as I think it is? Were you triumphant? How was Auntie? Did you give her our regards?

Karim could not resist giving them a full account of his successes, only to hear Jalila repeat them in exultant notes to other people, his grades inflated, his teachers made to sound more impressed than they had been. To listen to her, anyone would have thought that the whole city of Dar es Salaam was awestruck and enthralled by his presence. When he protested that he was just glad to have survived the year unscathed, she winked at him and smiled. Enjoy the adoration, Ali said. Jalila loves you.

At the beginning of his second year, he moved in with his mother and Haji. They had worn him down with their invitations and their affection, and the university room had grown to feel a little oppressive. Although living with three other students had seemed like an adventure at first, eventually this one's carelessly tossed dirty clothes, that one's endless chatter, the unpredictable outbursts and niggles, and his just not being able to get away when the talk was stuck on banal banter became tiresome and irritating.

He settled down easily in the house. The front door was never locked during the day and was often left half-open, so he came and went as he pleased, keeping out of the way of the gloomy old man. There was a garden gate that was entered through the carport where Haji kept his van. It was kept locked except for the days when Juma came or when Haji brought home something bulky, a bag of charcoal or a sack of rice that was going at a price too good to miss or a basket of mangoes that he could not resist. Haji had one key to that gate, and the other hung on a hook inside the back door.

The window in Karim's room overlooked the garden and faced southwest, so the light in the morning was silky and mellow, turning hard in the afternoon and then soft and amber in the twilight. He put his desk beside the window and often sat looking out and musing absently or watching Juma as he went about his tasks. Juma always went into the house when he arrived, but only downstairs to see to the old man. He moved about with the accustomed air of a longtime employee. Sometimes the old man came out into the garden and sat on a bench, looking on or dozing while Juma pruned or weeded. At other times the two sat talking for a while, too far from Karim for him to hear even the softest murmur. From his window, he saw that they were comfortable with each other, sometimes exchanging grins or even shaking with laughter. He never saw the old man behaving like that with anyone else, not even with Haji.

Toward the end of that year, the cleaning woman, Farida, fell ill and could not come to work. His mother was forced to wash their laundry and clean the house, which was not to her liking. She ignored as much of the housework as she could, sweeping the yard and the hallway but leaving the bathroom they shared upstairs and the bedrooms to look after themselves. After a few days Haji began to complain.

The bedsheets smell of sweat, and there is dust everywhere, he said.

Karim's mother shrugged and said, Don't exaggerate. When it became clear that Farida was not coming back, her illness forcing her to take to her bed, Haji suggested to Raya that she should employ someone to replace her. Somehow she could not find a person who suited her. In the end, Haji bought a washing machine and had it installed in one of the outside storerooms. Karim understood that the washing machine was the prize of this contest, something his mother had wanted for a long time and Haji had resisted. For some little time, the washing machine became a topic of conversation for Raya and Haji. How silently and cleanly it does its work. That was Raya. What a racket it makes when it spins, but now we are a modern household. No more backbreaking washing, never mind the expense. That was Haji, turning his defeat into mild sarcasm. Karim did not partake, taking their bickering to be a kind of affection.

At first the solitude of his room made it possible to work without distraction, and the months passed comfortably. And the long bus ride to and from campus, which sometimes took over an hour, allowed him to see more of the city. But by the end of the year, he began to tire of the daily journey. He missed the company of other students, their hectic camaraderie and silly antics that he heard about only afterward and felt excluded from. He did not stay for evening events because he knew that Haji and his mother did not like his coming home late. Neither said anything, but the few times he did stay on he came home to a locked door and a dark house and had to knock for admission. The door was always locked after the radio sessions in the reception room had finished and the old man's companions had departed. When Karim returned late, Haji opened the door without speaking and turned away with a soft grunt, leaving Karim to lock up. It was so unlike his usual manner that it felt like a rebuke. Karim determined that when he returned for his final year he would stay in a campus room again. He put in a request at the required time before he returned to Unguja for the summer but did not tell Haji and his mother. He would please himself on that matter and did not want to have to argue his case or appear ungrateful.

## 3.

Several days after Karim returned to Zanzibar for the summer, Badar was sent to work for the Mistress. It was just before the beginning of the fasting month, and he and his father waited under the tree by the roadside for the bus to town. When it came, the bus was full of passengers and piled high with gunnysacks, and bundles, and baskets on its roof rack. The conductor, who collected the fares and supervised the loading and unloading of the sacks and baskets, leaped down from his seat and ushered Badar and his father in, badgering the other passengers to squeeze up and let them sit. He himself stood on the rear running board, leaning into the bus with one arm looped round the post that supported the roof, or sometimes sat at the feet of the passengers. It was an old bus, an open-sided flatbed truck with housing and benches built on top. Canvas sheets were tied up in rolls along the sides, ready to be lowered when it rained.

The growl of the engine, the rattle of the vehicle parts, and the noise of the tires on the road silenced everyone except the conductor, the ton-boy, a lean young man of eighteen or so, who kept up a chatter like someone possessed, addressing the passengers as well as people on the roadside when the bus slowed down. It was a long ride, and it was already past midday when they arrived in the town. Badar followed behind his father as they walked through the crowded lorry park and down a main road thronging with cars and bicycles and pedestrians and traders and noise, through dust and heat and petrol fumes and the roar of motor traffic. They walked past houses with shops and offices at street level and balconies overhead, and then through winding unpaved lanes with broken gutters and piles of rubble and building sand until, like an unexpected relief, they came to a wide dusty open space.

There were houses around three sides of the clearing and a mosque on the fourth side. It was much grander than their village mosque, with a blue-tinted wall across one side and a glimpse of treetops in the enclosure behind it. A decorated metal archway ran across the top of the open gate. They walked past the mosque and stopped at a neat and prosperous-looking two-story house a short distance beyond it. A covered drive ran along the side. One panel of the front door was open and a curtain billowed across the opening. His father, who had not spoken one word to Badar since they'd left home, stepped up the narrow walkway from the road and knocked on the closed panel. He called out hodi to announce their arrival, and then called out again. It seemed a long time before someone came.

The man who came to the door was elderly. His head and chin were clean-shaven, and he was dressed in a gray shirt and dark trousers. He stood at the door of the house for a moment without speaking, a frown on his hairless face, squinting in the glare, then he raised his arm in greeting and pulled the curtain aside for them to enter. Badar caught his left foot on the doorway as he went in, which he knew meant the house was a place of unhappiness. He stepped out of his sandals and left them on the doormat.

The man showed them into a large room just inside the front door, which had a thick carpet and large sofas with velvet-covered cushions scattered on them. Badar felt dirty and dusty, and as he sat down on the sofa nearest the door, he tucked his feet out of sight. Framed pictures hung on the walls: two were of groups of people, some sitting and some standing behind them, and one was of an enormous mosque with several minarets. A large radio with ivory-colored knobs stood on a low table in a corner beside a reading stand with a copy of the Koran on it. He could tell it was the Koran from the scrolled writing on the red cover. The room had the mingled aroma of old incense, tobacco smoke, and something else he could not identify, something warm and rich. His father did the talking, asking after the man's health in deferential tones and then making polite conversation while the host hummed and nodded in reply and slowly released his frown. All of a sudden Badar realized that they had stopped talking and were both looking at him. He thought he had missed an instruction and waited anxiously to be rebuked. Then they both rose to their feet, and he rose too. You'll stay here with Uncle Othman, his father said, pointing to the man they had come to visit. He did not look at Badar as he said this.

His father shook hands with Uncle Othman, and without another word to Badar he turned toward the door, with the man following to see him out. Badar was too surprised to ask questions. Was his father instructing him to wait until he came back, or was this where he had been brought to work? He had told Badar the previous day that he had found work for him in town. There was to be no more school for him. There was no money.

He heard the words of farewell—You are welcome. Please visit us next time you are in town—and then the man his father called Uncle Othman returned to the room. He looked at Badar without speaking for a long moment, and then he made a clucking, impatient noise and said, Come.

Badar picked up his bundle and followed Uncle Othman through the house. On the right were two doors, one open, through which he saw several chairs and a table laid with plates and glasses. Opposite the open door was a third door, which was closed. They walked through the hallway to the garden at the back. A woman in a faded old dress and headscarf was sitting on a low stool before a brazier in front of the door to the kitchen, which was in a separate low building behind the house. I have the boy here, Uncle Othman said to her, then he turned back and left Badar there.

The woman looked at him for a moment, her face slender, her eyes wide open and glowing, and a slow, lazy smile grew on her face.

What are you called? she asked.

Badar, he said.

She nodded and said, That's a nice name. Sit for a moment while I finish this.

She was making sesame bread, spreading the soft dough with her right hand and handling the skillet with her left, with which she also scattered a handful of sesame seeds into the pan. She rinsed her right hand in a bowl of water by her feet and wiped it on her dress, ready to scoop another handful of dough. She did this methodically, unhurriedly. He liked sesame bread, its plumpness and slight stickiness when warm, but he had not seen it being made before or realized how messy the process was. He stood watching, so absorbed that she had to tell him again to sit down.

The place where he stood, between the kitchen and the back door of the house, was covered with a thinly woven bamboo roof. There were two chairs and a table beside him, and he wondered if that was where she was instructing him to sit. Instead he sat on the floor, to avoid any possibility of causing offense. Alongside the kitchen and in the same block were three other doors, all closed and two of them bolted, the padlock on the first one hanging open in the latch. Between the two padlocked doors was a concrete trough with a water tap. Beyond the covered yard was the paved garden, with bushes and neat cultivated beds against the surrounding walls. Nearest to him was a bush he had never seen before, covered in blue flowers.

The woman looked up as he sat down. How old are you? she asked.

Fourteen, Badar said, although he was still in his thirteenth year. He was almost at the end of it and felt justified in stealing a march on fourteen.

He sat silently in the yard whose bamboo screen cut out the worst of the early afternoon sun and through which a small breeze blew, and waited. Every now and then the woman looked toward him. She was still smiling, though not at him, perhaps at something else that amused her.

He had an inkling of his situation even though nothing had been said to him. This was where he had been brought to work, probably to serve this woman. He wondered if she was Uncle Othman's wife, or maybe his daughter. She said something softly, almost in a whisper, perhaps speaking to herself. Badar sat in that space between the kitchen and the house, his bundle between his feet, and watched as the woman, now finished with her bread-making, rose from her stool and went into the kitchen itself with the plate of sesame breads, which she put on a tray under a kawa cover. There was another dish already on the tray, and when she lifted its lid, Badar smelled a bean stew and his stomach rumbled with yearning. She stood for a moment, her hands idle on the kitchen counter, and then she sighed. Perhaps the sigh escaped her unexpectedly because she glanced quickly toward Badar, but he lowered his eyes before hers could make contact. After a moment, she took the tray inside the house and came out again to fetch a bowl of rice and salad greens.

He heard a man's voice calling out cheerfully, I'm home. After some considerable time, during which he heard the sound of metal on crockery and the voice of the man who had announced his arrival, the woman came back out with the tray, now carrying dirty dishes, which she put on the table. He saw that in the meantime she had changed into another dress and taken off her headscarf. Later he discovered that the old dress and the checked headscarf tightly knotted at the back of her head were her working clothes. She pointed at the stone trough against the wall of the kitchen block.

That's where you'll do the washing up. The bucket with the soap and the scourer are behind the kitchen door. Come now, wake up, she said, smiling again. Be careful you don't break anything.

He went to the sink and began to wash the dishes while she went inside to fetch some more. There was some rice left over, which she put in a metal enamel dish, pouring over it what was left of the bean stew. She set the dish to one side on the kitchen counter. She put the rest of the sesame bread in what he thought was a cupboard but later found out was the fridge. She instructed him to stack the wet plates on the table under the bamboo screen to drain. When all this was done, she stood for a moment looking around in case she had missed anything, then pointed at the enamel basin with the rice, which she had put on the kitchen counter.

That's for you. Eat. I'll come back just now, she said, heading into the house again.

He sat back down in his spot on the floor and ate. He was very hungry. It was his first meal of the day, and the food was delicious. After he finished eating, he washed the enamel basin and sat down on the floor once more to wait for her return. She came back out soon after that and opened the first door in the kitchen block, the one with the unlocked padlock hanging from the latch. This will be your room, she said, switching on the electric light. Clean it up, but first clean the kitchen and stack the drained dishes on the counter. When the coals have cooled, you can clean the brazier and put it away over there in the corner. Make sure you lock up the kitchen. After that you can sweep the yard. You'll find the broom in your room. Now, come with me. The door at the end is the washroom for your use. There is a shower, so get yourself cleaned up after work. You'll find the key in your room.

By the time he was done, it was midafternoon. An empty clay jar stood in a corner of the room with a pair of leather sandals beside it. A bamboo basket with some cleaning rags in it stood beside the door as well as the broom he had used to sweep the yard. Inside a wooden trunk against the back wall, he found a rolled-up mat. He took it out to the yard to shake off the dust and to check for bugs and then spread it out where it would catch the sun. After that, he sat on the trunk in the room at the back of the silent house, excited despite his misery. Distant street noises reached him, and the muadhin's calls to prayer surprised him. He had forgotten how close they were to the mosque.

He was to be their servant boy, their boi, he understood that now. It was so sudden, and no one had explained. In the bundle his mother had given him before he left home, he found a vest and a pair of shorts, and some coins in a knotted rag. He was still dressed in his school clothes, a blue shirt and khaki shorts. He used the shower as instructed and returned to the room to wait, not sure what else to do.

Later he heard voices in the yard, the Mistress and the cheerful man he had heard arriving at lunchtime. The man had already gone back into the house when Badar went out to retrieve the mat. The Mistress was preparing supper. Badar did what she instructed him to do in a daze, following her into the house with a tray of food while she brought in the fruit and a jug of water. A tajwid was broadcasting on the radio in the front room, a recitation of the Koran. Badar put the tray on the side table as he was told to do and was then sent back outside, where he waited for a long time until the Mistress called him inside. The men had moved to the front room for their coffee and radio.

When he was alone on the mat in the storeroom that night, closed in and in the dark, he felt a panic cutting through his misery.

He sat up in alarm and heaved for air. He was too old for sobbing in the dark, but he could not stop. After what seemed a long time, the nausea eased, and he stretched out on the floor mat and tried to sleep. He remembered his father sitting silent and sullen on the bus, then striding in front of him past the blue mosque. He remembered his look of rage, his last words to him. His mother bent over the bananas she was peeling for lunch.

He knew she was not his mother. She had told him so herself, although he knew it already because he had a different father's name than his brothers and his sister. His name was Badar Ismail. He learned that when he started school. His brothers and sister were the children of Mohamed Rashidi, whom he thought of as his father too but knew was not. Even before he started school, he understood he was different from his brothers and sister. Perhaps he did not really understand at first but felt the difference, in the way he looked, in the way he was spoken to at times, in the chores he was required to do, in the way that he was somehow always last. When he was six years old, on the first day at school, the teacher took the register and asked each of them to stand up as she called their names so she would know them. Badar Ismail, she called, and no one stood up. She called again, Badar, are you here? Stand up. And he stood up. That was when he heard his full name for the first time.

Afterward, he asked his mother about his name.

We took you because your real mother died when you were a baby, his mother said. Kipindupindu they called it. Many people caught it, and some of them died, but we did not know what the disease was. People would feel unwell, and the next day they would be gone. It was cholera. Even today that word makes me tremble.

They told us it was because of dirty water, that was what caused it. Since then, it has been back to punish us every year, but that was the first I knew of it, that time when your mother went back to her Maker. Your mother was a relative on my mother's side, the stepdaughter of my aunt, so not a blood relation at all, his mother said, but I had known her since she was a child. Your father brought you to us. There was no one else who wanted you. There was nowhere to send you. Your real father brought you to us and then left to look for work in the port in Mombasa. That was what he said. After that, he disappeared. He was troublesome like that, a restless man. No one even knows if he is still living. Perhaps he went to sea and never came back. Perhaps he has passed away. Men are like that when they wish to please themselves. They go away and give no thought to the misery they leave to the women. He was always quarreling, that man, and even quarreled with his family, who wanted nothing to do with him after that, or with your mother or with you. Your people did not want you. What else could we do? We had no choice but to take you.

He was six years old when she first told him that story, and after that she told it to him more than once, without adding anything to it. He cried every time she told it. He felt so dirty. She tutted at him when he cried and wiped his tears with her fingers, but then later she would tell him again. We did the best we could for you, and God will reward us.

She stopped wiping his tears as he grew older and told him to bear life's burden without grumbling. That was what everyone had to do. He thought of her as his mother and could not imagine the real one, whose name he did not know and did not ask. He never thought of his real father, even though he carried his name, Ismail. He knew only the father who was not his father, and he was afraid of him. He did not look too deeply for the reason. He was just afraid. All the boys were afraid of their fathers, and he did not know if his fear was any different from theirs.

His father frowned when Badar crossed his sight and sometimes made a small evasive movement if he came too near. He scowled if Badar cried after a tumble, or if he raised his voice or sometimes even when he spoke in an ordinary way. He did not do that with the elder brothers who were not his brothers, or with his sister who was not his sister, even though she raised her voice often and muttered discontentedly at any rebuke. It was Badar who effortlessly vexed and exasperated him, and whom he often waved out of his sight. His father was not the only one he irritated, but he was the one Badar feared the most, and not because he hit him or even threatened to hit him. It was his scorning unhappy eyes. His father often sat in silence when he was at home, cross-legged on the floor in his room, sometimes with his palms on his temples as if his head was hurting.

His mother sometimes said, You are an insolent little rascal. He did not always know what he had done to be called that. More usually she scolded him, Next time I call you, you come to me and don't run off to play with your friends. Do you think I'm your servant? At other times she shouted at him, You are my burden. Then unexpectedly she stroked him and called him my heart, but he felt that he was an affliction to her. When she needed someone to run an errand, it was usually him she called for, Run down to Thabit's and buy me a tin of tomato paste. There were moments when he saw a look of distaste on her face, which made him cringe with shame.

His brother Sefu did not become irritated with him. He was tolerant with everyone and often moved away quietly when voices were raised. People sometimes said, Poor Sefu, as if there was something sad about him or something lacking. Omari, the other brother, was insolent and jumpy with everybody except his father, and even with him Badar felt that one day soon he would refuse to obey. Omari was always mocking and laughing, making out that his cruelties were just high spirits and not malice. Then there was Aysha, their sister. She was a year older than Badar and had bullied him since he could remember. A few weeks before, in front of her mother, she accused him of peeping on her when she was dressing, crossing her arms on her budding chest as if to cover herself from the memory. Despite his protests, he saw that her mother could not disbelieve her, and later he knew from his father's hard look that she must have told him about Aysha's accusation.

Lying in the silent storeroom in the dark, he wondered if that was why he'd been sent away, because of Aysha's accusations. He wondered if he would ever be permitted to return. He did not know any other place in the world but the village. He had been cast adrift by the only people he knew. Was he only able to think of the unkindness of his time with them now? There had been happy times too, with the other boys, walking to school together down the country road, playing football on the open ground, or just sitting in the shade telling stories.

He had allowed himself to think that the family's irritations with him were no worse than their irritations with one another, but he saw now that they must have disliked him very much. Had he not known that for a long time? Aysha scorned him, calling him Mchungulia, the Peep, at every opportunity, and before that she had had other names and was always sharp-tongued with him. Omari's name for him was Mkojozi, because he used to wet his mat when he was younger. He had been too frightened to go to the outhouse in the dark. In the end, they could not wait to throw him away. It was something he had feared would happen one day. He had known, had felt their dislike at times, in looks, in words that just failed to be checked. Get away from here, you little goat pellet, Omari would say, accompanying his words with a slap or a cuff on the head. He often hit Badar, sometimes deliberately waiting to ambush him with a punch to the belly and then standing grinning over him while he writhed on the floor. Omari was the first person he learned to hate. Really, he was not completely surprised that he was sent away.

The night's silence deepened with that thought running through his mind. Then, in the darkness, he saw a figure segmented like a worm, white in color with a smiling human face. He could still see it when he closed his eyes. It moved its bulbous head from side to side, its eyes dark blue and round like marbles. In all the years that this figure had come to him in the darkness, he could not be sure what that shake of the head meant. Was it commiseration or mockery? It was the earliest figure of his nightmares. It came to him always as it did on that first night in the Mistress's house, unsummoned and serving no purpose. There was something liquid about its shape, as if the segments were viscous and gelatinous. It seemed to be wriggling, about to move, but it did not move. It hovered at an indefinable distance from him, seeming near but also on the edge of an invisible horizon, looking on with that ominous smile. When it had first come, he had been too terrified to fall asleep, certain that if he did so it would slide nearer and smother him. In time he lost that terror but was still made anxious by its presence so close to him. It made him conscious of how soft his body was and how brittle his bones. He knew that if he waited long enough, it would slowly recede and eventually extinguish itself, but he was not always able to wait long enough and sometimes fell asleep in its presence, which is what happened that night. As he fell asleep, despite the anxiety about the figure in the room with him, he felt a small stir of anticipation for what the next day would bring.

## 4

Fauzia knew her mother's anxious look well. Khadija fretted about so many things, about footsteps on the stairs no one else heard, about voices in the street at night, which to her meant armed robbers, about shortages, about violence, about the brutality of the world, and Fauzia knew that she also worried about her. When Mama was in the grip of one of her panics, no amount of soothing reassurance from Fauzia could shake her out of it. Her terror sometimes infused Fauzia, and it was a struggle to resist. Only Ba could reassure her mother, and even that was not an uncomplicated task.

Mothers worry all the time, Ba said, but never in front of Mama. They see danger everywhere. It is an instinct, I expect.

Sometimes her father sat listening to Mama in her anguish, his chin in his hand, unable to say anything to reassure or placate her, unable to say the ugly words that would make her stop, unable to do anything but leave her to her sorrows.

Fauzia knew the reason her mother worried about her. She had had the falling sickness for three years in her childhood, and her mother had not lost the fear that it would one day return. She had not had an episode since she was six years old, the week before she started school, but a decade later her mother still worried. She tensed if Fauzia suddenly caught her breath or if she sighed unexpectedly, as people sometimes do.

That was one of the first signs, her mother said, heavy breathing and then dizziness and a fall. It was heartbreaking to watch you. Your eyes went up into your head. You screamed with fright, whipped your head back and forth as if you wanted to snap it off. Afterward you could not remember anything.

Fauzia hated these descriptions of her childhood illness, and when she was older, she went out of the room as soon as her mother started, covering her ears.

When she spoke that way in front of Baba, he always interrupted her. Now, Khadija, there is no need for that again. You and your worries, they are bad for you, Musa told her, chiding her, smiling to soften his words.

Her mother did not like to be interrupted in this way, even if it was done with a smile. I can't help being anxious, she would say. This is how God made me.

Very well, be anxious, there's no need to blame God, Musa would say, and sometimes that worked, and they exchanged smiles and moved on, and sometimes it did not and the exchanges continued.

It's not doing you any good, he would say. That kind of talk is no help to you or to Fauzia. Don't you see how your worries unnerve her and make her fearful? Look how well she has grown. She has been for checks, and there has been no return of her illness. She is better, can't you see? Look how well she is doing at school. She is such a clever girl. In a few years, she will begin a career where she can look after herself. It does not do any good to be anxious about her. It will make her feel an invalid.

It doesn't matter how many times you are right. I am her mother and if I want to worry, I will. I do my best to keep these things to myself. I can't help myself. I'm not strong, you know that.

It's all right, Fauzia told her mother. Just don't worry so much. I am well.

Yes, I am a worrier, her mother said. I don't know why. My mother must have been in a fright when she gave birth to me.

Fauzia discovered that one way of reassuring her mother was to tell her about what she learned at school. Khadija had not been able to spend long at school herself, and not only did she take pride in her daughter's progress, but she took pleasure in the elimu za dunia that Fauzia related to her. Seeking elimu za dunia, a knowledge of the world, was an obligation our Maker had placed on us, she said. So when Fauzia told her what she had just learned about the planets and the revolution of the earth, or something like that, Khadija listened with rapt attention, asking questions and sometimes demanding illustrations, and waiting for follow-up information next time she returned from school.

They took me out of school when my mother was ailing, she told Fauzia. It wasn't sudden. She was ailing for a long time, poor Mama. She could not eat properly, I don't know why. It got worse as time passed, until one day she could not swallow anything but the thinnest soup. The doctor at the hospital told her there was nothing he could do. There was no medicine for whatever she had. They took me out of school to look after her and Baba, who was also poorly. His knees were swollen, and it was agony for him to walk. Then later his sight failed and he had to be led everywhere. He was so frightened by his blindness. He had nightmares that he was dead and woke up weeping like a child. There was no money for help, and it was my duty. Well, I was denied, what else can I tell you? They took me out and there you are. They had several years after that before God gave them rest. Now, tell me again about that train that goes under the sea. Aren't they afraid that the water will just flood in one day?

When Fauzia learned about the digestive system of the cow, she could not wait to share the news. A cow has four stomachs, she told her mother, who frowned skeptically, but Fauzia was prepared. She had diagrams and illustrations and detailed descriptions. A cow is like a factory, she said.

Mashaalah, her mother said at the end of her daughter's presentation. No wonder they produce such mountains of dung! I don't think goats have more than one stomach, though. Look at their little pellets.

Some nights when Fauzia was a lot younger, her mother had come to her room and stretched out on the floor beside her bed, humming and singing softly while Fauzia looked on and listened. Her room had a view of the sea, and her mother thought it was the loveliest room in the house. At night Khadija shut the window but opened the shutters, because she could not bear to leave windows open in the dark, in case something came in. A bat once flew in and frightened Fauzia, and another time she heard a lemur calling nearby, and when she leaned out of the window, she saw its wet eyes glowing from the roof gutter. Khadija's terrified scream was enough to frighten the lemur away. After that she always shut the windows at night.

When the moon was full, the tide was also in, and Fauzia would hear the roar and the slap of the waves on the shore, hissing on the sand and then hitting the seawall. The shutters were open, and the glow from the sea filtered in and brightened the room. On those nights, she loved seeing her mother lying on the floor in the room, and sometimes she came down from her bed and lay beside her. Sometimes she fell asleep right there on the floor, and Khadija had to pick her up and return her to bed.

Khadija made all Fauzia's clothes as well as her own. Fauzia's best dresses were made of poplins and silks and polyester her mother selected for their pale colors and floral designs, because she thought they made her daughter look happy. She made them with ruffled sleeves, with stitched lace around the neckline and sometimes around the waistline. Fauzia's everyday dresses were unadorned pink and blue, sometimes pinafores. Her mother also made her cream or white blouses to wear with the pinafores. Her mother's own dresses were all made in the same style, ankle length, square neckline, using light green or blue material with intricate foliage or floral patterns.

Fauzia was three years old when she was diagnosed with the falling sickness, so she did not know what was said and done, except what her parents told her. The first doctor they saw had warned her parents of the possibility of recurrence. He said it was vital to avoid the shocks that could trigger an episode, as if it was Musa and Khadija who ran the world and could keep its cruelties in check.

That was what Khadija said, although not to the doctor. Do you think I can tell the world, Hey, no more shocks from you? When Khadija asked the first doctor what had caused the sickness, he said no one knew for certain. Other people were less hesitant in their opinions. Some told her it was God's will, like with madness, and nothing could be done about it but to pray. Some others said it was a sacred disease, and those who suffered from it were blessed, God's chosen. Some said it was a punishment for the sins of ancestors, or was caused by the evil eye, or by a head injury during birth. The episodes were especially bad during the rainy season, no one knew why. Khadija avoided taking Fauzia to crowded places, lest she lose control of her bladder and bowels when she fell. Fauzia did not remember that. It made her feel a great shame at first, even though her mother told her it had only ever happened at home. Fauzia knew it had not happened the last time she had an episode, the week before she started school. She had shuddered and trembled and felt dizzy, and then she had fallen on the floor. It did not last long. She had spluttered for a few seconds, and then she must have passed out. She had come to in her bed with her mother kneeling beside it. It's over, it's over, she had said.

Fauzia dreaded her first day of school, because her mother had warned her that anxiety must have brought on the attack, that she should take care because if she shamed herself, the other children would laugh at her. But later she remembered only that dread during the night, and the teacher smiling as she called out her name in class the next day. Then everything had progressed so easily that afterward she could not recall very much of those first few days. She had taken to it all so happily, it was unbelievable.

# 5.

There were times . . . there were times when Khadija wished . . . it was sinful to think like that, she knew, and Musa told her so as well. It was sinful to wish . . . she could not even complete the thought in her mind. It was sinful to wish that her daughter was other than the way God made her. It was not up to her to pick and choose what was granted to her. She could not get over the thought that it was her fault.

Fauzia was a beautiful girl, slender and clean-complexioned, taking after her father. She was a little shy as well, so she had taken something from each of them. Or maybe she was not shy, only hesitant, her head tilted to one side as she watched you. Even as a child she did that, angled her head to one side as if she was an adult listening carefully, when she was too young to be listening to anything with that kind of attention. Perhaps she was wrong, perhaps children understood things in a different way, even when it seemed we thought they understood nothing and needed everything explained to them. She had suffered from small ailments: a cough, an earache, stomach pains. She had a high temperature after vaccinations for measles and chicken pox and fell ill with typhoid when she was a baby, the ailments of childhood that cleared up in time, alhamdulillah. But when she was three years old came the sickness, the falling sickness, and it soiled and soured Khadija's life and filled every minute of it with anxiety. At times Khadija watched her daughter with dread. She tried not to let her see her watching, or if she did, she quickly wiped her frown away with a smile. She worried about Fauzia and could not get over the fear of a return of her sickness. It was not just Fauzia. She often had the feeling that something bad was waiting to happen to them. It was a feeling that lived in the back of her mind even when she was not aware of it.

What could it be that tormented her like this? She was an ungrateful woman, a silly sickly woman, that's what she was, a grumbler. She was not strong. She had not been strong enough to nurse her own baby, and the baby she gave Musa was afflicted. She had not even been able to feed her and had to give her to someone else to be nursed. Then she was not strong enough to give Musa any more children. He said it was not her fault, that she was not to think like that, but she knew it was her fault. They took the farm away in the same month she lost her first pregnancy, although by then they had been living through several weeks of terror and violence from the uprising. Two years later, she lost the next one, and it took so long for the bleeding to stop. The blood leaked out of her for weeks. Every time she thought the bleeding was over, she would feel a warm trickle down her thigh and knew it had started again. It was her fault. Her womb was not blessed, her body was not strong. It was ten years before she was pregnant again, and that was when Fauzia came. Khadija struggled with the delivery, and after that

Musa and she both said no more, and the doctor gave her the Pill. It was God's will. He who knows everything knows best.

The doctor they saw at the hospital told them there was nothing he could do for Fauzia and that they should look for a specialist. Where were they going to find a specialist in the misery of that time? In the meantime, he prescribed a pink liquid that he said would make Fauzia sleep. It certainly did not stop the panic the girl experienced, or the falls and the terrifying thrashing of her little body. In the end, Musa made inquiries of his sister Sahar and her husband, Mahmud, who lived in Mombasa, and they told him about a doctor who specialized in children's illnesses, so they took Fauzia to her, Dr. Sharifa, an Egyptian doctor. Dr. Sharifa told them there was no medicine to make the disease go away completely but that she would give them pills to help calm her when they saw the signs. Fauzia had only one episode after that, the one just before she started school, and the pills helped her then too. For a while she continued to have some tremors in the night, but then that also passed. Fauzia went back for tests every year at first, and then every two years. It was private treatment and expensive, but what could they do. At least they could stay with Musa's sister and cousin and spare themselves a little expense. Dr. Sharifa was much the best doctor in the world and the treatment worked, much the best ever, may God give her strength, but she was expensive. Musa said they could afford it, but Khadija guessed he had had to borrow money to pay for the trips to Mombasa.

Khadija watched with gratitude as Fauzia thrived. The years passed, and she watched her daughter with less anxiety and with growing hope that she had outlived the sickness, as Dr. Sharifa had said she might. Khadija worried that Fauzia would grow old unwed because of her affliction—people had long memories when it came to finding a bride—but in her teens she was radiant and blooming. She was such a serious girl, so like her father, the same stride, the same way of looking with lowered eyebrows, though Fauzia was uncertain and hopeful whereas her father often seemed past surprising, but she was still young, while he was of an age when a man is expected to be wise. He was much older than Khadija when he married her, almost twice her age, and was now in his midsixties. He was gentle in everything he did, and that, too, was something he had passed on to the girl in some measure. Khadija knew, though, that some of Musa's serenity was a form of resignation to the way life had turned out—the loss of his first wife and child, the loss of the farm—and that his air of calm was a way of stilling the nerves, a way of coping with an unpredictable world. Fauzia could not possibly have that kind of knowledge yet, but she did have a small measure of his serenity. So, no, she did not worry as she used to that the illness would return, but she still worried that others would remember it and warn men away from her. They would be afraid that the illness could be passed on, and how was she to know that it would not? No one seemed to know for sure, not even Dr. Sharifa.

She worried about everything, Musa told her. Yes, she was a worrier, she did not know why. It was part of her feebleness. Her mother must have been in a fright when she gave birth to her. Yes, she must have been. Poor Mama.

# 6.

This is the reception room, she told him on his first full morning as she showed him round the house. You start here every morning. Open the windows to air the room, get rid of the tobacco smells. That's Bwana Waziri, he smokes like an old engine. Plump the cushions on the sofa and the chairs and straighten them out. As you see, sometimes they end up on the floor, as if one of them was going to sleep there. Wipe the frames of the pictures on the wall with this duster, wipe the radio and the mirror above it, dust all the surfaces, including the kursi, she said, pointing to the reading stand. Only pick up the Koran with the cloth covering it, not with your bare hands. Then tidy up the cups and saucers and take them and the ashtray out to the kitchen.

She stopped for a moment in front of the photograph of the mosque Badar had seen the previous day when he arrived with his father. The Blue Mosque, Istanbul, she said when she noticed his interest, and after a moment she sighed. Come now, here on the left is Baba's room. You do this room next. Knock on the door like I just did in case he is in. Don't barge in. He won't usually be in first thing in the morning, but knock anyway. Make the bed like I showed you and sweep the floor. He has his own bathroom in here, and that is to be cleaned thoroughly every morning. Don't touch anything else, do you understand? Anything. On the right here is the dining room, but you know that already. Wipe everything down and sweep the floor every morning. If anything is spilled on the tiles, you get the mop and give the whole floor a clean. This is the cloakroom, you clean the toilet and the basin every day, make sure there is a dry towel on the rail and the soap dish is not crusted up or wet.

Upstairs there was a large room facing the front that was the Mistress's, its windows shuttered to keep out the morning sun. An underwater light filtered in and gave the room a stillness and composure Badar had not experienced before. At one end of the room was a large bed with a trellised headboard and a mosquito net frame. A double-doored wardrobe stood beside the bed, and a dressing table beside that. The rest of the room was furnished with a sofa and an easy chair that faced a television in one of the corners. In the other corner was a small table with a telephone on it and a vase full of the blue flowers he had seen in the garden. The room had a mingled odor of fragrance and warm skin. The Mistress stood silently beside Badar, and he wondered if she guessed how much he relished the ease and luxury of the room.

This is the guest room, she said, walking across the landing to a room whose window overlooked the garden. My son Karim stays here when he is attending the university. Across there is the bathroom, to be thoroughly cleaned every day and the floor mopped. After that you can come to the kitchen to help me. Today you can peel the fruit for lunch. Later I will show you how to serve at the table.

The dining room furniture was made of a wood Badar could not name, but he could see from its grain and luster that it was of a noble variety. The floor was tiled in blue and gray, with a shine he had never seen before. He thought it was from some kind of polish, but later found out that the tiles were of a special stone. She had to teach him everything, how to mop the tiled floors so there were no smears, to make the beds so there were no creases, to clean the bathtub and the shower so they glistened, to dust the furniture and sweep behind corners to make sure there were no spiderwebs, to set the table, and to wash the pots properly—Not greasy as you left them yesterday.

Bwana Haji, her husband as Badar now understood, came home for lunch, and they ate together: Uncle Othman, whom they called Baba, Bwana Haji, and the Mistress. He waited in the yard by the back door as instructed and went in only when the Mistress called his name. He could hear Bwana Haji talking and laughing but not what he said. When Badar was called, he went in to clear the dishes and saw that Uncle Othman had already left the table. The Mistress was on her feet, organizing the dishes for Badar to take out to the washbasin. Bwana Haji was leaning back in his chair, a toothpick in his mouth. He sat forward when Badar entered, his face quick with curiosity. He had tightly curled hair, bright brown eyes, and mobile features that Badar thought completely agreed with the cheerful voice he had overheard earlier.

Hey, young man, Bwana Haji said with a big smile, what's your name?

Badar, he said, his hands laden with soiled dishes.

Sawa, Badar, wait for me when I come home from work this afternoon, Bwana Haji said. Don't go wandering off somewhere.

Where is he going to wander off to? the Mistress said. He doesn't know anyone or anything. Can't you see how frightened he is? Let him get on with his work before he drops the dishes.

Frightened of what?

Of you for a start, I should think, the Mistress said. Booming at him like that.

Of me? Don't be silly, Bwana Haji said, laughing. No one is frightened of me. You don't know the mischief young people can get up to. Haya, Badar, wait for me, yes? Don't go to sleep and don't go wandering off anywhere. I want to show you the shop where we get our groceries.

Bwana Haji talked to him as they walked, naming the roads so he would know his way. The grocer's shop was not far, just a couple of streets away. He introduced Badar to the grocer, Fadhili, and explained that the household had an account at the shop. This young man is Badar. He works for us, he said to the grocer, who nodded and smiled. Fadhili was a short, stocky man in a dark blue shirt and saruni, clean-shaven and glossy-skinned. His smile was so broad it almost grew into a chuckle, and Badar smiled back, grateful for the smile and too naive to recognize a shopkeeper's professional good humor.

All the goods in the shop were tinned or dried. The pulses and grains were arranged in a row of boxes in front of him, rice, millet, lentils, red and white beans, making a pleasing color pattern. Tins of tomatoes and butter and sardines were on shelves behind him as were tins of jam, labeled with pictures of yellow and red fruits unfamiliar to Badar. On other shelves were packets of biscuits and tea, matches, razors, and condensed milk. A large can of kerosene was kept apart near the doorway so it would not taint the ghee, and the sugar and the flour were in tubs beside the grocer's seat. Compared to Thabit's kiosk back in Badar's village, the shop was overflowing with tempting goods.

A short distance beyond the grocery was another shop, which sold fresh produce: fruit, onions, spinach, okra. It was much smaller than Fadhili's, and its owner, Hamisi, did not have the same oily gloss of health. Flies buzzed around the bin outside the shop, nuzzling the discarded skin of mangoes and pawpaw pips. As they walked back, Bwana Haji explained that Hamisi's produce was of good quality even if his business was small and his shop untidy. For meat and fish, Bwana Haji himself went to market once a week.

At first, the Mistress wrote out a list for him to give to the grocer. After a few days, she stopped bothering with the list and just said what she wanted, and Badar went round to the shop for it—a packet of tea, a kilo of wheat flour, a tin of tomato puree, half a kilo of sugar. The shopkeeper wrote down the purchases in his book and explained that it would all be settled at the end of the month and that was that, no need for him to worry. A woman came out from the back of the shop as Fadhili was explaining this and stood silently in the doorway. Her face was angular and sharp-edged, her brow creased in a frown, and her eyes shone with a brittle light. Badar looked away from that hard-bitten gaze and asked Fadhili for a packet of cigarettes. The Mistress had given him money to buy them for her. She was a secret smoker and did not want the cigarettes put on the account. The grocer knew who the cigarettes were for and was discreet in the way he handed the packet over, cupping it in his turned-over palm and slipping it to him. Badar did not glance at the woman as he left, but he felt her eyes on him.

The Mistress followed him around for the first few days to see that he was doing his chores as she had trained him. She was patient and did not snap or chide when he was slow or made a mistake. Take your time, she said. There's no hurry. Don't be afraid. She did not say he was her servant or explain what arrangement was made with his father. She gave him instructions, and he called her Bibi and obeyed as if everything was already clear to him. She showed him how to use an electric iron and how to clean an electric oven, which was something he had never seen before. When he did well, she smiled.

Five days after he came to work at the house, Badar met Juma the gardener. It was the first day of the fasting month. Juma kept his tools in a tub in a corner of the storeroom next to where Badar slept. In there he had a hoe, a fork, a broom, a machete and shears, various pots and sacks, twists of rope and string, several watering cans, and a coil of water hose. Another corner of the storeroom was occupied by the washing machine, which Badar was also instructed to operate.

When Juma arrived for work, he took off his kanzu and kofia and folded them away carefully in the cupboard beside the washing machine. He then swapped his leather sandals for rubber ones cut from an old tire, changed into his sleeveless shirt and cutoff shorts, and selected the tools he needed to start that morning's work. He was a gnarled old man whose face was weathered with age and labor and whose arms and legs were sinewy with muscle. Badar addressed him as Mzee Juma, because it did not feel right to him to call an elderly man by his first name.

Am I your grandfather? Call me Juma, the old gardener said, frowning, his growl exaggerated in a pretense of anger. Then he smiled and held out his hand. It felt to Badar as if he was gripping untanned hide.

Juma liked to talk, and when his work was done—or sometimes even before, because the Mistress left him to his own devices and treated him with indulgence—he would sit out of sight of the house in the shade at the back of the kitchen block and roll himself a cigarette. He did that even though it was a fasting day and it was not permitted to smoke during the fast, or to eat or to drink, but Juma had stopped caring about that, he said. In this city not everybody was a Muslim, only he did not want to offend the people of the house, so he smoked out of their sight. Njoo mtoto, he said on that first morning. He patted the ground beside him and waited until Badar settled before he began.

At first it was questions.

What are you called? Juma asked brusquely.

Badar, he said.

Where is your home? he asked.

In the country, Badar said.

Where in the country?

When Badar told him the name of the nearest town to their village, Juma said, That's not far. I know that place, it's only just down the road.

Badar shook his head in disagreement but did not say anything. It felt far to him, a whole morning's ride on the bus.

Do you want to know where far is? Juma asked. I'll tell you. Far is a thousand days' walk from here. Can you count to a thousand?

Badar did not bother to answer. Of course he could count to a thousand. He was nearly fourteen. He was intrigued, though, by the idea of walking for a thousand days. He wondered if that meant walking through the nights as well.

Do you know where you would get to if you walked for a thousand days? To the other side of the world, and there is no coming back from there. Do you know anyone who has come back from the other side of the world? So there you are! Far is the dark, endless sea where ships are driven in storms and where huge fish with bulging eyes and enormous jaws live. The fish we know never go into that dark sea, or if they do then that's the end of them.

Juma stopped and looked inquiringly at Badar, who did his best to look credulous. He did not want to spoil Juma's story, but he was familiar with the world map. He was not yet sure whether Juma was trying to entertain him or himself.

Sometimes those monster fish lose their way and come to our side of the world, Juma continued. I don't expect you've ever seen one, have you?

Badar shook his head. Perhaps the old man was taking him for someone much younger, who could be frightened with stories of monsters with bulging eyes.

I didn't expect so, Juma said, relighting his roll-up, which had gone out while he was playing at monsters. How would you see such sights in the country? Do you know how far fish travel? You don't, do you? Wanahama. They don't stay in one place. They travel all over the world, except to the dark sea where they only go by mistake.

Juma paused, perhaps tiring of his own drivel, and gave Badar another long look. He grinned suddenly and slapped Badar on the thigh, then took a long draw on his cigarette before it went out again.

Have you seen those great shoals of sardines that come every year? Dagaa. They come from a long way away, hundreds of miles away. Ask them, where were you last week? They'll tell you Madagascar or Maskati. Have you asked them? You haven't seen them! It's because you're a country boy, but still you must have gone to the sea at some time. Well, you'll see them when you go up the coast, not here in the city. It was after those sardines that we came.

Where did you come from? Badar asked, when it seemed as if Juma was waiting for him to.

From over the hills there, Juma said, waving an arm behind him. Only the men and the older boys came. Oh that was a long time ago. We camped there on the beach. Every day was exciting— fishing, listening to the stories the men told, sometimes there were songs and even drumming if the neighboring people did not object. Then one year we did not go back, and my father decided to stay here and fish, and I went to work for the bwana in there.

Uncle Othman? Badar asked.

Is he your uncle? I didn't know you were related, Juma said, smiling. Yes, him in there, I've worked for him since I was about your age. He was a farmer then, a landowner. I was working on his land when the young master was born.

Bwana Haji? Badar asked.

What is this Bwana Haji? Everyone calls him Haji. Yes him, I have known that one since he was a baby. I know this family very well. And now you have come to look after them.

Juma came to work in the garden on Thursdays. There was always a moment or two on his garden day when he called Badar to sit beside him for a while and listen to one of his stories of long ago. Whenever he saw Badar sitting idly, perhaps resting between chores or just hungry and bored during the long fasting day, he waved him over and gave him a task in the garden beside him while he talked about the plants and their nurture, about the season for mangoes, about the best care for sweet potatoes, and in inspired moments he lost himself in reminiscences of his youth. Badar saw the Mistress watching them with her suppressed smile, which he had at first mistaken for disapproval. Her name was Bi Raya, he now knew, and he thought her beautiful.

Mzee wangu, she said to Juma, her voice languid and teasing, let the boy get on with his work.

He did not seem to mind that she called him Mzee. He's a clever boy, he's done all his work, Juma said to her. Now it's time for him to keep me company and learn about the world.

Are you getting tired of listening to me? Juma asked Badar.

No, he said, which was true.

Everyone gets tired of listening to me. You will too, he said, grinning.

In those weeks of the fasting month the Mistress did not rise until late in the morning, when Bwana Haji had already gone to the pharmacy and Uncle Othman was in the reception room, reading the Koran aloud. The Mistress explained to Badar that Baba read several suras of the Koran each day during Ramadhan. By the end of the month, she said, he will have read to the end of the holy book, unless the new moon is seen early. Sometimes it appears after only twenty-eight days. You are not to go into that room until after Baba has finished reading. You have plenty of other jobs to do.

Badar could hear him reading for hours on end. He was usually finished by midday, and then he went to the mosque for the Dhuhr prayers. Everyone became more holy during Ramadhan. In the afternoon, the Mistress began preparing the meal for the breaking of the fast. That was one of the many pleasures of the fasting month. You had all day to imagine the food on which you would feast after sunset, although anything felt like a feast at the end of a day of hunger. Every evening there was some combination of fried fish, parathas, beans, green bananas in coconut sauce, and always a dessert. Badar had never seen such plenty. Not all the food was consumed in the house. Some of it went to neighbors, and they in turn sent some delicacy to the house.

After their meals, people went outside and strolled the streets, or spread a mat in the clearing and played cards and talked. Young people were allowed to stay out until late, and they ran around in their energetic games without rebuke. Badar went out there too and looked, hovering at the edges of the groups he was not yet bold enough to join. Night after night it went on like that, days of hunger and heat followed by a feast and then that joyful mingling. The month passed quickly, and he grew reconciled to his new circumstances quicker than he had imagined.

At the end of the month, the house returned to its regular routine. In the morning, Bwana Haji left for work soon after breakfast, which for him was an orange peeled of both skin and pith and then sliced, half an avocado, and a slice of mango. It was Badar's job to prepare that for him. He washed that down with a cup of black tea with one spoonful of sugar. The Mistress had a slice of bread and two cups of milky tea. Uncle Othman went out to a café for his breakfast. Badar cleared the table and washed up, and then went to clean the downstairs reception room, which was the domain of Uncle Othman, Bwana Haji, and their visitors. The Mistress did not go in there except to burn sandalwood in the incense burner every few days.

Badar sensed, in a way that helpless people can, that Uncle Othman was cool toward him. He knew without being told that he was not to address him as Uncle Othman, but he never learned to address him in any other way, so could only wait to be addressed. Badar knocked on his door every day, as instructed, before going in. Uncle Othman made his own bed, and there was very little tidying to do except when the bedding needed changing. He cleaned the bathroom, rolled up Uncle Othman's prayer mat and put it away, replaced his empty water glass with a fresh one, and did not touch anything else. Then he went upstairs and made the Mistress's bed and swept and dusted everywhere, including in the guest room, which as the Mistress had explained was always to be kept ready for when her son Karim came to stay. He wiped and scrubbed the bathroom until the basin and the tub and the toilet gleamed. When that was done, he swept the yard and the front terrace, and went to the grocer's when required. He derived unexpected satisfaction from these tasks.

One gardening day Juma said to Badar, You look at that Haji, always talking and full of himself. He wasn't always like that. There was a little mischief in him at times, but he was a quiet, obedient boy, a good boy. Nothing like this yabber yabber big laughing man he is now. I saw him grow up and go away to school and then leave the farm to come and live in the city and work here. That was when he grew into the man he is now, here in the city with our lady mistress. After many years, his father became tired of farming, and when his Bibi passed away, he sold up. Maybe other things, too, had become tiresome for him. Anyway, he moved to the city and bought this house for himself and his son. My own boy was living in the city then too, an electrician, so we came to live with him, me and my lady wife. When Haji heard that we were here, he asked for me to come and look after their garden. These people are like family to me. When they need anything, they ask.

Now I want to hear from you, Juma said some days later. I want to hear everything about you and your village in the country. Who brought you here to look after these people? Was it your father?

Badar hesitated. He wanted to say that he did not have a father, only a name, and a father who was not his father, a shithead who threw him away. He wanted to say that he was not here to look after anyone, but to obey and skivvy as required. He saw in Juma's eyes that he had seen his hesitation.

First of all, tell me your father's name, Juma said. Is that all right or is it a secret? Do you mind telling me? Or tell me if he was born in the country or if he moved from the city. Is he tall or short? If you don't want to tell me, don't. Otherwise, just begin where you like.

After a moment Badar said, His name is Ismail. I don't know where he was born.

Juma leaned back slightly, his gaze fixed on Badar, pondering, then he said, Ismail? Does he have other names? Or only Ismail?

I don't know, Badar said. I only know that name.

All right, was he tall or short?

I don't know, Badar said.

Juma frowned. After a moment he looked away, and Badar involuntarily sighed with relief.

All right, tell me about the village, Juma said after a silence, turning back toward Badar and speaking lightly, smiling encouragement, moving on.

It's not even a village really, Badar said, sneering like a townsman.

Never mind about that, tell me about it, Juma said.

There is a clearing under the mango tree by the roadside with a kiosk on one side and a small mosque on the other, Badar said. That's Thabit's kiosk. The mosque is built of stone and mortar and is whitewashed every Ramadhan. It was whitewashed just before I came here. When the whitewash is new, it gleams in the dark. It's nothing as big as Msikiti Zambarau round the corner, just a small country mosque.

If it's a Muslim village, I expect it's the biggest building there, Juma said.

Yes, Badar said. The village houses are small, many of them just huts, some of them sticks plastered with mud. You can't see all of them from the road. Between the houses are the vegetable gardens and the cassava rows and fruit trees. If there is a meeting or something like that, it happens under the mango tree by the roadside. People sit there to wait for the bus to town or to sell produce to passing bus passengers or to talk or just to see if anything might pass by. They go there under the tree even when there is no reason to be there.

Did you have power? Electricity? Or is the village still in the dark ages? Juma asked.

There is power, but only near the road. Once you step away from the road it is oil lamps. When it is properly dark and the night is in, most people go inside. Then you hear noises you do not hear in the day.

What noises? Juma asked.

Rats scratching in the rafters and cats chasing them, lemurs crying and moaning. You hear mongooses squealing in the dark and mosquitoes whining all night. When it rains, the smell of latrines is everywhere.

You miss it all, don't you? Juma said, laughing at him. You tell it well, I like it. I used to live in the country, remember? I know all about that. Tell me about the man with the kiosk. What was his name?

His name is Thabit, Badar said. His kiosk is the only shop in the village. He has power there in his kiosk. There is always someone hanging around the kiosk when it's open, chatting or passing the time. Thabit does not have a lot of customers, but he always has people hanging around. He only opens at certain hours, otherwise he locks up and gets on with other things. He looks after the mosque.

All the grown-ups talk to him and he talks back to them, and he reports us to our parents if we are bad. He has sugar and a very large belly which he swings from side to side as he walks—Badar got up to demonstrate—so big that he can never walk in a hurry. We laugh at him behind his back, but no one says anything to his face. If he catches you, he knuckles you on the back of the head and then reports you to your parents. Well, that's how it was anyway.

Badar also remembered but did not tell Juma that Thabit had a Sony transistor radio that his son who worked at the city docks brought him. He had picked it out of the garbage on the cargo ship he was unloading, or so he said. No one really believed that story, that someone would throw a radio in the garbage. It was in a brown leather sleeve that was perforated around the tiny speaker, and it had a shiny folding aerial. It must have been damaged, because it could receive only the local station. Thabit did not allow anyone to touch his radio, but he was happy to put it on and let people listen to the news or the football scores, and he always tuned in to the record-request programs.

Badar remembered their house, which like the mosque was built of stone with a lime mortar rendering, so it was a solid building unlike some of the other houses in the village. He had heard his father say that he'd built it himself, but Badar did not think he meant with his own hands. It was possible, though, because he was an important man in a way Badar was not sure of, and it could be because he had unusual skills like house building. There were many things about his father he did not properly understand. He knew that his father's field was productive and that he owned a share of the kiosk. He certainly led the prayers in the mosque sometimes, and when he spoke, the other grown-ups listened to him. He was related to a holy person who was no longer living, a cousin or an uncle about whom he spoke reverently at times. It was said this relative had bequeathed some of the holiness to Badar's father, who had a way of speaking that made him sound as if he was translating from sacred words or quoting from the Koran. He spoke like that when he wanted to give weight to his opinion perhaps, but to Badar that voice sounded like a rebuke. He could not remember when he started to think of him as a shithead.

At first Badar could not always suppress memories of the village and the boys he used to play with. Sometimes he positively invited them in and then suffered heartache in the loneliness he was not yet fully accustomed to. He had only been one of the troops in the boys' group, because the bigger boys decided what they would do or believe. The small boys obeyed and ran after them like a herd.

Those early days at the Mistress's house were so full of new things, so free from rebuke, that in time he did not think of his family or the village as much as he had at first, or if he did it was to feel disgust at the abrupt way he was thrown out. He did his best to suppress any thought of his mother or his servant state, and fell on his mat tired but safe each evening. He had a washroom to himself at the end of the kitchen block, with running water and a flushing cistern. He had a room to himself with an electric light. His chores were numerous but light, and he always had enough to eat. The terror of the first nights slowly began to recede.

The Mistress kept an eye on him to make sure he did everything right, but she did not scold him when he made a mistake. She waited for him to own up and then gave him a rueful smile and sometimes tutted softly. She let him sit nearby when his most urgent chores were done, and occasionally she spoke to him, just chatting about the rise in the price of flour, or how scarce vanilla pods were this year or how she preferred to cook with charcoal but it made such a mess of the walls that she had learned to use an electric oven and now used charcoal only in the yard. Once, out of a reverie, she said, The Blue Mosque, isn't it beautiful? I hope you'll see it for real one day. I don't think I will. She spoke about these things without strain or emphasis, talking in her usual leisurely way. He listened without asking questions, and at times she paused and looked at him, learning him. In the early afternoon, after Bwana Haji had gone back to work and Uncle Othman had gone for his customary rest, she smoked a cigarette— she smoked only one a day out in the yard and afterward went upstairs to lie down and read her magazines or watch television.

Uncle Othman rarely said anything to Badar or looked directly at him. He pointed at things he wanted Badar to do: remove a used cup, close the door. If Badar was not quick enough, he snapped his fingers to hurry him, but he did not speak to him. Sometimes he made a small irritable noise like a soft hiss when Badar was nearby. He was a neat man both in appearance and in the space he occupied, which he always kept orderly. He was not a smiling man, and his scowls and bulging eyes made him look frightening. Badar thought there was a sadness in the old master's habitual silences and gloom. He was drawn to sadness and could not help noticing it in people.

Bwana Haji was quite the opposite. His voice rang through the house, and it often had a smiling undertone to it. He started talking as he stepped through the door when he came home for lunch and did not stop until it was time to return to work. He erupted in sudden laughter in the middle of his stories, and his laughter made his listeners laugh too, or at least smile. In the evening, he sat with his father in the reception room, listening to the news and talking in a loud voice. Neighbors who lived nearby joined them, drinking coffee from a thermos flask and smoking cigarettes, although Bwana Haji himself did not smoke. The visitors did not go beyond the reception room except to use the toilet in the cloakroom.

Unlike Thabit's transistor, Uncle Othman's radio received the local station as well as the Kiswahili Service broadcasts from the Kenya Broadcasting Corporation, the British Broadcasting Corporation, the Voice of America, Radio France Internationale, Radio Cairo, you name it. It was Bwana Haji's task to retune the radio as each station completed its bulletin. When the listeners were interested in an event, for example the news of the Srebrenica massacre or the assassination of Yitzhak Rabin, Bwana Haji changed from station to station to compare reports. To Badar, much of what he overheard from the radio was news from a world he had only a vague understanding of, from bits and pieces picked up at school and from rumors, and what he heard was not always comprehensible. Every so often voices were raised in debate among the listeners, and at times they became heated. Bwana Haji's voice usually rose above all the others. Badar came to recognize them and tell them apart as he sat within earshot in case he was required. Unless otherwise summoned, Badar entered the reception room only to take in a fresh thermos of coffee.

Bwana Haji was usually the first to leave and go upstairs to the room he shared with the Mistress. The visitors did not stay long after that, and when Badar looked in before he went to bed, he saw Uncle Othman sitting alone with the radio turned down. The voices murmured to him while he sat unmoving, frozen in fixed thought, his face immobile and distant as if he was listening to someone he knew well who was in the room with him.

With the Mistress, Bwana Haji was soft-spoken and restrained, not the yabber yabber big laughing man as Juma had it. If there were no visitors, they sat in the yard or the garden in the late afternoon or early evening before supper. Badar heard their murmuring conversation but he could not make out more than the odd word. Sometimes the Mistress looked round to see where Badar was before she leaned forward to say something to Bwana Haji in a lowered voice. Badar waited for their exchange of smiles as they spoke and could not help smiling too, even though he could not hear what they said to each other. After dark the mosquitoes arrived and forced them inside, and in any case Bwana Haji had to be at his station by the radio.

To Badar the Mistress was beautiful, especially when she had just risen from her afternoon rest and was dressed in a loose, thin gown that sat well on her and clung a little to parts of her body as she moved. Her hair was often uncovered and tied back, revealing the clean line of her jaw, her high cheekbones, and her dark brown eyes that seemed to glow. It was in this garment that she played her part in the fantasies he tormented himself with in his darkened room.

Bwana Haji gave him money every few days, small amounts that he passed to him when no one was around, looking away as he did so. They were not regular payments, gifts rather than wages, given casually. Sometimes Bwana Haji slapped him lightly on his shoulder when he passed him or poked him playfully in the ribs to make him jump. What is this Bwana business? Call me Haji, he said.

# 7.

Karim came back for two weeks in August to finalize his accommodation arrangements. He took a taxi from the port as agreed, and saw that the household had acquired a servant, a boy of about fifteen or so. At first, when the boy opened the door for him, Karim thought he was a relative of the house who was there on a visit. How are you? Are the people of the house inside? he asked, and the boy said, Karibu, they are inside. The boy reached for his small suitcase but Karim told him, No, no, there's no need.

His mother must have heard him arriving because she came down as Karim stood waiting in the hall. She held out her hand for him to kiss, smiling, and he took it with a big smile of his own, ducking his head toward the hand, exaggerating the gesture but not making contact.

What a nice surprise. Come upstairs, she said. Badar will make us tea.

He put his suitcase away and cleaned up, then he went to his mother's room. She was sitting on the sofa, leaning back, waiting for him, smiling as if she had last seen him only the day before. That was her way, unhurried and patient, listening when he wanted to talk but just as content to sit silently with a magazine on her lap while he read the newspaper. Strangely, her silences often made him want to speak, as they did just then. He talked about the upheavals in the government after the recent election violence, speaking with some heat about the abuses of the security forces.

It doesn't seem to end, election after election, this same chaos, he said, sitting upright and speaking with distress. The police provoke the violence. They beat people up in the streets, and when they resist or retaliate, they call it a riot and clamp down on any campaigning or other activity. That is the time when the count gets fudged and the election is stolen. That is what has happened every single time.

Karim went on talking as the boy came in with the tea tray and put it down on the table. His mother nodded at the boy with a smile. After the boy left, his mother poured the tea and then sat down again, gazing at Karim with one of her lazy smiles while he resumed talking. The price of everything has gone crazy, he said. The simplest thing costs thousands and thousands of shillings, like we are using joke money. It's impossible, as if there is no one in charge of anything. I know there are powerful countries in the world screwing us all the time, but we make it worse for ourselves with inattention and panic and incompetence. All these cruelties . . . Oh well, talking doesn't help much.

It will come, a better time will come, she said, a little surprised at his passion and eloquence. Tell me, did you visit your grandfather? Is he well?

Karim shrugged, sensing a diversion.

He seemed the same, he said. Or maybe a little older and groaning more loudly than before. You should hear him talking about the state of the country. He told me to ask you why you don't send him something. I assume he means money.

I'll send him something, she said.

After a while, when a silence fell between them, Raya asked, Do you think of your father?

Karim started with surprise and then grinned. Where did that come from?

I've been thinking about it, she said.

I used to, at times, but you were there with me, he said.

She smiled ruefully but did not speak for a moment, and when he did not continue, she said, her voice breaking a little, I wasn't there very much. I did not know any other way, I did not know how I could get away and start again.

There was also Ali, he said carefully, evasively, not wanting to say anything bruising.

He is a good brother, she said.

He could see that her eyes were glistening, that she was trying to say something to him. The truth was that he did not often think about his father, just now and then, and at those times he thought to himself, What did he do that was so bad? Why is it something we never talked about? What are you keeping from me? He never said this to her, but it came to him at times. He felt that there was something shameful being kept from him but he did not feel he could ask what it was. He would have to one day, or maybe not. He sipped his tea, and just that small act broke the spell and he began to talk again with some animation about the reports that were coming out about the fraudulent elections.

When Haji came home, he greeted Karim with raucous delight, making Raya laugh. When did you arrive? You should've told me, I would've come to collect you, Haji said.

Later that evening, Karim saw the boy helping his mother in the kitchen and then he saw him collecting the dishes after supper and washing up, and the next day sweeping the yard and cleaning the bathroom. So, a servant then, but that did not mean he was not a relative. Some households did that, sent for a poor relative to skivvy for them, but he did not expect that of his mother and Haji.

The following morning he heard Haji calling for him but he was too sleepy to reply. He got up presently and went downstairs for a cup of tea before taking a shower. The boy was in the kitchen, and as he passed Karim a mug of tea he said that his father was asking for him, to give him a lift on his way to the pharmacy.

Do you mean Haji? He is not my father, Karim said, and he saw the boy wince. He laughed to see him so jumpy. Hey, what's your name again? he asked.

Badar, the boy said.

The battle of destiny. Who gave you that name, your mother or your father? I bet it was your father. I expect he wanted you to be a hero, Karim said, and then chuckled but did not explain.

I thought you did not want a servant in the house, he said to his mother later that morning, but she shrugged and calmly changed the subject.

The university is not open yet, is it? she asked.

No, I've come for a short visit, he said. Did I not tell you? I'll be moving back on campus when term begins, and I wanted to make some arrangements.

She regarded him without speaking for a moment and then nodded. You did not tell us that, but if it is your wish, she said. We liked having you live with us.

I liked it too, he said. I liked it very much. This is my final year and I want to concentrate on my studies. The bus journeys took so long and sometimes I was late for events and classes. I can get to the library when I need to on campus. Anyway, it's already paid for, part of the scholarship. I'll come and see you often.

Of course you will, she said, but he could see that she was disappointed.

Haji was much less restrained. He remonstrated with Karim at length but managed to do so with his habitual good humor. Why do you want to waste your money so you can live like a farm animal?

It's not my money, the scholarship pays, Karim protested.

All right, it's not about money, but why live in a sweaty crowd, eating rubbish and garbage, going to the toilet in front of everyone? How can you concentrate on your work with all that noise around you? What are you up to really? Is it a woman? You are up to some mischief, aren't you? You can tell me; I won't tell your mother. Come and live here and let us feed you up. Then you'll have even more fire for your woman.

Karim just smiled, and Haji slapped him on the shoulder and poked him in the ribs. You filthy goat.

Karim wondered about the boy. Ali and Jalila did not have a servant, nor did Karim's grandparents. He was not used to servants.

The boy did not act like a servant. The servants he saw when he visited people's houses were usually silently industrious, eyes cast down on their tasks, except for the odd one who had been with the household for years and had probably raised its children. He saw quite quickly that the boy, though discreet in his manner, was somehow without diffidence. In his unobtrusive way, he looked and listened to what was going on. Karim wondered if he was simply naive and self-effacing but unable to contain his curiosity, or if he was a watcher, an eavesdropper, a future mischief-maker. Karim's mother treated the boy with surprising gentleness, he thought, as if she liked him, and why not. It made Karim curious. Haji was his usual bubbling self with the boy, teasing him and making him laugh. Only the old baba was grumpy, but he was also like that with Karim, who generally kept out of his way.

One day, looking out of the window into the garden, he saw Badar sitting in the shade with Juma the gardener beside him, both looking very comfortable and at ease with each other. Badar was leaning back against the wall, a newspaper open in both hands. From the front-page headline Karim recognized it as the one he had been reading the previous day and had thrown away in the waste-paper basket. From the way Badar glanced toward the gardener every so often, Karim guessed that he was reading it to him, or telling him about what he was reading. Juma was leaning forward, one knee drawn up, head lowered in concentration, listening. It was a picture that made him smile, youth informing the elder who probably could not read. Karim stood at the window for a few minutes, watching them. Badar turned the page over and he and Juma exchanged a smile. Then Juma looked up for a moment and saw Karim at the window. Badar turned around too, and when he saw Karim watching, he folded the newspaper and put it down on the ground, as if he had been caught in improper possession of someone else's property. Karim waved to them and stepped back, amused by the boy's sensitivity.

Badar can read, he said to his mother.

Are you surprised? He went to school, she said.

He was reading a newspaper. In English. The one I was reading yesterday. He was reading it to Juma and probably translating because I don't expect Juma understands English. How many years was Badar at school?

She was silent for a long moment, and Karim thought she looked watchful. He finished primary, she said softly, reluctantly. I don't really know. Did you hear him read? He could have been pretending.

They were sitting in her room after supper. Haji was downstairs on radio duty. Karim's mother felt around her on the sofa for the TV remote, and when she found it, she looked up and saw Karim sitting silently, waiting. She said, What is it?

Karim shook his head in puzzlement. I'm curious, he said. Why is he not at school? He looks alert and bright, and he is reading a newspaper in English. Why is he here working as your servant when I have heard you say you do not want a servant in the house?

She smiled one of her languorous smiles and said, Those detective books you read are giving you ideas. You think there is a mystery.

Well, there is a story anyway, he said, smiling too, but becoming silently tense at her familiar evasiveness.

I'll tell you one day, she said, clicking the remote to switch the TV on.

Give me a clue, he said sharply, restraining himself from taking the remote from her hand, surprised at his own persistence. He had never before tried to insist with his mother, not about something she was unwilling to talk about. He felt his lower lip tremble with suppressed irritation.

She turned back to him, her head a little to one side, regarding him for a moment. She clicked the TV off and pointed downward with the remote. It's their business, she said, and Karim understood that they were the old baba and Haji. The boy's father is a relative of theirs. He did something bad and Baba Othman threw him out. He chased him away. That boy is his son. He doesn't know he is related. They won't tell him.

Raya waited, giving him time to retreat from that moment of tension. He guessed that she had seen his lip tremble, and it probably made her think of how that had happened when he was a child, how he would become unruly in his sulks and sometimes burst into tears. Why won't they tell him? he asked, calming himself.

She said: His mother's relatives looked after him and they—she pointed downward again with the TV remote—paid a little money to help. It was Haji who gave them money, secretly, because Baba Othman did not want to know. But then the relatives did not want to keep him anymore so they brought him here.

Why did they have to make him into a servant?

It was his idea to make him a servant, Baba Othman. He could not make himself turn the boy away but he made him a servant to punish his father, I think. He hates that boy's father.

What did he do? The father, Karim asked.

I don't know. It's not your business. Don't busy yourself with other people's affairs. Sooner or later they will work it out among themselves, she said, and clicked the TV on.

## 8.

Yes, when he came to stay, Badar recognized him at once. Of course, he knew he would come sooner or later. There was the instruction always to keep the room ready to receive him, but he also had something of his mother in appearance, those melting eyes. Then there he was, a broad-shouldered, lean man of about nineteen or twenty, dressed in a checked shirt and jeans and smiling broadly. It was a friendly and obliging smile, as if he was sure of his welcome, as if he knew he was certain to please.

Badar was in the backyard when Haji came home but even from there he heard the delight with which he greeted Karim. It was then that it occurred to him that there was something alike in them. He thought that Karim was Haji's son, but found out that he was the Mistress's from a previous marriage. He is not my father, Karim told him, and Badar thought he had said something annoying or intrusive. Then he asked for his name, and when Badar told him he said, the battle of destiny, whatever that meant. Then he said that thing about his mother and his father, them wanting him to be a hero. It sounded like he was laughing at him, making fun of a servant named after a hero.

When he saw them together later that day, Badar could tell how fond Haji was of Karim, touching him, bantering with him, putting his arm around his shoulder. In Karim's manner there was something restrained, a hint of control in his cheerfulness where Haji was open and unreserved with his laughter. He was taller than Haji, but not by much, and muscular where Haji was wiry. So really, the more he saw of them the less alike they seemed.

On his first gardening morning after Karim's arrival, Juma provided some more details. The Mistress is from the islands and the young man still lives there, Juma said. Haji went all the way to Zanzibar to find her. The young man comes here to go to school and sometimes stays, then when school closes he goes back to Zanzibar. Haji treats him like a son, takes him with him everywhere when he can, showing him off. He is a good young man, he seems like that. I expect he gets on with people, clever too, a reader of books, otherwise he wouldn't be at that big school.

Juma looked at him as he said this, as if unsure he had made his case. Badar saw no reason to disagree, but he wondered if Juma was holding something back. He would wait for him to tell him in his own good time.

Karim knew people in town, and nearly every day went out on his own, sometimes not coming home until the evening. When he was not out, he stayed in his room reading, or he sat in the yard with a newspaper or talking with his mother. When they were together like that, Badar kept his distance. Sometimes Badar saw him standing by the window of his room looking out at the garden deep in thought. In the evening he sat in his mother's room watching television with her. They seemed to have a lot to say to each other although it was mostly he who did the talking. Badar could hear the low rumble of his voice while he sat downstairs within call of the reception room. If Haji was with them upstairs, their voices were lighthearted and laughter dominated. Karim did not sit in the reception room and did not have much to do with Uncle Othman except to greet him and make minimal conversation with him at mealtimes.

On the first Friday during his stay with them, Karim came down from his room just after midday, dressed in a kanzu and kofia, on his way to prayers. It was so unexpected. Badar realized that he had assumed that with his jeans and sports shirts, his university education, his English newspaper and TV, his shunning of Uncle Othman's radio crowd in the reception room, Karim would not be a praying man. When he appeared, dressed for the mosque, it was as if he was in a costume. He was smiling, pleased with himself.

Aren't you coming to the mosque? Karim asked Badar, in a voice that made clear he was joking.

Badar was too surprised to say anything. He had just finished laying the table for lunch and was about to wash and prepare the fruit. The Mistress looked up from her work and silently inspected Karim as if she was not used to the sight of him. Then Karim waved cheerfully and went away to Juma'a prayers. Badar passed by the mosque every day, maybe several times a day on his errands. *Msikiti Zambarau* said the metal scrollwork above the gate. He had taken the color of the building to be blue but everyone called it the Purple Mosque. Perhaps once the walls had been purple. He heard the muadhin calling in the heat of the day and in the darkness of night—and was always woken by the call at dawn—but he had not gone in there. He did not have decent enough clothes, and in some other way he did not feel clean.

Through the open gate he had caught a glimpse of the terrace under the large spreading trees and the water cistern for ablutions. Fronds of young palm and bougainvillea blossoms were visible above the wall. The courtyard looked cool and peaceful and he was curious about what lay beyond. Back in the village they had been required to attend for prayers every Friday, and at other times too if they were unwary enough to be around when the muadhin called. Until he was eleven, on every afternoon except Friday, he had had to attend an hour-long Koran class at the mosque before the alasiri prayers. He had a kanzu and kofia for the mosque, but his departure had been so sudden that he had not had time to pack them and had left them behind. Haji never went to the mosque and Badar had never seen the Mistress praying. Uncle Othman attended on Fridays and sometimes for the early evening prayers, otherwise he prayed in his room. He had a mat in his bedroom and at the appropriate times he interrupted whatever he was doing and went inside to say his prayers. In all the months Badar had been a servant, no one had told him to go to the mosque, so he had walked past the Msikiti Zambarau and never gone inside.

After Karim left, the Mistress said to Badar, Go if you want.

I don't have a kanzu, he said.

The Mistress looked at the shabby servant trousers he had inherited from Haji and could not suppress a smile. You are beginning to outgrow those too, she said. The next morning Haji said to Badar,

Come with me. They drove to town in Haji's van and stopped on a street at the back of the market. He was to be measured for a kanzu. The tailor's shop was a small room with a battered wooden door that must once have been painted green from the flecks that remained on its striated folded-back panels. The shop opened onto the road and was just big enough for the tailor's sewing machine, a cutting bench, and two chairs for his customers or visitors. There was enough room for Badar to step inside as instructed while Haji stood outside the doorway. The tailor expertly measured Badar with his eyes before he cut the material and held it against him to check, talking all the time with Haji about something else altogether. It'll be ready on Wednesday, he said.

There you are, Haji said cheerfully on the way back. No more excuses. I have a kofia I can give you. Next Friday you will go and say your prayers. When you accumulate sins, let it not be through our neglect.

Haji was pleased with himself and talked about their trip to the tailor at lunch and even made Uncle Othman smile or perhaps smirk, his eyes glowing briefly before they slid away. Badar wondered if it was the thought of a sinner brought back into the fold that stirred him but he guessed it was something more sinister than that, some mockery. Karim was not there for lunch but he must have been told about the kanzu because the following Friday, to the Mistress's amusement—her suppressed smile—Karim came downstairs early and waited for Badar to appear in his new kanzu and kofia. At the mosque, they performed their ablutions at the cistern in the courtyard and went through the great door into the deep calm of the carpeted prayer hall. Karim signaled for Badar to sit beside him as they listened to the sermon and then rose to pray. The sermon that day was on the virtues of forgiveness. When they rose to pray, the sala was far longer than the Juma'a prayers in the country mosque, perhaps because it was led by a proper imam who knew the long suras by heart whereas in the village whoever was pushed forward to be imam was likely to keep it short rather than embarrass himself by fumbling a verse. Afterward Badar was not sure if he was to continue beside Karim while he greeted people or if he should make his own way back to the house and to his duties. Karim turned to look for him and waved him closer, and Badar felt an unexpected protectiveness in this summons and hurried up to him.

Karim stayed for three weeks. Their visit to the mosque was midway through that time. On Saturday morning, as Haji was getting ready for his weekly trip to the market to buy meat and fish, he asked Karim to come along. The van was in the drive with the motor running when Karim called out for Badar to come as well.

I have to clean the house, Badar said.

Don't be stupid, you can do it later, Karim called out, beckoning vigorously.

Haya haya, get a move on before the fish is sold out, Haji said, adding his summons to Karim's.

The three of them sat on the front seat of the van with Badar in the middle. At the market Haji went from butcher to fishmonger to fruit seller, greeting people and being greeted back, laughing and bantering as he led Karim and Badar around. After that trip to the market, whenever Karim was on his own in the garden and Badar was nearby, he waved him over to sit with him. Badar did not approach unless he was summoned and then he sat and listened as

Karim talked. Sometimes he asked him questions. What class did you reach at school? What school did you go to? Did you like it? How did you end up working here? Did your father bring you? Badar answered as best he could, pretending not to understand when the questions were touchy. Mostly Karim talked and Badar listened. His voice often had a hint of amusement, as if he knew that what he was saying was news to Badar and that he was bound to find it absorbing, to learn something. It seemed at times like a performance for Badar, who enjoyed it and did not mind the teacherly tone. Sometimes the questions were to do with what Karim had said, as if to check that Badar had understood. Unafahamu? Do you understand? When Karim spoke to him like that, Badar felt included, felt that he was not expected to sit silently while he was lectured, although that was exactly what he did, sit silently while Karim talked.

I've just finished reading this story about a man who had everything, Karim said, holding up the book. Well, perhaps not everything, but he was from a noble family, had a good job in the government, and was respected. This was in Russia many years ago. He had a wife, not beautiful but also from a noble family and with a good portion, with whom he lived in a comfortable apartment. He had rich friends and was welcomed in what they called society, a man content with his life. Then he began to sicken. He went to see the most famous doctor in the city of Petersburg, who could not find anything wrong with him but gave him some harmless medicine to make him happy. It did no good, he became more ill with each passing day. He consulted other doctors but could not get any better. He was sure he was ill but no doctor could find out what his illness was. He lost his job, his friends deserted him because he was always moaning and groaning, his wife left him, and in the end he took to his bed and just lay there, smelling bad and waiting for the illness to finish him off. The only person who remained loyal to him was his servant. How do you think the story will end? Will he die from a disease no one can diagnose? Perhaps one he has stubbornly brought on himself? Or will the servant bring him back to health in some way? What do you think?

I don't know, Badar said.

I don't know, Karim mimicked in a childish voice. Make a guess. Show some spirit. Can't you think for yourself?

The servant looks after him and he gets better, Badar guessed, stung by Karim's mockery.

I thought you'd pick that one, Karim said, laughing. You want a happy ending. No, he dies and the servant disappears with what few valuables were still in the man's house. He robs the dead man.

He held the book up again for Badar to see, and he read the word *Tolstoy*. Sometimes Karim talked to him about something on the news or a friend he met in town and the film they went to see. Once Karim knocked on Badar's door and told him to run an errand to the pharmacy, to take a paper Haji had forgotten, and another time sent him to the baker's to buy a cake for his mother. Some mornings he sent him out for a newspaper.

One day Badar asked Karim what he meant when he mentioned the battle of destiny after asking for his name.

Badar, Karim said, reaching out to chuck him under the chin. That's the name of the first battle Muslims won. You are named after a memorable day.

As the end of the three weeks approached, Badar overheard Haji remonstrating with Karim about staying longer. Did he not see how much pleasure he brought his mother with his visit? Did he not see how much pleasure he brought to all of them? Anyone could see how much he, Karim, enjoyed living in the city. Why not stay a little longer? Karim just laughed and bantered away Haji's intensity. On the day he was leaving to return to Zanzibar, Karim gave Badar a detective novel. This is good, he said. I think you'll like it.

After Karim left, Badar was desolate and overwhelmed with loneliness. He wept silent tears in his room as if he had lost his dearest friend. He was surprised by the force of his distress and a few days later he wrote a letter to Karim that he never sent. He knew that the name Karim meant *generous*.

Karim was back in Dar es Salaam a few weeks later to begin his final year at the university but it was more than a month before he came to lunch with his mother and Haji. It was perhaps to make the point that he was his own man, living his own busy life. On the day he came, lunch was fried perch, sesame bread and yogurt, and salad greens. The Mistress pointed to the sesame bread. That's Badar's work, entirely his work. He'll be a good cook one day, she said, and smiled at Badar, who stood grinning beside her.

## 9.

She met Hawa in secondary school. They sat next to each other on the first day in the new school, not by choice or arrangement, just by chance. Take a seat, girls, the teacher said as they walked into the classroom from the assembly hall. They had not met each other before, and they sat quietly side by side on that first day, listening to the teacher's instructions, carrying out the exercises they were asked to perform, silently passing a pencil or a ruler as the need arose. After that there was no reason not to sit together for the rest of the day and for the days that followed.

On that first day, most of the girls were cowed by their new school, except for those who already knew one another and formed themselves into groups. Neither Fauzia nor Hawa knew the other girls well, so their attachment was out of need to begin with. At break they walked out of class together, after school they walked their separate ways home. It took Fauzia and Hawa a couple of days to get beyond shy smiles and hesitant questions, but they were soon more at ease together.

A little less talking there, the teacher admonished them in maths class, although it was Hawa who was doing the sibilant whispering rather than that they were talking. The exercise was how to calculate a gradient. The teacher had written on the blackboard: *The gradient is the change in height using the* y *coordinates divided by the change in width using the* x *coordinates.* She explained this with a couple of diagrams and then handed out a worksheet with four problems for the class to work on.

What is she talking about? What is a gradient? Hawa whispered urgently, which is when the teacher looked up, located the source of the whisper, and after glaring for a moment said, A little less talking there.

In the meantime Fauzia had already used the coordinates to calculate the gradient of the first problem and had drawn the diagram as the worksheet instructed. She positioned her notebook so that Hawa could see what she had done, and after a discreet check to make sure that the teacher was not looking, Hawa copied Fauzia's diagram in her own notebook. Maths, it became clear, was not one of Hawa's strengths, although she was not ready to admit defeat. After every tormenting maths class, she asked Fauzia to take her through the exercises again so she could get the hang of what she was supposed to have learned. Her strength was in English. She knew words Fauzia had never heard of and she could use them without any visible effort. Their English teacher, Maalim Saada, sometimes put a short list of words on the board and invited the class to write a sentence or two using each of them: *spontaneous, apposite, disparage, fervor.* For many of the girls the meaning of the words was sheer guesswork. The spontaneous man arrived late. He was apposite as usual. He did not bring his disparage. He remembered to wear his fervor. Even when they knew the words, they exaggerated their ignorance because it made them laugh, the teacher too, and in the end Hawa would be called to read out her sentences and all would be explained.

Her reaction to her aunt's misery was spontaneous. She said the words that were apposite to her distress. Don't let that foolish woman disparage you or make you feel small. The fervor of her reaction calmed her aunt.

Excellent, Maalim Saada said, now explain what each of those words means. Tena pole pole, don't rush.

Within a few days, Fauzia and Hawa were walking home together after school, and a few weeks later they were meeting in the afternoon and walking by the sea, sometimes on their own and sometimes in a larger group of girls. They called at each other's homes and became known to each other's mothers, and in Hawa's case to her younger brother. They were so unlike each other, and sometimes people remarked on that. Hawa was a chatterbox when she got started and Fauzia was often silent. Hawa was outgoing and robust, even assertive, where Fauzia was reticent and withdrawn, perhaps seeming timid next to her friend. Nevertheless within weeks they were inseparable.

What is that smell? Hawa whispered one morning in class.

Fauzia stiffened. Her period had started earlier that morning and she thought that was what Hawa was smelling. Her mother had told her when the bleeding started a few months ago, Sometimes you'll smell something when you're bleeding. Dab a little perfume on your wrists. That was what Fauzia had done before coming to school.

What smell? Fauzia asked.

Perfume, Hawa said. I know that perfume. You don't usually wear perfume to school.

Hawa's reputation as a talker in class was growing, and the teacher put a pause to this exchange for the time being. It was near the end of school anyway, and on their way home Hawa returned to their conversation. That perfume, I recognized it, Hawa said, smiling at her cleverness. What is it called?

I don't know. My mother buys it from someone who blends the perfume herself, Fauzia said, relieved by the direction of the conversation.

My mother must buy from the same person, Hawa said. When I smelled it earlier, it reminded me of something, I couldn't think what it was at the time. My ma puts that perfume on the kangas in her wardrobe, and there is a picture she keeps under them. It was that picture that your perfume reminded me of.

Picture of what? Fauzia asked.

I'll show you, Hawa said.

When they were at her house, Hawa showed Fauzia a studio photograph of a man standing behind a seated woman holding a baby in her arms. My auntie Yasmin and uncle Kassim, Hawa said. They lived in Tanga on the mainland. They were traveling by bus from there to Dar es Salaam when their bus had an accident, and they were killed. I was about five or so, and when my mother told me about the accident, she said they had passed away. They were no longer alive. I did not understand no longer alive then.

Hawa paused and looked at Fauzia to see if she understood this moment of not knowing. Fauzia nodded, and Hawa continued, smiling, making light, Then in Koran school I learned about another idea of death, which is that life continues with no end until the Qiyamah, the last hour, when everyone will die and then come alive again. Smell the photograph, that's the perfume. I don't remember anything about them, only what my mother tells me sometimes.

New acres opened up before Fauzia in secondary school. She read whatever came her way and was not discouraged for long by concepts or ideas that baffled her. With the ones she found difficult, she persevered with a feeling that she was engaging with an adversary, until she could understand them in exhausted relief. Getting the hang of contours on a map was one of those, and even when she thought she had grasped the concept of surface tension, the calculations baffled her. When she felt she had persevered enough to arrive at a resolution, she rewarded herself by rereading something that had given her pleasure in the past. History classes absorbed her, and what she read about what her textbook called the Age of Exploration made such an impact that she never forgot the devastation that befell so many peoples during the heedless cruelties of that age.

Her father was not a big reader but he liked to browse through his one-volume encyclopedia, or books about debates on Islamic principles and movements, about disputed forms of the maulid or the liturgy. In years gone by, he told Fauzia, these debates aired on the radio, but now there were no longer any debates, just lectures and admonitions. He also liked to read geological and geographical summaries of the earth and the universe, with diagrams and pictures and maps. His English was elementary, and the pictures and diagrams helped. Don't you find it reassuring to think that some-one knows how this world works? He whispered his blasphemy out of Mama's hearing. Mama had no doubt who it was that knew ex-actly how everything worked.

Fauzia, too, found these books engaging and relaxing, potted bi-ographies of the world, as Hawa called them. Her father bought her a battered secondhand copy of *Selections from the Shahnameh: The Epic of Kings*, and she returned to it often. She even wrote a play based on one of the episodes in the epic for her and her school fel-lows to perform, but no one else was interested, so it stayed unused in her exercise book. Her father also bought her a pocket dictionary of quotations, which she found to be unexpected fun. She loved the reputation she had as a serious student even if, as they grew older, some of the girls found something to mock in that.

She loved school and school loved her. She was aware that some of the other students struggled with the work but she was still sur-prised when they asked her to show them how to do a task that seemed uncomplicated to her. She was flattered by these requests and tried to help, but she also found that she enjoyed doing so. The teachers always expected her to know the answers to their ques-tions. Let us ask Fauzia to explain this poem to us. Now Fauzia will demonstrate how to complete this algebra problem. She was made bolder by what she learned and by her success in learning. She was rewarded with praise and responsibility, all of which she took in her stride with self-effacing modesty. She did not fully believe it was deserved.

You are a saint, Hawa said in disgust.

When they were sixteen, the two girls persuaded their parents to let them visit Hawa's aunt in Dar es Salaam during school holidays. Fauzia had not left Zanzibar since she was eight, for her last trip to Mombasa for a medical check. For Hawa it was the first trip off the island. They were to stay for two weeks with Hawa's aunt Mwana and her husband in their apartment in Kariakoo. It was to their wedding that Aunt Yasmin and Uncle Kassim and their baby were traveling when they were killed in the bus accident, Hawa explained.

Aunt Mwana met them off the ferry herself, and even in the chaos and aggression of the disembarking crowd she had no trouble recognizing them. With those eyes, she said to Hawa, you could only be your father's child. She was tall and slender, ever so slightly stooping as if she was self-conscious about her height. She was wearing gray trousers and a short-sleeved pale mauve blouse, the dress of a professional city woman. Neither of the girls had ever seen their mothers in trousers and would have been shocked to do so. To complete her city appearance, Aunt Mwana had her sunglasses perched on her head. She hugged both girls and then held them away from her for a moment, admiring them. What beautiful girls, she said.

In the short taxi ride to the apartment she chatted as if she had known them for a long time, asking for their news between pointing out landmarks. The apartment was on a side street off the busy main road, one of two above a row of shops. They entered directly into an airy and bright living room, with a cluster of sofas at one end and a dining table at the other. Four doors came off the room, three of them open. That one is your room, Aunt Mwana said. It overlooks the road and the traffic can be noisy during the day, that's why the door is shut.

The table was laid for lunch and Aunt Mwana's servant—my helper, she called her—was standing smiling by the open kitchen door, waiting to bring the food to the table. Aunt Mwana looked at Fauzia for a long moment and then tilted her chin toward the scarf that covered her head. Do you need that in the house? she asked.

Hawa had disposed of hers as soon as they boarded the ferry, folded it away in her bag, but Fauzia had not been so brave. She took it off now, embarrassed as if she had been caught doing something inappropriate. Aunt Mwana did not stop to eat with them. Zubeda will give you lunch, she said. I have to go back to work now. I only took time off to meet you at the ferry. Eat your lunch and have a rest. I'll be back after four and then you can tell me all about yourselves.

Early that evening, Aunt Mwana's husband, Saleh, took them all for a drive to the seaside where they stopped at a café for snacks. Saleh was a short, plump man with a careful, unhurried manner. He ordered more samoosas and pastries than they could eat and they had to take a lot home with them. Tomorrow we'll go to the movies, he promised.

On Sunday Aunt Mwana and Uncle Saleh took them to the country to meet another family who she said were relatives of Hawa's father. During the day the two girls went walking round the city. They had to walk only a short distance from their building to be in the city center. There were crowds of people everywhere, the main roads heavy with traffic, drivers hooting each other into a frenzy. They walked on pavements shaded by tall buildings, taller than anything they had seen at home, past clothes shops, shoe shops, furniture shops. A man stopped them in the street and asked, Where are you two beautiful girls from? And Hawa replied, We are angels on a flying visit to earth. They went into cafés for a cold drink, into bookshops and the British Council Reading Room. They sat there for hours browsing the magazines, and went back more than once during their holiday. With what was left of their pocket money they bought two magazines to take home with them. They pored over those magazines for months after their trip, and were always on the lookout for more that they could borrow from friends whose relatives traveled back and forth. Hawa read little else but those magazines for several weeks. She begged her mother to make her dresses in the styles she saw in the magazines, and she listened to British pop music on the radio whenever she could. She loved the magazines with their photographs and stories of disco parties and beautiful actors in their millionaire mansions, their limousines and airplanes and swimming pools.

When they were younger and people asked Fauzia what she wanted to do when she grew up, she said, I don't know. When they asked Hawa, she said she wanted to be rich and pretty and to travel to Switzerland.

You should read your schoolbooks, not just these magazines, Fauzia said to Hawa. We were asked to read that chapter about ocean currents for geography.

I don't have to. The teacher will tell it to us in class anyway. I'm not a book rat like you, she told Fauzia. Despite scoffing at schoolwork, Hawa was proud of her friend's bookishness. You will be a doctor one day, she said more than once, as did other people. In the world they lived in, becoming a doctor was the loftiest learned ambition, more esteemed than finance or the law, both of which were thought to require some degree of crookedness.

I don't want to be a doctor. I want to be a teacher, Fauzia said.

When Fauzia made this reply, Hawa did not bother to conceal her mockery. She did not care very much for teachers or for school-work. The main purpose of school for her was to be with her friends, and to get through her work without excessive strain or reprimand. It was not that she did not care at all. She hated being found wanting or being scolded but she was not interested enough in what she was required to know. Homework tormented her. Geometry and algebra were a nuisance. The pollination of plants was boring, especially the diagrams. Surface tension was incomprehensible. What do I care about coffee growing in Ethiopia? Or the life history of a frog? Or that horrible periodic table? Why do I need all this useless knowledge? Agriculture in the Middle Ages, honestly!

Often Hawa required that Fauzia be nearby when she had work to complete. She could not face this rubbish on her own, she said, but really Hawa just loved company and kept up a steady chatter while she worked. Every afternoon between two and four the two of them sat at a table in one or the other's house and did their home-work. Hawa grumbled about the stupidity of the work she was required to do, and Fauzia did what she could to assist her. The result was that Hawa often received good grades for her homework and then an unexpected test or examinations exposed her. The activities Hawa most enjoyed were map work and English. She could draw freehand a fairly accurate map of the world's continents and popu-late it with major cities and even a river or two, and put a star beside each of the cities she intended to travel to. She excelled in English, and not because she tried hard in it—it just came easily to her. Sometimes she spoke English all day, which was another of her antics.

Fauzia was not sure when the English-speaking started. Maybe it was the magazines in the British Council Reading Room, or it was just because she was gifted in the language, or it was to do with the tourists who were coming in increasing numbers. It was the early nineties, and the government was now fully awake to the possibility of tourist money, so foreign exchange regulations were relaxed to allow foreigners to come and spend their cash and to encourage foreign investment to provide for their comforts, and to enrich the revolutionary barons with well-earned commissions. Wherever they came from, the tourists mostly seemed to speak in English. So maybe it was the tourists that provoked Hawa, or maybe it was the films on TV, or the serials from the United States with their paved and glittering city streets and the gilded vaulted halls into which American people strode. Or maybe it was footage of crowds of half-naked dancers in low-lit clubs whose flashing teeth and flying hair made Fauzia feel as if she was a deprived creature who lived underground. It was not difficult to be seduced by all that. Some people watched those TV serials without the sound, just glorying in the spectacle of such wealth and oblivious self-confidence.

They finished secondary school when they were seventeen. Hawa was a beautiful young woman bubbling with charm and laughter. She was not interested in any more schooling and went to work for a travel agency. It was the start of her ambition to travel the world, she said. Fauzia, composed and tranquil by all appearances, made her way to college. She had become more certain about her desire to make a career in teaching. Some of her teachers suggested that she could think more ambitiously but she was calmly adamant. It was what she wanted to do, to encourage and inform, and to be with people. Her father said that teaching was a noble profession, and if it was good enough for Aristu and Ibn Sina, it was certainly good enough for Fauzia binti Musa.

Hawa was not so convinced. In an ideal world, you might be instructing intelligent, hardworking youths who are destined to become responsible citizens of the world. But you are not living in an ideal world, and the crowd you will be teaching will be like the herd that we were schooled with or something like them, rude, uninterested, bored, and uninformed. Take a look at our teachers. Do they remind you of Aristu or Ibn Sina, whoever they are?

Aristotle and Avicenna to you, Fauzia said smugly, just to needle Hawa.

Thank you, smarty-pants, Hawa said. To me our teachers do not look anything like Aristu or Ibn Sina. They look like struggling and tired aunties, coping with willful and obstinate teenagers. Welcome to your future.

Despite these differences, they remained friends and were in each other's houses several times a week, exchanging stories and gossip, although it was mostly Hawa who provided the latter. Fauzia sensed Hawa's growing sophistication in her manner, in her speech, in the stories she told her about escorting tourists to hotels, booking them on tours, hiring cars for them. It was a different world from hers. At times Hawa spoke English as if it was her only language, and that made Fauzia smile.

# 10.

At the approach of the second Idd since Badar came to the house, Haji took him to a store in town where he had him choose a shirt and trousers. Up until then he had two pairs of trousers that had once belonged to Haji, a shabby pair for work and another that he wore when he went out, and the kanzu Haji had had made for him to go to the mosque with Karim. He still had his old school uniform, but that was now too small for him. He kept it in memory of the brief time he had spent in school.

Let's get you something smart, Haji said.

It puzzled Badar that Haji should show such kindnesses to him. In his own way, Badar liked being without, he liked wearing shabby secondhand clothes because it reminded him of his lowly condition and allowed him to indulge in warming self-pity when he needed to. It nurtured his subdued feeling of grievance at the way things had turned out for him. Haji's kindness made him wonder, was he just as he seemed? A good man doing a good deed for his servant? He had caught a smiling glance now and then, and thought it well-disposed, but there was something else in it, a wonder, a reflection as if at a memory. He would have liked to have asked, Why are you smiling like that? but he dared not. Haji was always ready with a quip or a joke and it was not possible to say to him, Why are you being kind to me?

Everyone gets new clothes for Idd, Haji said on the way to town.

He bought himself a pack of socks. Haji wore shoes and socks when he went out rather than sandals. He hated the feeling of grit between his toes, he said. After the store Haji drove them to Ocean Road where they stopped at a café on the beach. It was raining hard and they sat under the café awning, watching the dark clouds coming in and the rain pitting the restless surface of the sea. Haji ordered fruit juices for them and chatted amiably with the owner as he seemed able to do with everyone they met.

You should go and see your people in the country during Idd, he said as they drove back.

Badar was guiltily silent. He had been enjoying his outing until then.

They were good to you, Haji continued after a while. Did they tell you . . . about your father? Did they tell you . . . anything? You know, like who he is? Did they tell you about him?

She told me his name is Ismail, my mother did, Badar said, not thinking it was necessary to repeat the rest of the ugliness his mother who was not his mother had told him, that he was a restless troublemaker no one wanted to know. He was on the point of asking Did you know him? but Haji yawned suddenly and said, Well, you should go and see them during Idd.

They did not speak again during the short ride home. As they approached the house they passed a group of boys Badar sometimes sat with and he waved to them. They all cheered satirically, which made Haji laugh uproariously and beep his car horn. When they reached home, Haji parked the van in the carport and on the way into the house he patted Badar on the shoulder. Inside he made Badar try on his new clothes for the Mistress to admire. She smiled benevolently and said, You look very smart.

On the day before Idd, when there were so many dishes to cook, the Mistress showed Badar how to prepare the dough for mandazi. Gradually she was expanding the range of dishes he could cook. She was a skilled and fastidious cook and did most of the work herself, often only asking Badar to slice the fruit or peel and crush the ginger or to hand her a utensil or a jar of something, but every now and then she taught him a new dish. She issued her instructions one by one as Badar carried them out: First wash your hands, then shell a handful of cardamons into a jug of warm water, measure four cups of flour into a bowl, add one cup of white sugar and mix, strain the cardamom water into a dish and add the yeast, and when nicely bubbling, add to the flour and sugar and then apply some elbow grease. Leave to rise. He did all this so precisely and successfully that she gave him another job while he was waiting for the dough to rise, which was to soften and warm the sugar for the caramel. That came out well too, and the Mistress clapped her hands in unaccustomed animation and pronounced Badar a born cook.

After lunch on the third day of Idd, as Badar was clearing away the dishes from the table, Haji said to him, When you've finished that, get your new clothes on. We're going visiting.

Uncle Othman made a small noise of disdain as he sometimes did when Badar was the subject of attention. Sometimes the small noise sounded like the beginning of a spit. He was unsure this time if it was the new clothes or the visit that Uncle Othman was scornful of. Badar presented himself a little while later and it was only when they were in the van that Haji told him they were going to see his family in the country. He had already guessed as much. It was after four when they pulled off the road into the clearing. There were people sitting under the tree and some of them stood up and began to approach when the van pulled up. Badar saw his father who was not his father among the people seated, and Thabit the kiosk-keeper among those who were approaching, swinging his bloated body from side to side as he advanced.

Haya, Haji said with a sigh, jumping out of the vehicle and heading toward the approaching men with his hand outstretched. Badar stepped down too and headed toward his father, who was now on his feet waiting for them. When Badar was near enough, his father held out his hand, and Badar took it and kissed it. Haji shook hands all round, saying Idd Mubarak every time he did so. Thabit slapped Badar on the back and said, Look at him, he's only been away a few months and see how he's grown, and wearing trousers as well. City life must suit him.

His father gestured for Haji to sit with them and said to Badar, Go and greet the people of the house. He meant Badar's mother. He meant Badar was only a boy and was not to sit with grown-up men.

There were some boys looking on from a distance, and as Badar left the group of men under the tree they approached, calling out to him, shaking hands, punching him on the arm. He was happy to see them. They walked with him to within sight of his old home, and he saw Omari sitting on a stool by the front door. The heavy rain of the season had stained the outside walls of the house with mud. Mkojozi, Omari cried out as soon as he caught sight of him. Bed wetter. Then he and the boys who had accompanied Badar laughed as if it was a very funny joke. To Badar it came as a shock. He had become unused to that name.

He went inside and the house felt darker and smaller than it had before. He greeted his mother, who was sitting on a prayer mat in her room. She was not expecting him and had not heard him enter the house. For the first few minutes she could not stop smiling as she asked question after predictable question. How are you? Are you well? Is everyone well? Are you living peacefully with your good people? How tall you're growing! Such nice clothes! He gave her the bundle of notes that Haji had given him as a gift for her. She took the money with a small, humble nod and whispered thank you twice. She slid the notes under her thigh and out of sight. After what seemed only a few minutes one of the boys called from the front door of the house to say that Badar was wanted. You must come and see us again, do you understand? his mother said.

Haji was waiting for him beside the van, Badar's father standing nearby. Then as Haji shook hands with his father, Badar saw that he passed something to him during the handshake and saw his father lower his head slightly and then put his hand in his kanzu pocket. On the way back Haji was silent at first, only smiling to himself every now and then. Badar was distracted by his own thoughts. His father's coldness was not unexpected although he would have been grateful for a smile. The shithead. Omari's taunting was a surprise but only because Badar had got out of the habit of expecting it. Another shithead. It was his mother's muted welcome that was un-

expected. There was something—he hesitated with the thought—
something submissive in her manner. It did not feel right to give
her money, as if she was needy, but that was what Haji had said
to do. Then she had taken the money with subdued gratitude as if
she was a petitioner.

After some time Haji said, Wasn't that a good thing to do? Did
you remember to give your mother what belonged to her? I expect you were very pleased to see your friends. Were you happy to
see your old village? That's country life, eh, sitting under a tree all
day long.

Badar shook his head silently. That was not how it was. Everything was difficult and everyone was poor and had to work hard.
He knew that now, after years away living with prosperous people.

I know about living in the country, I grew up there, but once the
city bug gets you, you can't live like that anymore, Haji continued.
You can't sit under a tree for hours like that. You'll feel that life is
passing you by. You'll feel lazy and worthless. What I mean to say
is I would feel like that. It would drive me out of my mind.

It was getting dark as they approached the town. After another
long silence, during which Haji yawned several times, he asked,
How old are you?

Sixteen, Badar said. He was looking forward to being seventeen.
He liked the sound of seventeen.

Ah, too young to drive, Haji said. Never mind, we can get round
that. In a couple of months we'll take out a provisional license for
you. I know someone who can help us.

# Part Two

## 11.

He wants you, Hawa said to Fauzia, leaning toward her and whispering in mock excitement. Just see the way he looked at you, the adoration in his eyes, the love in his smile.

Don't be so stupid, Fauzia said, smiling herself.

That was seconds after they had walked past Karim in the street. Karim's smile was tentative, and then he frowned as he looked away. Fauzia was not sure if she had smiled back although she had meant to. She knew who Karim was but she did not know him well, just as he knew who she was, and of course she had seen him looking at her just as he had seen her looking at him. He had even spoken to her twice. The first time was when she went to Shirini Textiles to buy material for a dress her mother was making for her and he was there ahead of her. Go ahead, he said. I'm just waiting for someone. He smiled as he spoke and made a welcoming gesture with his hand, ushering her forward, very sure of himself. The second time he spoke to her was in the street when he said hello as they passed one another and there was that assured smile again. She was certain she smiled back that time, or she may even have smiled first. This time his smile was uncertain, and she wondered if Hawa's presence had made him self-conscious.

Fauzia and Karim had seen each other before those encounters, of course. He must have been back and forth during vacations but she had not really been aware of him although she probably had seen him. She would still have been in school uniform when he first went away, a regular, skinny fifteen-year-old, withdrawn, harassed by self-doubt and by an anxious mother, in the midst of her own distractions with studies and examinations. She had not yet become curious about men in the way Hawa was from early adolescence, or maybe in her self-effacement she did not look at men, to avoid misunderstanding. She did not want to see their indifference or disdain. There were so many good reasons to take no notice of men.

There's no adventure in you, Hawa liked to tell her.

There's enough in you for both of us, Fauzia told her.

There was also her father's health to occupy Fauzia's mind and daily life. It was soon after she finished school that Ba's pains began. It was likely that he had been suffering for a while and keeping silent. That would be just like him. Then late one afternoon, on his way upstairs at the end of a day's work, he was forced to sit on a step, heaving for breath and wincing with pain. The moment passed and he continued climbing, but Mama had seen him gasping on the stairs and had heard him call in alarm. She did not allow him to make light of the event nor did he seem inclined to, and he agreed to attend the clinic of Dr. Khalid for a consultation. Under interrogation from the doctor he admitted to several months of chest pains that did not last long and went away when he rested. It's just old age, he said, but the doctor diagnosed angina and prescribed exercise—a brisk walk every day—and regular checks. He also prescribed medication to be used only when the pain did not recede of its own accord. The treatment brought him relief but for Mama it was another burden to add to the ones she already carried.

Fauzia started at the teachers college, and with it came excitement but also the adjustment to new study routines and teachers and friends. And now she had not only to help her mother but to cope with Mama's new forebodings about Ba's health. So she had enough to think about without paying too much attention to Karim's comings and goings.

Still, you could see in the way he walked the congested streets back home that he thought himself enormous, a success. He walked with his head high and his eyes roving, as if looking to be acknowledged. That was what Fauzia guessed. He had returned from the university with a First Class degree to a town, now calling itself a city, where such an achievement *was* enormous.

She herself was also in a different frame of mind. College had been good for her and had given her a new confidence. She discovered friendship and a social ease. She was popular! She turned nineteen in the final year of her studies, and was posted to a school in town for her internship. That was when she began to notice Karim, how he walked the streets, so self-assured, as if expecting a cry of recognition from someone, a soft smile ready on his face when that anticipated outcome came about. That was how he seemed to her, handsome and bursting with confidence. Of course it was possible that she was wrong, that she was too quick to judge and the appearance of self-assurance was really a mask to disguise his uncertainty.

She was not sure, and she wondered if he was aware of how his swagger looked, understated though it was, if perhaps he imagined that no one could see through his self-regard.

She did not think these thoughts with hostility or dislike but with wonderment and interest. She said his name to herself, silently, to try it out, and sometimes she saw him as she lay in bed waiting to fall asleep. She tried not to build fantasies on such meager signs but she still found pleasure in imagining how it would feel to be with him, to lie with him. She did this secretly, not even mentioning to Hawa that she was attracted to Karim, so she was surprised by Hawa's mischievous remark, as if she was found out in something she thought she had succeeded in keeping hidden. It was quite pleasing to think that Hawa was right but her predictions and forecasts were sometimes wild and playful.

The school where she was doing her teaching practice was right around the corner from the travel agency where Hawa worked, and sometimes they walked home together after work.

Everything is dead at this time of year, Hawa said, already sophisticated about the travel movements of tourists. It's all to do with school holidays in Germany and the UK and Italy. Those are our main countries, although now we are beginning to get some interest from France too. The important ones are those three. They are the ones we do business with. Nobody from Asia or the Middle East comes here for their holidays. They all go to Europe, Paris, London, Milan, and the Europeans come to us—well, some of them. Americans only come here to learn Kiswahili so they can understand how to get on with their Black people, who of course only speak English.

It's the trouble with these things, Hawa continued after a moment's reflection. They thought they could just kidnap these people, bring them from wherever in Africa, make them cut down the forests, dig up the stumps, plow the land, nurture it, nurture it with their dungs and their tears, and then when all was sweet and luscious, the gross unwanted laborers would waste away, wash into the ground, and leave the good people in peace.

Hawa, where do you get this stuff? Nurture it with their dungs and their tears!

I keep my eyes and ears open, Hawa said sternly. Which is more than you do with your novels and poems. I get this stuff from all those magazines you think are such rubbish, while you read your Victor Hugo and Rabindranath Tagore. What was that book you used to go on about? Rostum and something.

Fauzia smiled. *Shahnameh*. It's actually Jane Austen at the moment, which is probably even worse. Last week I heard something on the radio—

Oh yes, the BBC World Service, Hawa interrupted with a jeer. Some of us only tune in to serious radio stations.

About the woman who was awarded the Nobel Peace Prize, Fauzia continued, ignoring the interruption. And they read something from her book *I, Rigoberta* something. The man on the radio called her book a testimonio. I love that word, that claim to truth. Do you know, I don't think I've ever got over that chapter, that class, when we read about how the Spanish invaders tricked the Incas and then slaughtered them for centuries. Rigoberta Menchú, that's her name. She is from Guatemala, not Peru, but the radio item made me think of the class when we read about the Incas.

Anyway, you keep your eyes open and learn all about school holidays in Germany and the UK and why Americans come here, much more important.

You are turning into a sarcastic little intellectual, Hawa said, making a disdainful face.

Is that a compliment? Fauzia asked.

Why would I compliment a wimp like you? But I like this brittle fighting tone. It sparks me a little too, Fauzia wetu, Hawa said, and the two friends walked on, bickering mildly, just as Karim was walking toward them in the other direction, from the office where he had been assigned since his return from Dar es Salaam. So although they had seen each other before, and even spoken, now it was as if he had never seen her before. He made eye contact and immediately shifted his glance away, as if he had looked where he should not have looked.

It was a flash, a moment, and then it was past, only it wasn't, because something sparked in her too, and she walked past him smiling. I know him, I used to know him. Who is he?

It was then that the glances began, which Hawa had noticed and gleefully teased Fauzia about. He wants you, she insisted. You agree? And unless my eyes deceive me from reading all those magazines, I think you want him.

What kind of way is that to talk? Want what? You think I don't have any self-respect, Fauzia said.

Hawa cackled in derision. Who could ever accuse you of that? I mean it's time to get you two talking, and then, you know . . . carrying on.

The two friends laughed at the thought, because neither of them had got to that stage of experience yet. From then on there were other such encounters, and not by chance but as a slowly growing obsession. Karim frequently returned to the street where he had encountered her returning home from school, and she did not hurry away when they caught sight of each other.

## 12.

He thought about her, that is, he imagined her in his own time when she was not there, and when he should have been paying attention to other matters, to the report he had to write on the last visit to the new pump installations in their target village locations, to the expense forms for the van drivers who were not directly employed by the department and who had to be paid out of another budget. He was still new to the job, yet instead of putting his mind to arriving at a fuller grasp of issues that were vital to his future career, to making his way in the world, he found himself thinking about Fauzia. He saw her face, the way her brow ran down her profile into her lips, how her chin made such a delicate curve, how her eyes smiled. He had seen her several times in passing, but these were only distant and imperfect sightings. In his own time, he imagined her and studied her in full.

He walked the streets where he thought he might see her, and when he did, he only smiled and said hello, and sometimes he even looked away as if he did not care. He did not know how to get near her or approach her or find out about her. He understood that something was not right about this hesitancy. He did not want to make a fool of himself. He was not unattractive, he was smart, and he did not want to cheapen himself by getting things wrong. He should be more bold, he had every right to be bold. He did not know anyone who spoke about a woman in the words he wanted to speak of Fauzia. He knew songs, and stories of mythic love, but nobody he knew used such words in real life, not Ali to Jalila, not Haji to Raya. He sat in the downstairs room that Ali and Jalila still kept for him and thought about her and fell in love with her, without once having spoken meaningfully to her. He did not know how to show her how much she had enveloped his life.

Nevertheless, these two clumsy lovers did meet, and over time their smiles grew broader as they passed each other, and their glances more lingering. Sometimes they exchanged greetings if they were close enough when they passed. After several weeks of these politely admiring exchanges, from which there was no retreat once they began, they met by chance at an open-air concert during the music festival. It was the first night of the festival and the ground where the concert was held was packed with people standing shoulder to shoulder. She had gone with Hawa, who had also arranged a clandestine meeting there with her manager at the travel agency, with whom she was contemplating having an affair. Suddenly Fauzia realized that Karim was standing beside her, and seconds later Hawa was gone. He leaned closer and said something to her, which in her excitement and with the noise of the music she did not hear, but she felt their shoulders touch briefly. She glanced at him and he gave her his bright, assured smile, and she was ready to fall into his arms.

He stayed beside her for the rest of the evening, listening to the concert, then wandering around the stalls when the musicians took a break, and at the end of the two hours when the crowd dispersed, he walked her home. It was not far, and on the way he asked her if she was interested in seeing a film that was being shown at the Old Fort the following night. On their third meeting he held her hand as they sat on a bench on the promenade. It was nighttime, the streetlights were dim, and he was being discreet with his holding, so Fauzia let him hold her hand and did not whip it away in embarrassment.

After a brief silence she asked: Which office is it you work in?

Development, he said.

Is that what you studied at university? she asked, changing her grip so she could have more of his hand.

Yes, I suppose so, I studied geography and environmental studies, he said.

Oh well, that's not too far from development, she said. Environmental studies sounds like development.

He also changed his grip on her hand, then after another silence he said teasingly, This means you are my girlfriend.

Yes, Fauzia said, smiling.

They met like that for several weeks, and shared embraces and kisses. He spoke of the triumphs he had achieved at university, how it was there he began to think about the possibilities that lay ahead. Everyone in the world is talking about the environment, there's a future there. He cajoled her into a little boasting too, in a way she had not dared to speak to anyone else before except her ba and mama.

He spoke about the thoughts that troubled him, about the father he had never known except in stories his brother Ali told him, about how his mother left him behind when she went to live in Dar. How she never spoke about his father, and how her silence made him imagine shameful cruelties in their lives, and fear that somehow his mother could not love him because of that.

I used to wonder why people have children if they can't love them, he said. I still think that, but I can also see how my mother is now and I know she must have been unhappy before and needed to escape. She doesn't really talk to me, even now, and certainly not about my father. Do your parents talk to you? Maybe parents don't talk in that way, or maybe that comes later.

There isn't always the need to talk, she said. My father has never been a big talker, at least not at home, but it doesn't always feel necessary to hear him talk. Now he is ailing and I wish he would say how he feels. I think he is being brave or something like that, trying to make light of his pains. Or maybe it's to reassure my mother, who worries about him and about me and about everything. So she does plenty of talking for all of us. She hovers over me, my mother. Fauzia paused for a moment and then she made the decision. I had the falling sickness when I was a child, she told him. That's why my mother hovers over me so much. Well, that's one of the reasons, the other is she's just such a dedicated worrier.

It was the first time she mentioned the falling sickness to him. She did not know how he would take it, whether he would think she was blemished and begin to pull back. He did not speak but sat looking at her, waiting for her to continue.

Sometimes I want to get away from it all, from them, to do something unexpected, something strange, but I daren't, Fauzia said. I haven't even dared speak this desire until this minute.

You should do what you wish for, he said, his voice sharp with conviction. You should be brave.

I will do my best, she said, smiling at the stern face he made.

Even though they were discreet, their meetings were soon known to everyone, and in the end Jalila spoke to him. Are you serious about her? she asked. Otherwise you are only going to make her unhappy and will not be doing her reputation any favors. This is not the land of romantic magazines, you know. People talk.

Well, yes, I'm serious, he said, smiling with a little embarrassment. I mean, yes, I like her very much.

Do you love her? Jalila asked irritably. What do you mean you like her very much? Is she special to you?

Yes, I love her, Karim said, shouting to cover up his confusion.

Do you want me to go and speak with her mother? Jalila asked.

Hey, not so fast, Karim said, laughing. Are you talking of marriage?

So it's not serious, Jalila said, her face deadpan.

Let me think about it for a while, Karim said placatingly. Let me get used to the idea. It's a big thing, isn't it, getting married?

It's a big thing messing about with a young woman's reputation if you are not serious about her, said Jalila.

I *am* serious, Karim said. But why so fast? I'm only twenty-three. I don't have any money. Where will I find the dowry?

You said you love her, Jalila said, softening and smiling.

Of course I love her, Karim said defensively, as if refusing an accusation, reluctant to be drawn in by her mushy tone.

Then we will find a way, Jalila said, and she blew a kiss at her brother-in-law.

# 13.

Afterward, smiling with delight, Mama told Fauzia, Jalila came to make inquiries about you and whether you would look kindly on a proposal from her brother-in-law Karim. Isn't that wonderful? He wants you. That will be one worry less, Fauzia's mother said.

Fauzia did not speak for a moment, savoring the news—Karim had already asked her himself—and trying to fight down her irritation at her mother's last remark. What do you mean one worry less? Did you think no one would want me?

Well, it's just one worry less, Mama said placatingly.

You were worried because I'm twenty and not married? It's not like that anymore, Fauzia told her mother. We don't have to get married at fifteen years old lest people call us spinsters. It's not like it was in your time.

I did not get married when I was fifteen, her mother said, speaking in her wounded voice although she was not really wounded. It's true, people used to marry earlier in my time. You know very well that I was older than fifteen when I married.

Fauzia did know it very well because her mother often told her the story. She was eighteen and living in the country, looking after her parents, who were both unwell. She had been doing that since she was fourteen, when they took her out of school. There was a man her father knew, a farmer who lived nearby and who sometimes stopped at the roadside shop near their house for a coffee. She had no idea that their neighbor Musa was interested in her. When her parents told her that he had asked for her hand, it was a complete surprise. He had been married before but his wife and baby both died during childbirth. That was all she knew. Musa never talked about it, although his sister Sahar, the one who married her cousin in Mombasa, told her that the baby was stillborn. He mourned his wife and child with respect and waited for a year before asking for her. She could not leave her parents but agreed to a betrothal, and they waited for two years until her mother passed away, followed soon after by her father, before they married.

How old was Ba? Fauzia asked. She knew already, but Mama looked so happy talking about her marriage.

He was forty, a radiant and handsome forty, she said. A young woman of your age should be married.

Fauzia knew that her mother was not anxious about her age but about the falling sickness. When it comes to a marriage proposal, people have long memories and worry about whether something like that can be passed on. Her mother had been worrying about that for years, so Fauzia understood her relief at Karim's proposal, but she wished her mother had not made it so obvious. She wanted to tell her that she had told Karim about her childhood illness.

They had discussed it again when he spoke to her about marriage, and she had told him all she knew. She had asked Dr. Khalid and he said it was possible for the illness to be passed on, but now medical knowledge about it was much advanced.

Now I know everything, Karim said, so there's nothing to stand in the way of our happiness.

Fauzia suppressed the joy she felt at Karim's proposal, both because it was more decorous to do so until her father gave his approval and also so as not to appear desperate for it, not to tempt fate. Hawa was not so restrained. She drew up a balance sheet to keep Fauzia focused, as she put it.

We can agree he is handsome, she said.

Of course he's handsome, Fauzia said.

Exactly, otherwise there would be no point. I think you're about the same height, she said. You don't want a husband who is shorter than you. That would just look silly when you are walking to board a plane or going into a shop or something like that. You are quite tall so it's lucky that he is as tall as you. He has nice hair, I like the way he has it bushy. I haven't heard him speak at length but you have. Would you say that his voice is deep and clear, not one of these snufflers . . . and at the same time gentle and respectful? His eyes when he looks at you . . . I've seen them, so full of longing.

You are just making this stuff up as usual, Fauzia said.

Maybe his eyes always look like that, Hawa said, laughing at Fauzia. Karim with the longing eyes. He looks eager. His nose is good, not too fleshy, with a firm edge at the bridge, a good ledge to rest his spectacles when the time comes, and he has a strong chin. I like that he is slim and athletic-looking. He looks strong, will probably turn out to be a sturdy performer. He hasn't got a beard, which is also good. It would only hide that strong chin, and I don't think it would complement those longing eyes. What are you waiting for? He has a good government job in the Department of Something, Interior or Transport or whatever, and one day he'll be a minister. I think you should ask him to show you the apartment where you'll make your home. You can't allow yourself to be taken in by those longing eyes. I'm not saying he would want to deceive you, far from it. He just might be too eager to hold off for proper arrangements.

We'll wait and see what Ba says, Fauzia said.

If I were you, I would not leave it all in your ba's hands, Hawa whispered, lowering her voice to speak these rebellious words. I would find out a few things for myself and make my own decisions.

What makes you think I haven't already? Fauzia said. Don't be so doubting.

For a couple of days there was some back-and-forth going on out of earshot. Her mother was all tremulous smiles, so Fauzia guessed that Ba's inquiries were proving satisfactory. After those few days they spoke to her together, Mama and Ba, telling her about the proposal and saying that they were willing if she was.

Does his mother know? We have not heard from her, Mama said. I am not sure if she has given her consent. I would like to know if she has been consulted. It really should have been she who spoke to us. I would not like it if my child was to marry without consulting me.

You worry about everything, Ba said. I know it would be more seemly if she had given her blessing but it's his business, not ours, to see to that. I am sure he has spoken to her and received her blessing.

To Fauzia her father said, You must satisfy yourself that you wish to have him as a husband. You must feel proud of yourself, of what you have achieved and of what you are capable of. I want you to be sure that this is what you wish. If it is, we'll invite him to come and meet us here at home. I have asked about his family, but you must meet him and talk to him and then he'll be able to tell you more about himself. He lives with his brother's family and he has a good job. People speak well of him. We are content if you are.

It was clear that Ba was not aware of their meetings, and Fauzia did not tell him she knew about his family. She wished he would come, so that she could be near him again and see how that made her feel. She did not want to seem malleable and obedient, without an opinion or volition, just another mute daughter laid out for deflowering. It was to herself that she did not want to seem like this, not that she thought her parents were forcing him on her. She knew what their preference would be, to settle the matter and consign her to the bliss of earthly security, but she also knew that they would want that only if she were agreeable and convinced that the marriage would bring her happiness, making Fauzia the convinced one, not her parents. There was no way of guaranteeing that for anyone, and that was a very good reason to approach her future a little cautiously, but she had been with Karim long enough to know he was what she longed for.

A day was fixed for an afternoon visit and invitations were sent out to Karim and to Jalila, the emissary of the proposal. Ba excused himself without further ado: too much work at the shop and he did not want to intimidate the young man with his age. Karim wore a light blue shirt and dark trousers, looking unostentatious and correct for the occasion. His sister-in-law, who was only a little older than him but who outranked him by a mile in the circumstances, being already a wife and a mother and now visibly pregnant with her second, had probably advised him on the appropriate tone to strike on this first meeting. When they entered the home, she gently pushed Karim ahead and then followed behind. Fauzia was already in the sitting room, seated on the sofa. Karim was ushered toward the armchair, Ba's throne, while his sister-in-law and Fauzia's mama shared the other sofa. Karim kept his eyes slightly lowered and in the direction of the matrons' sofa. Fauzia had to suppress a smile at the drama of it all.

The usual greetings followed between Mama and Jalila, while Fauzia and Karim remained silent. Are you well? Is everyone at home well? Are the children well? Oh, it is only one, but soon there will be another, alhamdulillah. I heard that your neighbor Bi Nuru is unwell. Is she better now? She has been unwell for so long, poor thing. Do you know if her sons have been told? Will they be able to come? Have they fixed the water problems in your area? Are they doing anything about that? You have been carrying buckets of water to the kitchen upstairs! You shouldn't be doing that in your condition when you have two strong men in your house. Oh I'm glad to hear it was not you carrying them, of course not. What can you say? Nobody cares if we live in the dirt like beasts.

These exchanges, mostly flowing from Mama, who was the more nervous of the two women, went on for a few minutes. Then Mama glanced at Fauzia as she rose, an excited spark in her eyes. She suggested to Jalila that they go fetch the tea from the kitchen. Karim glanced at Fauzia and a sigh escaped him. He started in surprise. He had not meant to sigh like that. Fauzia laughed and so did he.

They can go on like that all day, she said.

Yes, he said.

A brief silence fell between them. They exchanged glances that said they knew that their time alone was likely to be short. A few seconds later, Karim looked Fauzia fully in the face and she returned his gaze.

Will you? he asked, with a knowing smile, confident that she would.

If I will . . . she said, and then waited for a long moment before continuing. You know I will. If I will . . . Where are we going to live? You live with your brother at the moment. Where are *we* going to live?

*We* will rent a flat. We'll look for one together, he said. If you want . . . if you will.

She nodded. My mama wants to know if your mother has given her blessing.

He nodded. I don't think she really cares. I spoke to her on the phone and told her about coming today. You know she lives in Dar es Salaam. I asked her if she wanted to be here and she said it was our business and not hers. She's like that, she says she does not want to interfere. That's how she likes to see herself, but I think she does not really care. She is content with her life. So I suppose you can tell your mama that she has given her blessing. In a way. Has your mother given her blessing?

Yes, Fauzia said. She can't wait to have everything tied up.

Karim rose from his throne and went to the sofa. He sat beside

Fauzia and leaned forward to kiss her, but just then they heard Mama's voice approaching and he hurried back to his chair. They shared a smile over their narrow escape and that was more or less that.

To her mother's dismay and her father's skepticism Fauzia refused to allow a dowry to be set. She was not being purchased, she said, but was agreeing freely to a marriage. She knew that Karim would not have the money for a dowry and would be forced to rely on relatives, his brother Ali, who probably did not have anything much either, or more likely his mother in Dar es Salaam. She said no dowry to reduce expectations, to say she did not want anyone to go to needless expense, and to dampen the obligation her parents might feel to stage extravagant celebrations in return. Her mother feared it might seem arrogant to abandon the tradition, as if they were saying they were so wealthy they did not need the money, or that the groom's money was somehow unacceptable. It was, after all, meant as a safety net for her in case of any misfortune. It was nonsense to say it was to purchase her.

Fauzia did not expect any misfortune and she did not think her father would fear that people would say they were too wealthy to accept a dowry. Her father's hardware shop provided them with a living but not much else. No one could mistake him for being wealthy. Nonetheless, her father did not think it prudent to refuse the dowry, and if it was meant as a gesture of independence, then it was impulsive and perhaps a little high-handed. He knew these were different times, he said, but did they have to give up everything, their customs, their ways? It was on the tip of Fauzia's tongue to say, Why don't you keep the money then, as so many fathers do?

but she stopped herself in good time. She knew it would hurt him if she spoke that way, which was not at all how she spoke to him usually. Instead she kept silent and refused to be drawn into a discussion. Her father made an early retreat but it took some time for her mother to give up, and even then she was not entirely reconciled and could not conceal her disappointment when someone asked about the size of the dowry as it was customary to do.

Fauzia does not want a dowry, she told whoever asked. She does not want any extravagance. She says it is not what modern women do. We are just old-fashioned enough to want a celebration for our daughter's wedding.

Fauzia had not said anything about modern women but she kept the peace.

The refusal of dowry was a relief to Karim, who indeed would have had to borrow from his brother to be able to pay it. His mother had already volunteered a contribution from Haji, but Fauzia's decision made all that unnecessary. Instead Karim used the gift from Haji and his mother to commission a set of bangles, a pendant and chain, and a set of earrings from a goldsmith in Dar es Salaam, but he kept this gallant act to himself and his mother, whom he had recruited for her expertise in matters of jewelry. When it was ready, he went to Dar es Salaam to collect it, but he did not say anything about it to Ali or Jalila. He feared they might think him sentimental or foolish for buying it when he had so fortunately been relieved of the burden of a dowry.

While he was in Dar es Salaam, he stayed overnight with his mother and Haji. Karim had to put up with the usual teasing from Haji about the right food to build up his vitality for the big day, and had to refuse repeated offers of money to help him set up their new home.

We haven't even found a flat yet, Karim protested.

Find one and let me know how I can help, Haji said. There's no need to be so proud.

The flat Fauzia and Karim found in the end was two large rooms on the top floor of a tall old house near her school. It had its own bathroom. The last flight of stairs was narrow and the wooden floors were uneven in places, but the rooms were airy and it was all they could afford. Haji helped them with the deposit. They made haste to secure it before anyone could talk them out of it, promising themselves it would not be their home for long.

It was a small wedding, just as the bride and groom wanted it. It did not suit Fauzia's mother, who had insisted on a biriani banquet for the guests, whatever else was done. It does not look good, she said to Musa. It makes us seem like misers.

Musa rented a house in the country for the day. He hired passenger vans to take the wedding guests to the house by the sea, and paid for musicians to play for them. Another van brought the biriani specially prepared by a famous restaurant and its accompanying salads and delicacies, as well as the staff and equipment needed to serve the food. Mats and rugs were spread throughout the downstairs of the house and on the wide veranda overlooking the sea. Rose water was sprinkled on outstretched hands and incense burners gently perfumed the rooms. There were only a few guests, as the bride and groom preferred, but the richness of the food and the elegance of the service mollified Fauzia's mother to some extent.

Musa suddenly fell ill a few days after the wedding. It happened in the mosque, as he went down to do the sujud in the third rakaat of the Maghrib prayer. He lowered himself to his knees and groaned as he bent forward to touch the floor with his forehead, subhana rabiyala' ala, and then stayed like that as the rest of the congregation sat up for the attahiyat. Then slowly he fell sideways onto the lap of the man praying beside him, who broke his prayer and with a gasp of surprise wrapped his arms around him to prevent his head from hitting the floor. Not everyone in the congregation noticed the collapse, as prayer is a moment of deep communion to the exclusion of everything else, but those who did immediately said assalam alaykum wa rahmatu llah and hurried to Musa's aid.

He regained consciousness after a few minutes but was very dazed. As the alarm subsided, someone left to fetch a car and someone else who knew Musa accompanied him to the hospital and stayed with him until he was seen by a doctor, who immediately admitted him for observation. In the meantime, the driver of the car went to Musa's house to tell Khadija and take her to the hospital. He was already in the ward when she arrived, hitched to an intravenous drip and still very confused. He kept repeating, I don't know what happened, I don't know what happened. Khadija fetched a chair and sat silently beside his bed. She took his hand in both of hers and stroked it without saying a word.

He was sent home after two days, at the insistence of Dr. Khalid, whose clinic he had previously attended. The hospital was not a safe place to be if it was not necessary. It was overcrowded and patients were in danger of sharing their infections. Dr. Khalid read the notes and spoke to the duty doctor. Musa had suffered a stroke, but it was likely from the test results and his relative alertness that it was a mild one. Dr. Khalid was happier for him to go home and be cared for there, much safer. Perhaps Musa was overwrought by the events of the wedding but maybe not. More likely it was a result of his longtime condition, an event waiting to happen. Now he would be put on a regime of treatment to keep him safe, or as safe as possible. It's all in His hands, Khadija added.

To her relief, Musa was not helpless. He could walk slowly, his voice was slurred but he could talk, he could eat small amounts and keep his food down. He could keep himself clean. He did all these things with difficulty, and sometimes she helped him just to save him the trouble. Dr. Khalid said that all these activities were likely to improve with time. To Khadija's alarm, Musa wanted to get back to the shop after a few days at home, but Dr. Khalid said no, not yet, let your assistant look after the shop for a while, and Musa had no choice but to obey.

*14.*

He had not been able to go to Karim's wedding because he had to stay behind to look after Uncle Othman. The Mistress and Haji went away for the night and returned on the early flight the next day. Badar imagined that the bride, whom he had not yet met, would be all smiles and glowing joy, as would be the groom, and that they would both look wonderful. He was sure, though, that his Mistress would easily be the most beautiful and glamorous woman there.

A couple of years after that wedding, the Mistress and Haji went to another one, this time in Arusha, up in the mountains. Again they left Badar behind to look after the house and Uncle Othman, but this time they were going to be away for several days. They left in a taxi to the airport, and after he saw them off Badar went to prepare lunch for Uncle Othman.

In recent months Uncle Othman had visibly declined. He had grown more morose and withdrawn, hardly leaving the house except for a walk before the maghrib prayer at the mosque. He barely spoke to anyone, not even to Haji or the Mistress. Badar was not sure what had happened to make him withdraw in this way, even from his beloved radio. More and more he seemed half-asleep or in a daze. When Juma came on his gardening days, he sometimes managed to persuade the old man to come out in the garden for a while. It seemed that he was the only one who could reach him.

Badar was by now quite capable of looking after the house and had few qualms about being left to look after the old man. In some ways, the new silences were an improvement, preferable to the tetchy summonses and the despising snorts, though Badar still did his best to keep out of his way.

Badar had become a competent cook working alongside the Mistress, sometimes taking over completely for her. He cooked the everyday dishes for the house, rice and pasta and stew and fish and sesame bread, though she still made the tricky ones. She cooked a variety of other breads, paratha, rice bread, and even the tinned loaf called boflo. When inspired or preparing a special meal, she made sweet dumplings, farne, fruitcake, fish katlesi, sambusa. When necessary or if she was in the mood, she could produce a proper feast.

Uncle Othman's tastes in food were uncomplicated, though, and well within Badar's expertise. He did not eat meat, disliked fried food, and did not have anything to do with any kind of bread. For lunch he had a small serving of rice and perhaps a bean stew or a filet of perch poached with a stem of ginger and thin slices of green mango. Or for a change he had his rice with a sliver of dried shark singed in a pan or with a simple tomato sauce. His lunch was always accompanied by a salad of bitter radish leaves. For supper he had a slice of melon or boiled squash sprinkled with ground almonds, or braised plantain in a thin coconut sauce, accompanied by a glass of water. Sometimes he did not bother with supper.

He no longer took his breakfast at the café with his friends. He had no breakfast at all, just a cup of coffee. The radio was no longer switched on in the evenings and there were no gatherings of neighbors and friends to debate the state of the world, just Haji talking while Uncle Othman sat in his deep silence, his son's voice swirling around him. It seemed that Haji did not take any notice and carried on talking. Sometimes the old man nodded or smiled. His smile, when it came, was often brief and unexpected. After a while he would begin to doze and Haji would hustle him to bed.

Badar always dropped his eyes in front of Uncle Othman or looked over his shoulder. He had learned to do that early on when he accidentally made eye contact and saw what looked like loathing in Uncle Othman's eyes. He never addressed him except in reply, and then he spoke in complete sentences. It's all right, Badar thought to himself, treat me like cow dung, I'm your slave. This was as far as his rebellion went. That was how, over the years, he had become used to Uncle Othman, by diminishing his own presence before him to one of mute servitude and deference. The soft tissue of his body learned to absorb the abrupt summonses and dismissals and the snorts of contempt.

In the absence of Haji and the Mistress, Uncle Othman took his meals in the reception room. While he was having his breakfast coffee, Badar cleaned his bedroom. Uncle Othman spent the morning in the reception room, dozing or staring into space. He returned to his room in the afternoon and dozed some more until evening, when he went for a slow stroll on his way to the mosque. Badar stayed within earshot while the old man was in the house and made sure that the thermos of coffee was full and by his side. He was probably drinking more coffee than was good for him.

So in the first few days while the Mistress and Haji were away to the wedding in Arusha, Badar did his chores in the usual way. He cleaned the old master's room as he had been doing for years. He washed the clothes Uncle Othman put out for the laundry, which in recent times included soiled bedding because he sometimes wet himself in his sleep. He did not say anything about the bedsheets to Badar, who took them away and washed them. The first time it had happened, Badar told the Mistress, and later that morning Haji brought home a waterproof cover for the mattress. Uncle Othman did not say anything about that either. Badar prepared the old master's lunch and then withdrew to his other duties, or in the afternoon he went out to meet with some of the young people he had become friendly with, or he stayed in his room with one of the detective novels he had become fond of since Karim had introduced them to him some years before. Later he prepared a supper tray for the old master, and when the time was right, he left him to his silence and went to his own room in the yard. Uncle Othman never forgot to lock and bolt the back door.

Badar had struggled to think of him as *Uncle* Othman even though he knew the title was only a courtesy. Everyone was uncle something or other, after all, and it did not mean how it sounded but Badar just could not think of him in that way. In his mind he called him Babu Mzee, the Old Man. He felt a menace in Uncle Othman's dislike and did not know why he was so stern with him. He wondered if it was because of a sorrow that was nothing to do with him. Once he had this thought he could not rid himself of it. He became convinced that the silent aura the Babu Mzee carried with him was tense with discontent and maybe grief.

When Juma came on his gardening day and learned that the Mistress and Haji were away, he glanced at Badar but did not say anything immediately, just gave him a look of curiosity or perhaps slight concern.

How are you managing? Juma asked, tilting his chin toward the house, by which Badar understood that he was referring to Uncle Othman.

I manage all right, Badar said, making light of the question. He doesn't take any notice of me. I do what he wants and he doesn't know I'm there.

Juma smiled sympathetically. He knows you're there, all right, he said.

A little while afterward, Juma went into the house to greet the old master, as he always did. Later in the morning when Juma decided it was time for a rest, he called Badar over to sit with him in the shade of the garden wall while he had a smoke. He is always fierce with you, he said to Badar, nodding toward the house.

Uncle Othman? Badar asked. He has been like that all along, as you know. Sharp words, abrupt, he doesn't speak to me otherwise. I don't know why he is like that, maybe he is just an angry man. Maybe he is like that with all people who work for him, except you. You have known him for a long time, you must know.

Juma was pensive and Badar left him to his thoughts. After a while Juma said: I started working for him when I was as young as you.

He was silent again after that, sorting through his memories. Then he said: He was quite young then, not yet thirty, just married and starting out on his farm. It was land his father bought for him. His father was wealthy, not as wealthy as some of these Indian lords but rich enough. On the road to Morogoro, that's where the land was, a little way after Chalinze. My father sent me to him because someone he knew worked there. He did mixed farming and he was eager and young and had many plans, always frowning, worrying about money, I think. That's what happens when people have money, they worry about it all the time. He was a small man, just as you see him now, but he was full of energy. All day long, going from one thing to another, dressed in shorts and boots like one of those English government people we used to have in those days, dashing from this to that as if nothing could wait. He became impatient if he thought you were working too slowly, yes he was abrupt if you were slow. He had cattle and raised chickens and sold eggs and grew pineapples and did market gardening. It was the chicken farming that brought in the money, the eggs especially but also the meat. I did not have anything to do with that stinking work. I was in the market garden, tomatoes, cucumbers, aubergines, spinach. When I started there, the crew leader must have thought that was the most suitable work for me because I was young but then I stayed in that line all my life. Every morning trucks filled up with eggs and chickens and vegetables and fruit and headed for Dar es Salaam. Every morning before it was even fully light! No, he was not very irritable then, no more than all these other people who want to make money quickly. I'm not saying he was a laughing cheerful kind of man, no, but he was not grumpy.

What happened then— Badar began to ask, but Juma cut him off.

Don't be in such a hurry, he said. Many things happened. That's how it is in life, many things happen. Well, first the young bwana came, our Haji. I remember when he was born. They had to wait for him. I was there for about nine or ten years before he came. The bwana and his wife Bibiye went on the pilgrimage, and when they came back, she had the son, so they called him Haji. He was a happy man then, yes. It was coming toward the independence years and everything was exciting, so many opportunities, so many plans. Yes, he was happy then, not a big laughing man like Haji is now, but he was happy. He laughed then, not that often, but he laughed.

Did Haji have any brothers? Badar asked as Juma seemed lost in the past. He had often wanted to ask that because the old man seemed to be Haji's only relative.

No, he had a sister, Juma said. She passed away when she was a little girl. It was a fever; I don't know what it was exactly. We just say it was God's will, you can't argue with that. It was about then, maybe, that Bwana Othman began to feel the burden of life, when his little girl had the fever and passed away. Well, whether it was then or not, the fever took the little girl, Saada was her name, may God have mercy on her soul. The fever also struck her mother but she recovered, or I should say she lived but she was not well. She tried hard, Bibiye, she always did. She was the better half, we all liked to say.

Juma was silent for so long that Badar began to think that he would have to wait another day for the next installment, but then he started again.

Those two, Bwana Othman and Bibiye, when you saw them

together you could see their love for each other, you could see it, but you could also see the sadness that had come into her life. She did not have the strength anymore. Everything was a struggle. It was the woman who went to the house to care for her who told us about how she was because the master said nothing even if you asked after our Bibiye's health. He just said, She's getting better. When she did come out again, she suddenly seemed so much older. She lingered for many years, maybe seven, but her health was gone, it was that fever, or maybe it was her spirit, her heart was broken. It slowed down the old master too; her illness. He was still working hard, organizing and instructing, but all that dashing around was now accompanied by frowns and a bad temper.

Juma's gaze was wandering round the garden as if he was casually looking for something, then he looked at Badar as if to see how he was taking in his words. Badar still did not speak. He was used to listening when he was with Juma. Then Juma said: In the end he sold the farm. After Bibiye passed away he sold the farm and moved here with his son.

Why did he do that? Badar asked.

Juma shrugged. You should ask Haji, he said. Maybe he was tired, maybe he had other reasons. Ask Haji, he'll be able to tell you.

Why would he tell me? Badar asked.

Just ask him, Juma said. He knows.

Do you know? Badar asked, intrigued by Juma's reticence. Usually he liked nothing better than to provide all sorts of gossipy details.

Juma shrugged. Ask him, he said again.

They sat like that for a while, leaning against the outhouse wall and evading eye contact. Badar felt that Juma was trying to tell him something, but he didn't know what.

Finally Juma said, Anyway that is how it was, and that was what Bwana was like when he was younger, but then life changed him and made him bitter like he is now. It has eased him to live with his son here in this house. He is grumpy but he is no longer hurrying after work and money, which is good for the human soul.

I can see that, said Badar. He is often silent, even with Haji and the Mistress, but he is not so irritable with them as he is with me. I think he just doesn't like me.

Yes, but that's your luck, Juma said. It's not your fault.

Badar pondered that for a moment. Do you mean you know why he dislikes me? he asked.

Juma grinned delightedly. I didn't say he dislikes you, he said. You said that.

Badar pondered some more, going over what Juma had told him, trying to find where and on what his recollection snagged, to guess at what game he was playing with him, what it was that he was trying to tell him. Why do you say it's my luck that he dislikes me?

I mean that you have not done anything to deserve it. You look like someone he dislikes, Juma said, still grinning.

After a moment's silence, Badar asked a question that had been lurking in his mind, formed from the things Juma had told him in the past: Did you know my father?

Juma chuckled and then sighed. Yes, I knew your father, and so did he, the bwana in there. Leave those worrying people to themselves. Keep your eyes open and your mouth shut. This is not a good place for you to be.

Badar was still not sure what Juma was telling him, what he was warning him against. He sat for a while longer, leaning against the garden wall, his imagination fixed on the sullen figure of the old man.

Will you not tell me what you mean? Badar asked.

Ask Haji, Juma said stubbornly. He will tell you.

He should speak to Haji when he returned. Or perhaps it might be better to let everything be buried by silence, to cut his losses and keep his mouth shut. Later in the evening when he was in the dark in his room in the yard, he thought about his father, his real, absent father, and fantasized his return. For some reason, with Haji and the Mistress away, he felt the presence of his father more strongly than usual. What had happened to him? It was better not to ask. His mother who was not his mother had made it clear he was a trouble-maker. He did not want to hear that again.

The following Tuesday, Badar served Uncle Othman a lunch of rice and a filet of perch the way he liked it, poached with green mango slices. When Badar came to clear the table, he found that Uncle Othman had barely touched the food, although usually it was one of the meals he relished. Badar cleared up in the kitchen and retreated to his room. Late in the afternoon he heard Uncle Othman leaving the house for his slow, obstinate stroll. He came home after evening prayers, and Badar took him his supper tray of plantain in coconut sauce in the sitting room. He noticed as he passed that the front door was already bolted, when usually it was simply left closed until the old man was ready to go to bed. He guessed it was a new quirk, or perhaps an anxiety because he was alone in the house. Badar put the tray on the side table without a word, waited a moment for any further instruction, and then retreated. Even with downcast eyes he had sensed a huff rising to a climax. When he returned a while later with a thermos of coffee, he saw that Uncle Othman had only picked at the food. He made to put down the thermos beside the supper tray when Uncle Othman let out an angry snort.

Take it away, he said in a growl, flapping his hand angrily over the supper tray.

Badar looked up into the glaring eyes of the old man, and for a moment he was tempted into mischief. Shall I get you something else? he asked in a voice of naive sweetness.

No, Uncle Othman said, flapping his hand in a rage.

What was that about? Badar said aloud to himself when he was back in the kitchen. As he was putting the plantain away in the fridge, he heard the back door being bolted too. Once again Badar retreated to his room, a little anxious about the meaning of whatever was going on, but reassured by the thought that the Mistress and Haji were expected back the following day.

Then everything happened at once.

In the morning, the back door was still bolted. Badar knocked to be let into the house, but there was no reply. His first thought was that something had happened to the old man, or maybe he was still asleep, which would not be at all like him. The Mistress and Haji were due back before lunch, and he needed to go to the market for fresh fish, but the key to the garden gate was inside the back door, where it was always kept. In the end he climbed over the garden wall and jumped down into the carport and set off for the market. He came back with a string of red mullet, which was Haji's favorite fish. The front door was still locked so he had to climb onto the carport roof and crawl his way to the garden wall before jumping down again. He had no idea what was going on but he thought it best to just keep going with the cooking.

As he was cleaning and dressing the fish, he heard Uncle Othman unbolting the front door, but the back door remained closed. When his food preparations were completed, he knocked on the back door again, thinking he would freshen the upstairs room for the Mistress and Haji, but still the door remained closed. So again he went over the garden wall and over the carport, and again he tried the front door and still it was closed. He stood in the shade of the carport, now thoroughly confused by what was going on, and waited for the return of the Mistress and Haji. He had a bad feeling that whatever was going on had something to do with him.

Uncle Othman must have been watching from the reception room because as the taxi drew up in front of the house, he opened the front door. Badar stepped forward from the carport to greet the Mistress and Haji, who looked tired. She glanced at him, an inquiring look, so perhaps the perplexity of the morning's events was somehow evident on his face. Or perhaps she was simply wondering if all had gone well in their absence. He smiled to reassure her and took their luggage upstairs. After that he went downstairs, unbolted the back door, and returned to the kitchen to finish the cooking and await instructions to serve. It was a long while before the Mistress came out and told him that she would serve the food.

Let me help you, Badar said.

No, you stay out here, the Mistress said with unaccustomed sharpness.

He watched as she went back and forth with the trays of food, looking grim. You stay out here, she said again as she took in the bowl of radish leaves, but this time she said it softly.

He waited for the dishes to come back out, his mind racing with confusion and some anxiety. It must have to do with something he had done. What had he done to upset the Babu Mzee? He went over the last few days but could not recall anything unusual that had happened to bring on such drama. Had it something to do with the previous day's lunch? Was the perch not cooked properly? The old man had hardly touched it.

After a while the Mistress brought out the dishes and left him to put the leftovers away and then do the washing up. When he was finished, he wiped the counters and closed the kitchen door. It was then that Haji came out. He must have been waiting. Badar had not seen him since he first arrived and was struck by his scowling face, so unlike his yabber-yabber-big-laughing-man style. Haji pointed to Badar's room and followed him there.

Badar now had a bed with a metal frame and a spring base. He also had a mosquito net, and a small table and chair as well as a mat on the floor. He opened the window on the back wall to let in the light. Haji sat on the old wooden trunk and pointed to the chair by the table. Badar sat down, tense in anticipation of whatever accusation he knew was coming.

Haji sighed. The groceries, he said, and waited. And then: You have been stealing groceries.

*15.*

She was a lovely little sister, Saada, she cheered everyone with her talk. She did not mean to but she was such a bright thing that you could not help laughing when such a small girl came out with something so grown up.

She was six years old when Haji was sent away to boarding school in Morogoro. They had to send him away. There was no secondary school nearby, and Morogoro was too far to go and come back every day. He did not think they wanted him to go away to school, but he was desperate to go. When it came to it, they had no choice, they believed too much in what they had been denied. They wanted him to study and win his freedom, find his own way in life. That was what his mother said, what she wished for him. His father laughed and said yes, let him go to school, maybe that will make a wiser farmer. He had every hope that his son would continue with the farm.

The school accommodation was overcrowded. The students came from far and wide and slept in bunk beds in long dormitories.

The food was plain and not always enough, but there was order, and all the boys were eager for what was on offer.

Anyway, while Haji was away at school, the fever struck his mother and his little sister. They called him home, but Saada was gone by the time he arrived. He was just in time for the funeral. At least there was that, he was there to witness and share in the grief of his mother and his father, that was not nothing. He was there for the reading and the prayers. Later when he came home properly during school holidays, he found that the fever had struck his mother again. She was very ill, so thin, so weak, so sad. Often now she could not even leave the house.

Next time he came home from school, at the end of the year, he found Ismail had come to live on the farm. Haji had not met him before, but his father explained that they were related. Ismail was the son of a distant uncle who had now passed away. He was about two years older than Haji, though his birth had not been registered so his exact age was guesswork. He looked maybe sixteen or seventeen, and was much bigger and stronger than Haji. He looked as if he had already seen a bit of life, and his smile was hard-bitten and with a cynical edge.

He was quiet at first, and it was hard to tell whether that was caginess or perhaps even a sign of respect for the master's son, but Haji did not hesitate. He took to Ismail as if he was a brother, sitting with him when he was not working or visiting him in one of the rooms in the storehouse where he slept. Ismail had not been to school and could neither read nor write. Perhaps it was that which made him aggressive and gruff, a defense against disregard, or perhaps he was just made that way. Haji was not put off and sought Ismail out anyway. For the short while that he was at home during the holidays, he became Ismail's informant about the great world. At least that was how Ismail made him feel. Where is Japan? Ismail asked after Haji had showed him where it read *Made in Japan* on the cutlass he was using to clear a path they were walking on. Haji did not know very much about Japan but he knew where it was on a map. When they returned to the farmhouse, he brought out his atlas and showed Ismail Japan and Siberia and California and all those other unlikely parts of the world. He also told him about the calendar of beautiful Japanese women in the barbershop in Morogoro. It was for the year 1977 and had been hanging on the wall of the barbershop for more than a decade. The barber loved the pictures of those women so much that he did not allow his customers to touch the calendar because he said they would make the paper grubby. He changed the page every month.

After that the atlas became the starting point for an endless stream of Haji's tales and teachings. He showed Ismail the cataracts on the Nile, the delta of the Amazon, and the chain of the Western Ghats, quoting whatever he could remember his geography teacher saying.

Why are the oceans in different colors? Ismail asked.

The white parts are frozen oceans, blocks of ice miles deep, Haji said. The green here is darker to show that the water is deeper. In some places it is so deep that no one has seen the bottom, not even with a submarine, or the creatures that live there.

Ismail was pensive for a moment. What does it say there? he asked, his finger hovering at a spot on the map.

It says Hamburg, Haji said.

I will go there one day, Ismail said.

When Haji was seventeen and in his final year at school, his mother passed away. She had been ailing for so long and her illness had grieved his father so much that her passing was a kind of relief, although he knew it was unforgivable of him to think like that. At the end of the school year, he came home to find that Ismail had moved into the house with his baba. Haji assumed that his father felt the need for company after his mother passed away. A short while later Haji left for college in Dar es Salaam, coming home for only a few weeks here and there. In the city he lodged with friends of his father who treated him like one of their own, and no one blamed him for preferring the city to the farm, all that mud and cow dung and chicken shit.

Afterward he blamed himself for not visiting more often. He blamed himself for not seeing, or not acknowledging, his father's sadness. He blamed himself for leaving his father alone with Ismail. He knew that Ismail was abrasive and difficult, and the older he grew, the more difficult he became, especially after Haji's mother passed away. He was foulmouthed and quarrelsome, and had begun to mix with some renegade youths in the district. They roamed in gangs and disrespected people and often got into fights with one another. Even his face had changed. It was full of scars, and it turned ugly at the slightest provocation, ready for battle. He grew a beard to hide the scars, which were not in fact a result of his constant altercations but from a cat. It used to creep into the house through the kitchen window and steal food, sometimes in broad daylight. Ismail was infuriated by this animal.

One day he locked the kitchen door, then went outside to wait until the cat climbed through the window. He slammed the window shut and went back inside. He let himself into the kitchen and closed the door behind him, armed with a thick stick with which he was going to bludgeon some sense into that animal. In its desperation, the cat tore strips off his arms and face before Ismail had the good sense to open the door and let it out.

Haji knew all this about Ismail but he also knew that he held himself in check in front of Baba. When Baba rebuked him about reports of his behavior, he sulked but was silent and did not answer back, not at first, as he would have done with almost anyone else.

Then at the end of his first year at college Haji came home for the vacations to find Ismail gone. When he asked his father what had happened, he made a face of disgust and waved him away. It was the woman who had looked after his mother in her last days, Bi Mgeni, who also did the cooking and kept house for Baba, who told him what had happened.

You know old Kigogo in the village, Bi Mgeni said. He came to see Bwana Othman to complain about Ismail. That young man had no respect for anyone. When the master scolded him, he answered back. He had been doing that but not rudely, so the master let it pass. This time I think Ismail had been smoking bangi and he snarled at the master like a mad dog, which put Bwana in a rage. When the master raised his arm as if to strike him, the young man held the raised arm by the wrist and laughed. Then he stormed out of the house and that same day he was gone. He stole the money the master kept in a cashbox in his office and disappeared.

It was about that time that Haji noticed that his father was losing interest in farming. He did not know if it was to do with the money Ismail had stolen or the disrespect he had shown, or if it was part of his father's general loss of interest in everything since his wife's passing. He began to complain bitterly of exhaustion and frustration with the government's interference and incompetence, and as soon as Haji had completed his studies, his father sold the farm. He gave him some of the money he got to buy into the pharmacy shop. With the rest he bought the house they both moved into.

They never heard from Ismail again but he must have talked to someone about Baba because word reached them that he was living upcountry somewhere in Kilosa way. Then one day a man they did not know called at the house to tell them about Ismail's orphaned child. The mother was the man's distant relative. Neither Baba nor Haji had had any idea that Ismail had married or had a child, let alone that his wife had passed away. It seemed that after the wife died Ismail left, abandoning the baby to his wife's relatives.

It was then that the man whose name was Mohamed Rashidi had first come to ask if they would take responsibility for the orphan since he was a close relative of theirs. Baba was adamant, he would not have that dog's child in his house, and anyway there was no one to look after him. In the end they came to an arrangement. Haji would pay the man and his family a sum of money every quarter for them to look after the child, on condition that they kept him away.

That arrangement held for fourteen years. Every two months Mohamed Rashidi came to the pharmacy to collect money from Haji for the boy's upkeep. Then one day Mohamed Rashidi came to him in some distress, saying they could not keep the boy anymore because he was becoming troublesome to their teenage daughter.

No amount of money was enough to make him continue the arrangement. Haji had to talk Baba into letting the boy come to them. Haji suggested that he could work for them, in the house or in the garden, and Baba agreed on the condition that the boy was kept in ignorance of who they were to him. It was understood that this was to be a temporary arrangement, until something could be worked out for him.

The boy turned out well it seemed, and lingered with them for four years. Now here he was, grown into a young man and a thief.

It had happened just the previous evening, Baba said. He had been passing by Fadhili's grocery shop on his way to the mosque, with no intention of stopping or anything like that, but Fadhili greeted him so effusively that he felt it would be unfriendly just to walk by without returning greetings. To make conversation, Baba asked if their account was in order. Was it paid up? Fadhili said this month's account had not yet been settled. It was Haji who usually settled the account, but since Baba was there and Haji was away, Baba thought he would deal with it himself. How much? Fadhili told him the amount and Baba in his meticulous way asked to see the full bill. Fadhili showed him the little notebook in which he recorded their orders. To his surprise Baba found quantities of rice, sugar, tea, and so on listed there that were greatly in excess of what their small household could consume. He looked at the list for the previous month and saw the same thing, including some items that he knew were never used in the house: tins of strawberry jam, for example. Did anyone in the house eat strawberry jam? Tinned sardines. He had never seen those at the table. Did anyone in the house eat tinned sardines?

I don't think so, Haji said. I'll ask Raya.

Never mind, Baba said. What about the rice and the sugar? Did you never check the items on Fadhili's list? Did you not see that there was more there than we consume?

No, Haji said. Fadhili always just tells me the amount and I pay him.

It's him, that boy, said Baba. Fadhili told me the boy just comes and asks for whatever he wants and he gives it to him. That boy has been stealing from us and selling those goods to someone. I don't want that thief and son of a thief in my house. Get rid of him at once. Do you hear me, at once. I don't want him in my house for a single day more.

That was how Baba met him when they arrived back from Arusha. He was shaking with rage. When he first saw him shaking like that, before he had told him about Fadhili and the account, he had feared that he was having some kind of an attack. He had been declining so much in recent months. After saying that he did not want Badar in the house for a single day, Baba sat in his accustomed silence, as if not another word would pass his lips. Haji went upstairs and told Raya, and they sat for a while in stunned silence.

He'll have to go. Where is he now? Haji said.

Getting lunch ready I expect, Raya said. Has Baba said anything to him?

No, he hasn't. What are we going to do with him?

Speak to him. See what he has to say for himself, Raya said.

Speak about what? Who could it be but him? Anyway, Fadhili says it's him.

Now Haji said to Badar again, the groceries. He waited. And then: You have been stealing groceries.

Badar frowned. What groceries? he asked.

What have you done with the rice and sugar and tea that you have been taking out of Fadhili's shop? Who helps you?

Badar was speechless, unable to answer, his tongue thick with shock as he understood at last what Uncle Othman was accusing him of, what he had been waiting to accuse him of. Haji, too, saw the shock and could not mistake it.

When he was able to speak, Badar said in a low, trembling voice close to a whisper, I did not steal any groceries. I have not stolen anything.

If not you then who could it be? Haji asked sharply, looking around the little room as if to find evidence of stolen goods. He rose from the trunk he was sitting on and opened the lid. He saw a red blanket, a rolled-up mat, and some books and old magazines. There was no other possible hiding place in the room, no cupboard or cabinet. He stood up and stepped back and forth a couple of times across the small space, took a deep breath, and said with less conviction: What have you done with it all?

Badar shook his head, not trusting himself to speak, while Haji glared at him.

Stay here, Haji said, and left the room.

I don't know what to think, Haji said to Raya when he was back upstairs. I don't think it's him. He looked stunned. I don't think it's him.

Then it's the shopkeeper, Raya said without hesitation. He's been cheating you because you've not been checking. Go over the bill with him, or bring it to me and I can check to see what we have used.

Haji shook his head. He will say that the boy took the stuff, he doesn't know what happened to it. He'll say that's nothing to do with him. Anyway, Baba wants him out of here, no matter what I think. I just can't believe that Fadhili would rob us like that.

And I can't believe that boy would do what he is accused of, Raya said.

I can't believe it either, but Baba says to get rid of him. At once.

Later that afternoon, when Haji had tired of the conversation and decided to take a nap, Raya went downstairs and made a pot of tea. She poured herself a cup and then knocked on Badar's door. When he came to the door, she saw that his eyes were bright. With surprise, with anguish, with hurt? She could not tell.

There's some tea for you in the kitchen, she said. Did you have something to eat?

He shook his head. I didn't have anything. Bwana Haji said to stay here. I didn't want to be called a thief, he said with small defiance. He looked at her. I have not stolen anything.

She smiled in that way he loved, as if she were trying to suppress it. I know, she said. Have a look in the fridge. Get yourself something to eat.

She heard Badar sigh as she turned away. She was halfway up the stairs when she heard a knock on the front door. Raya put her cup down on the step and went back down. She opened the door to see Karim standing grinning on the doorstep. Raya clapped her hands in surprise.

Hello, Ma, I thought I would come and greet my mother before

catching the ferry back, Karim said, taking Raya's hand and bringing it toward his lips without quite kissing it.

Come in, come in, she said. Come upstairs.

Haji had heard the knock too, and he appeared at the top of the
stairs and called out with familiar joy at the sight of Karim. Mhuni
we, what are you doing here, you vagabond? Did you bring Fauzia?

I'm on a training course, just a quick one, yesterday and this morning, Karim said. I'll be on my way back on the morning ferry so I
thought I'd come and see you before I go. Fauzia sends her regards.

You have made us happy, Haji said. You are welcome.

Karim listened silently as they told him of the day's proceedings
and all that lay behind them. When they had exhausted the urgency
of their telling, Karim spoke with an air of gravity, as if he was
passing judgment: Have you told him all this? Does Badar know
what you have just told me about his father?

No he doesn't, Haji said, making a face of contrition. Baba insisted he should not know.

Why not? Karim asked.

Haji shrugged. He did not want him to make demands. He did
not want him to say, I am a relative and I need your help. Actually,
there is a resemblance. He looks like his father, and I expect Baba
found that difficult. Ismail was such a great disappointment to him.

Karim shook his head. I think you should tell him, he said. You
yourself. You should've told him a long time ago. If you believe
him, then I think you should explain all this to him. Whether you
believe him or not, you should tell him. Then let him come with me
tomorrow until you work something out. I'll look after him. I'll ask
him if he would like to come with me once you've spoken to him.

So it was that Haji spent part of the afternoon in Badar's room, sitting again on the trunk. First of all, I want to tell you that I believe you about the groceries, he said. And Raya believes you too. Fadhili must have been adding things to the bill because I never looked too closely at what he put down there. Then when his cheating came to light, he passed the blame to you. Yes, I believe that is what he did even if we can't prove it. We will just stop this account and get our groceries somewhere else.

Badar saw the glistening smile of the grocer in his mind's eye and recalled the bitterness with which his wife had gazed at him. They must have taken him for a complete fool.

I want to tell you about your father, Ismail, Haji continued. Not the man you thought was your father but your real father. You knew that Mohamed Rashidi was not your real father, didn't you? You said they told you. Your real father, Ismail, was a relative of ours, which means you are too. That is why you are here.

Haji explained about what had happened between Uncle Othman and Ismail, the quarrels, the robbery, and the way Badar's life had been arranged after his mother passed away and his father left.

When Mohamed Rashidi returned you to us, Baba only agreed to let you stay on the condition that we did not tell you that you are related to us, Haji said. He would not let me send you to school. I should have tried harder. Baba was still very angry with your father, and he did not want you to live with us. Now he believes Fadhili and is very angry with you and wants you out of the house. It is not your fault. It is mine, but Baba is adamant. We will work something out. Do you understand? We'll work something out.

Badar listened silently to everything that had been kept from him. He nodded in acknowledgment when Haji asked him if he understood, and shook his head when Haji asked him if he had any questions. Is there anything I have not told you that you want to know? Haji asked. We don't know where your father is. Mohamed Rashidi told me that when he handed you over to them, he said he was going to Mombasa to look for work, but they never heard from him again. So he might be in Mombasa. I remember how much he liked to look at my school atlas. He wanted to know what is this place, what is that, I will go there one day. Maybe that is what he has done, gone to see the world.

Badar did not immediately get up after Haji left. He sat where he was for a while, working things out. He had not known if he was a servant or a possession, but he had known that there was something degraded about his circumstances. He had gathered it was to do with his father, his absconding father. Juma's nudges and grins had hinted at a mystery, and he had guessed it was something to do with his father, or at least the man whose name he carried, whom he already knew from his mother in the village was a restless, quarreling man. What good was it to him now to know who his father was, or what kind of vagabond he had become? It was time he began to think about what he was to do with himself.

It was not a new thought, but he had never had an answer to it. Now he thought that perhaps he could find work as a driver. Haji had taught him to drive although, lacking a birth certificate to prove that he was eighteen, he did not have a license. Or he could get a job in the docks, anyone could work in the docks. He was strong, he could do that kind of work. Or in a factory. This place was not good for him. That was what Juma had said, and now he knew why.

A short while after Haji left there was another knock on Badar's door. It was Karim, and from the look on his face Badar understood that he knew something of what had happened. He could not suppress the small rush of pleasure that rose through him as it always did when Karim came to visit.

How are you feeling? Karim asked.

Badar shrugged. How was he to know how he was feeling?

Don't let that old shit get you down, Karim said. Sometimes old people become mean because they can, because they know we have to obey them. I am going back to Zanzibar tomorrow morning. Why don't you come with me? Would you like that? I'm sure you'll like Zanzibar. Come visit. You can stay with us.

Badar stared in astonishment. Are you teasing me? he asked at last.

No I am not teasing you, Karim said, grinning. Come with me tomorrow morning, get away from here for a while.

So it was that several hours later Badar found himself on the midmorning ferry to Zanzibar, which he had never visited before. His Idd clothes, his kanzu, and his detective novels were in a shopping bag. He had said a quiet goodbye to the Mistress, who had given him one of her smiles and said, Now I'll have to do all the cooking myself again. At the last minute Haji thrust a bundle of banknotes into his pocket, and gave him a sharp smack on his left shoulder. Don't let this vagabond get you into trouble, he said. Don't worry, we'll work something out.

Once again Badar found that the direction of his life had changed without any effort on his part.

# Part Three

# 16.

The Tamarind Hotel was on the narrow street near the old ivory workshop, round the corner from the former residence of the French consul. The consul had lived there a long time ago, in the time when the Omani sultans still dealt independently with foreign governments, among them the British, the French, the Germans, and the United States of America. Later in the century, the British took over the sultan's affairs in order to advance progress and civilization. The sultan of the French consul's time was the founding patriarch, sire to many concubines and suriya purchased from as far away as Albania, Georgia, Cairo, and Abyssinia. The sultan shopped far and wide for his pleasures, and there were always people whose tragedies made them vulnerable to such commerce. With these women the sultan fathered scores of sons and daughters, all of whom became legitimate princes and princesses. He was husband to only one wife, but that union was childless.

Further down the road from the residence of the French consul, next to the palace complex which housed part of the Sultan's enormous family, was the former dwelling of a German merchant. One of the sultan's daughters, Salme, the one whose mother was a Georgian or a Circassian or possibly an Albanian concubine, made a famous scandal by having an affair with the German merchant whose name was Herr Ruete. Their liaison became impossible to hide after she fell pregnant, and with the help of the British mission, they escaped the feared wrath of her family on board a Royal Navy frigate, which took her and Herr Ruete to Aden. In Aden she was baptized, then she married the Herr and gave birth to a boy who died a few months later en route to Hamburg. They had three other children before Herr Ruete was run over by a tram in Berlin three years after their arrival in Germany. The valiant princess wrote a memoir of their daring love affair that became popular in Germany and Britain and provided some respite from her straitened circumstances. She made her life in Germany and lived there into her late seventies.

Nearby on the same road as the princess and her merchant were the houses of other Omani princes and aristocrats, many of them the sultan's descendants, or cousins and related families. Years later, after the overthrow and expulsion of the sultans, the houses became hotels for tourists, furnished and decorated to evoke that same perished era. The first signs of the tourist bulge became visible in the mid-1980s, after the easing of foreign exchange regulations. Cafés for visitors opened, serving burgers and chips rather than goat stew and mandazi and sweet milky tea. Gift shops sold textiles from India and leather sandals from China as if they were the work of artisans who lived round the corner. Trinkets like elephant-hair bracelets, bead mats, and carvings of animals unknown on the island—bushbucks, giraffes, elephants, oryx—were shipped from the mainland in large volumes. Hotels, which before were used mostly by visiting officials and journalists hopping over from the mainland to report on yet another outrage, began to fill up with holiday visitors. Foreign investors bought old buildings and transformed them into gilded fantasies of oriental luxury. New beachfront hotels were constructed for the anticipated mass arrivals. Enterprising people with large houses refurbished them to take economy guests so there was accommodation for all budgets. Local political grandees took their cut, and builders and the hardware trade flourished. Businesses appeared for which there had been no need before: tourist travel guides, car-hire firms, bars, boutiques, expensive restaurants. It was not that there were no visitors before. People were always coming and going, to Dar es Salaam, to Mombasa, to Nairobi, and later even to the Gulf and beyond. With tourism there were, suddenly, thousands of strangers, mostly Europeans, who did not speak Kiswahili and who went about their pleasures with frowning intensity, stretched out on sun beds in the blazing sun or bargaining for trinkets in the gift shops or stumbling in the lanes after a tour guide as he reeled off his half-fabricated stories ahead of them.

The konsol Faransa, as it was still known more than a century after the French consul lived there, had a large walled garden that had become a venue for fetes, music concerts, and even weddings. In the street around the corner from it was a tall, narrow building that once belonged to an Indian merchant family. They had since left for India or England or Canada, one or the other of those places where so many Indians found refuge after the postindependence panic which gripped much of Africa. The building was now the Tamarind Hotel. Its brochure described it as an exclusive upmarket boutique hotel in the heart of the old town. There was a small board above the door, its black background turned ashen and its white letters faded, which read *F. Kassam & Son, Contractor and General Merchant.* The board was old and weather-beaten, a relic left behind from another age, and intended to authenticate the hotel's boutique-ness, in some fashion. Beside the entrance was another, newer sign in copperplate with the hotel's name emblazoned.

At first, Badar was disappointed when he learned that was where he was to be a trainee. It was in the town, near where people lived. Was that what tourists wanted? Would they not find the closeness of the lives of unknown people suffocating, the opposite of what a holiday was supposed to be? Would they not prefer a beach or at least a swimming pool and a wide-open terrace where they could sit under a colorful umbrella and sip their drinks? He had seen pictures in the magazines the Mistress used to throw out, of half-dressed women running into the sea with rapturous smiles on their faces, and male and female bodies stretched out on beds by the side of enormous glittering swimming pools. Wasn't that what tourist ho-tels were meant to be like? Once inside, he saw that the hotel had its own attractions. Despite the absence of a pool, the rooms were styl-ishly furnished and the appointments, as the assistant manager told him, were luxurious.

The assistant manager was an unsmiling man with a narrow, gaunt face and a mustache trimmed into a thin line. That was Ba-dar's first impression, a starved face and a thin mustache. He thought that style of mustache made its wearer look fussy in a mean way, made him seem something of a fanatic for spending so much time getting that line of hair to be slender and straight. Assistant Manager Issa hardly looked at Badar for the first two hours or so that morning. He was too busy with guests and staff. Badar waited in the office as he was instructed to do, excited and anxious about these new events in his life. He smelled the breakfast that was being served somewhere nearby and heard the sound of metal on plates and a low murmur of voices.

There were three desks in the office. The largest one had a green leather surface and was clear except for a blotter and a telephone. On the wall behind the desk was a framed photograph of the president. A Charter Airlines calendar for 1998 hung on another wall, with Mount Kilimanjaro in the background and smaller insets of animals and planes in between the months and days. Adjacent and at a right angle to the big desk was a smaller one made of cheap varnished wood with a computer on it and a clutter of papers. The third table, which was set apart from this cluster, was slim and elegant, like the Mistress's dressing table. A large mirror hung behind it, facing the big desk. Badar was instructed to sit and wait by the third desk.

When Assistant Manager Issa returned to the office, he sat at the smaller varnished desk and tapped at his keyboard for some moments without a word to Badar. After a while he stopped tapping and looked up, first ahead of him through the open door and into the lobby, and then he swiveled his head slowly toward Badar, who guessed this was a performance to intimidate him, which it duly did. He shifted his glance slightly so that he was looking at the assistant manager's shirtfront rather than into his eyes, which in a brief moment of contact he had seen were hard with some kind of irritation.

What are you called? he asked in a brisk voice.

Badar, he said, even as he wondered at this curtness. Was the assistant manager always like this or was Badar to understand that he was an imposition? Badar did not at that time know how Karim had obtained the position for him. Karim had told him only that he knew someone who was a friend of the family who might be able to help, and subsequently announced that he was to be a trainee at the Tamarind Hotel and he was to go there the following morning and report to Assistant Manager Issa. He did not explain any further than that, and Badar did not ask any questions.

When Karim told him he was to be a trainee in a hotel, he guessed that he was to be trained as a waiter or maybe even a cook because Haji and the Mistress had so often praised Badar's cooking and encouraged him to think there was a future for him in that kind of work. After the unpleasantness with the groceries happened and he went to live with Karim, who said he could help him get a job in a hotel, Badar assumed it would be to do the same kind of work he had been doing at the Mistress's house, cooking, cleaning, serving. He was still wounded by Uncle Othman's venom, and too grateful to Karim to quibble about the arrangement. Karim's manner expected gratitude and Badar was happy to provide it and take whatever position Karim found for him. When Assistant Manager Issa began to instruct him in his duties, he found out that the Tamarind Hotel did not serve lunch or dinner, as there were so many restaurants and cafés nearby, and that his role would be to do whatever he was told to do.

So let's start, Assistant Manager Issa said, and ran his eye over him, head to toe. You will wear a white shirt and black trousers to work. You will wear shoes not sandals. You will acquire these items at your own expense. Do you have any experience in hotel work? I did not think so. We'll have to start you at the very beginning. First thing first, let's give you a little tour. Most of the guests are still in their rooms so we'll leave that for later.

The reception and lobby on the ground floor opened to a paved internal courtyard that was overlooked by a veranda with a cast-iron balustrade running all the way round. A tiny stone basin containing a trailing bougainvillea stood on a stand in the middle of the courtyard. Other plants in ornamental pots were distributed round the courtyard, cannas, poinsettia, hibiscus, aloe. Badar knew these plants because Juma loved to call out their names for him.

Your first job every morning will be to water the pots, the assistant manager said.

Badar nodded and followed Assistant Manager Issa through the courtyard and into the breakfast room, whose windows overlooked the patio. There were five tables in the room, two of them occupied by guests having breakfast. All the guests were European. One was a man on his own, a book open beside him as he ate, and the other table was occupied by an elderly couple who looked up briefly as they passed through. Beyond the breakfast room was the kitchen. He was introduced to the breakfast cook, Habib, and his assistant, Iddi, and the two cleaners, Maulidi and Chambo, all men. They worked only in the morning. The assistant manager pointed out the staff facilities, a small room with some hard chairs and a Formica table, and the staff toilet. In a corner of the staff area was a watering can, and Assistant Manager Issa pointed to it wordlessly. Pots must be watered first thing every day.

Later in the morning, once the guests had gone out and the rooms were being made up, Issa took him on another tour of the upstairs, pointing out the features, all rooms en suite (a new word to him) and air-conditioned and supplied with quality toiletries. He called out the rates for the standard rooms and the premier rooms as they went along, and the sums were shocking to Badar. The hotel had seven guest rooms, four premier on the first floor and three standard on the top floor, which also had an open but covered patio area, furnished with comfortable chairs and low tables where guests could choose to be served breakfast or could sit in the evenings to catch the breeze.

Badar found out that most of the guests at the Tamarind Hotel were older couples like the ones downstairs, people who wanted to be in the town rather than at the beach for part of their time on the island, who wanted to wander the streets and peer into shops and ask questions. Many were at the hotel for only two or three nights, a break from their safari holiday on the mainland, the assistant manager explained.

These are our typical guests, he said. Staying at the Tamarind is the serious part of their holiday. Here they rub shoulders with local people and eat street food, as they call it, and maybe get slightly upset stomachs. Then after this new experience they can return to their luxury beach bungalows and game lodges with a good feeling. Several of them have stayed with us more than once. We give them a discount if they return.

Assistant Manager Issa delivered his explanation with a deadpan expression, his voice slightly tinged with acid. At some point he broke off his instructions because a guest appeared unexpectedly, an elderly European woman who approached with an apologetic smile.

I think I left my book at the breakfast table, she said.

Badar stepped aside to let the woman pass. Assistant Manager Issa addressed the woman without a smile or change of expression. Good morning, madam. I expect it is still there.

To Badar that did not seem the right face or tone for a hotel manager or even an assistant one, so he made eye contact with the guest and beamed, and he saw how pleased that made her. The assistant manager gave him a long look before continuing with his instructions.

Smile if you have to but always speak directly. These people don't like cringing. They want you to serve them politely and then get out of their sight. Always remember, they are only tourists. It's just their money we want, not their love. Don't argue, don't answer back. Don't be cheeky. Don't stare at the men, especially when they wear stupid clothes. Don't make jokes and don't laugh out loud. Don't touch them!

Badar had had no dealings with European people before but he could not believe that Assistant Manager Issa knew what he was talking about. To him Issa's instructions sounded high-handed and mean. He sounded like a very bitter man.

Don't laugh out loud, Badar said. Why not?

They'll think you're laughing at them, Issa said.

The assistant manager dismissed him at lunchtime, at the same time as the other workers went off. He was to come back at seven the next morning, properly dressed and ready for a full day's work. With the money Haji had given him, later that afternoon Badar bought a white shirt and a pair of black trousers from a clothes shop in Darajani and a pair of shoes from a market stall. He had been living with Fauzia and Karim for two weeks by then. They let Badar spread a mat on the floor in a corner of their sitting room and sleep there. He had known when he arrived that he would like living in Zanzibar but that he could not stay with Karim and Fauzia for long. They led compact and contented lives, he thought, and their flat suited that well, with a large bedroom and a living space that included a kitchen and room for chairs and a table and a shelf for their books. He tried his very best not to intrude on their lives. Karim did not come home from the Development Office until late afternoon, shortly after Fauzia, so at the end of that first day at the Tamarind Hotel, Badar had to contain his impatience before he could parade his newly acquired finery for them. He told Karim about Assistant Manager Issa and how it seemed he was not to work in the kitchen as he had assumed he would.

This is better, it's an opportunity, Karim said. It's both work and perhaps a future. Learn everything they teach you and then see what lies ahead for you. You must work hard and make something of your opportunities, otherwise taking you away from that old man would have been a wasted effort. I don't know what would've happened to you. They would have thrown you out into the streets, I expect. From now on you must think hard about what you want for yourself in the future. You've plenty of time. You're only seventeen.

Nearly eighteen, Badar said. I don't know why you're laughing. Anyway, thank you for getting me this opportunity. I will do my best.

He really meant it too, and did not say thank you in a sarcastic way, even though at times Karim talked to him as if he was an ignorant teenager. He did not mind that Karim sometimes spoke to him like that, not really, though perhaps he felt a tiny wince that quickly passed when he remembered how obliged he was to him.

The manager of the Tamarind Hotel was Bwana Sharif Makame. He also owned a major share of the hotel and was altogether a very busy man with other enterprises to supervise, including an all-inclusive beachfront hotel, so Assistant Manager Issa told Badar. He came in on Badar's third morning and had him summoned from the housekeeping training he was receiving from Maulidi. He was working the first floor and Chambo was doing the top floor. Badar was scheduled to train with Chambo the next day. It was Issa's decision that he should learn all the hotel jobs, making up rooms, serving breakfast, sorting the laundry, in case of need.

Bwana Sharif was sitting behind his pedestal desk sipping coffee. He smiled and offered his hand without rising, and Badar went round the huge desk to shake it. He was in his late forties or early fifties, round-faced, sleek and athletic in body, smartly dressed in an expensive-looking shirt and dark trousers. It was plain to see he was a powerful man in every way. He held on to Badar's hand while he looked him up and down and then nodded.

How is your uncle Haji? he asked.

Badar had not known they knew each other. He is well, he said.

Sharif Makame nodded, glanced at himself in the mirror across

the office, and then waved Badar away. Give him my regards. Now
back to your duties, he said.

When Badar came down after the rooms were done, the manager was gone. Later he guessed that Bwana Sharif was who Karim
had meant when he said there was someone who was a friend of the
family who might be able to help.

Have you used a computer before? Issa asked him that afternoon.

Badar laughed in surprise and perhaps embarrassment. Where
would he have learned to use a computer? Issa had not inquired into
his past and for that reason Badar supposed he had been told something about him but it seemed not. What would a house servant, a
boi, have to do with computers? At that time he was not sure what
it was the computer did except that the assistant manager spent a lot
of time pecking at it. That afternoon he had his first lesson in log-
ging on and accessing the hotel inbox. Issa explained that was how
guests made reservations so it was important to keep a regular
check on the inbox. He showed him how to open the website page,
and there he saw a photograph of Bwana Sharif sitting behind his
huge empty desk. Then Issa showed him the hotel plan, and which
guests occupied which rooms. He showed him how to search the
internet. He did not take it all in at once, but he knew it was the
beginning of something exciting.

He had not spent long enough in school, just eight years of
elementary learning. There were just the Mistress's discarded magazines and the detective novels and the English-speaking programs
on the transistor radio the Mistress kept in the kitchen and that she
used to let him borrow in the evenings. He had understood the an-
nouncers on the radio well enough but now he was lost when guests

spoke rapidly or with an unfamiliar accent or using a fashionable word he did not know. When it came to speaking, he had no practice and no confidence, so talking to the European guests made him tense, his tongue felt thick and clumsy around the words, and at times he feared that he had the words in the wrong order. In his early days at the hotel, getting the words right was a greater source of anxiety for him than laughing out loud at his own jokes or staring at the tourist men or any of the other things Assistant Manager Issa had warned him against doing.

The guests had many questions and many requests and sometimes complaints about mosquitoes or the rain or the smell of the gutters in the old town. Badar put on a bright smile for them which he thought they preferred to Issa's sulky looks. He listened, kept his answers simple to avoid embarrassing himself, and did his best to meet their requests even when they were silly. What did they expect him to do about the rain or the heat or the mosquitoes or the smell from the gutters in the streets? They were in the heart of the old town, after all. Still he listened and sent in an additional fan and promised to change the mosquito net, and sympathized about the gutters overflowing with water. The rains have been unexpectedly heavy this year, madam. He overheard one guest saying to another that the smell reminded him of the smaller canals in Venice, and Badar wondered what that was like, Venice. The next time a guest complained about the smell in the old town he might ask, Have you had the opportunity to visit Venice yet? The canals smell just like this. Of course he never did, it was just an underdog's fantasy. Don't argue, don't answer back. Don't be cheeky. But there were many occasions when addressing the guests was unavoidable, and with practice his confidence grew and he lost his fear of speaking English. In fact he found a growing ease in it and even began to receive compliments from the guests, as if they had indeed expected him to stumble and stutter and mispronounce. He smiled at their condescension and chatted cheerfully and the guests smiled back and said thank you.

Assistant Manager Issa nodded his approval, his face deadpan, and gave him more responsibilities with each passing day. He did not ask Badar any questions about himself except in relation to the hotel. He talked exclusively about the hotel and those outside events that concerned its running. The other staff, all of whom were in their thirties, did not hesitate to ask Badar questions, but they were teasing and bantering questions that their ages over his youth gave them every right to. Badar teased back and laughed with them and they all kept their distances.

His duties came to include deputizing for the assistant manager in matters of daily management, ordering supplies for the kitchen, checking the rooms after they had been made up, dealing with minor guest concerns, a blown light bulb, an accident with a cup of tea, calling a taxi. All bookings and all financial management still had to go through Issa, but Badar asked questions and Issa answered: about the rates, the discounts and how they worked, the average length of stay, the promotions. When Issa was not there, Badar browsed the guest records, their names, their addresses, copies of their passports. Sometimes when he checked the rooms after they were made up, he opened the drawers, looked through the guests' clothes, carefully, so they would not notice. He checked out the little things in their bath bags and sniffed their perfumes and creams. It was fascinating to see what they took with them when they traveled.

Bwana Sharif dropped in once or twice a week and the staff buzzed discreetly around him. Badar fetched him a coffee while Issa gave him an update or discussed a problem. Bwana Sharif's face was open, a man without burdens. He was clean-shaven, his eyes lively and curious. He spoke rapidly, just short of curtly, and gave an appearance of eagerness and hurry, someone with much to attend to. His smiles came quickly and often in the midst of the teasing patter he kept up with all the staff. No one teased him back. Beneath the smiling talk there was something hard that demanded deference. Bwana Sharif did not give instructions to his assistant manager or ask to see the accounts or anything like that. He left the running of the hotel to Issa, or so it seemed to Badar in those early weeks. His appearances were brief but he always asked after Haji: How is your uncle Haji? Give him my regards, don't forget.

In addition to the Tamarind Hotel, Bwana Sharif was also the executive manager and part owner of a beachfront hotel, the Crystal Bay, and an adviser to the Ministry of Tourism. Badar was not sure what part he owned or who the other owners were. When he asked Issa, he waved the question away, foreign investors, he said, so Badar guessed there was something sharp about the arrangement. It was nothing to do with him. Even he knew that the tourist and hotel business was corrupt, but since that crookedness went all the way through it, no one was going to get into trouble because who was going to accuse whom? He had looked up the Crystal Bay Hotel website and marveled at its guest lodges and restaurants and swimming pools and its fun-loving tourists. Access to the hotel was restricted to guests and those invited by the management, in other words no locals. He hoped that one day Bwana Sharif would move him to the Crystal Bay Hotel.

One afternoon, when he came back to work after lunch—which was just a bowl of potatoes in a café—Assistant Manager Issa said to him, We have a day booking in room 5. He said this casually and did not look at Badar. He had been there for nearly two months then and they had not had a day booking before, so he was not sure what that was. When Issa explained that it was a booking until late afternoon, he thought he heard something in his voice, a kind of furtiveness in his tone. He made to look at the computer screen over his shoulder but Issa waved him back.

It's not entered, he said, frowning. It's complimentary.

As he said this he put his index finger across his lips for silence.

Bwana Sharif— Badar began in a whisper.

Issa shushed him crossly and then nodded, once again putting his finger across his lips.

Alone? Badar asked.

Issa shook his head. The guests are in the room already, he whispered. You'll have to clean it afterward. Maulidi and Chambo have gone home. We're expecting another guest on this evening's flight from Dar. He will be here around six thirty. Ramadhani will check him in but you must make sure the room is freshly made up before you leave.

Ramadhani was the night clerk who took over when Issa and Badar went home. Badar wondered why Bwana Sharif did not take his guest to the Crystal Bay, but perhaps there were too many people there who knew him and the Tamarind was more private. After

Issa left, earlier than usual as if to keep out of the way, Badar sat in the office with the door open as always and heard the guests who had spent the afternoon in their rooms to escape the heat making ready to go out for a walk or a snack. At around five, as he was worrying that he would not have enough time to clean the room, Bwana Sharif appeared at the office door, looking gay and refreshed. He stood there for a long moment, smiled at Badar, said a few words of greeting, waved his farewell, and left. Badar waited for twenty minutes more for the other person in the room to descend. At five thirty he went up to room 5 and knocked on the door. There was no reply. He knocked on the door again, and when there was still no reply, he used his passkey to let himself in. The room was empty. Whoever the other person in the room had been, they must have slipped out when Badar was not looking, perhaps when Bwana Sharif stood at the office door, blocking his view. The window was closed and the room smelled of perfume and of something sour, perhaps sweat or sex or the toilet. He opened the window, stripped the bed, and cleaned the bathroom. He brushed the rug and dusted all the surfaces and then fetched clean sheets from the linen cupboard, which was on the same floor. He hurried downstairs to fetch a clean glass and a fresh bottle of water from the kitchen. He was very quickly done, and went back to the office to wait for Ramadhani's arrival at six.

It was a struggle to keep all this to himself but Karim was out when he got home. He often went out in the evenings to meet with friends for an hour or two while Fauzia completed her preparations for the next day's classes. Badar was not sure if it was appropriate to tell Fauzia about the events at the hotel. In any case, she was busy with her schoolwork and looked up only to smile at him and tell him to make himself some tea if he wished. He made tea for both of them and browsed through an old newspaper he had already read several times, stealing a look at her now and then but pretending not to. He loved looking at her.

They had a light supper when Karim came home, and afterward Badar poured out his story to him, almost out of breath with excitement.

Karim laughed at him. You silly country bumpkin, he said. Don't you know what happens in hotels or what old goats like him get up to?

Of course he knew, he had heard people talk, but he had not had to go into a room and clean up after them. The silly country bumpkin comment wounded him even though it was said teasingly, so he did not say anything more.

## 17.

Fauzia made sure they talked about her falling sickness again before she came off the Pill, but it was Karim who asked, Do you think about making babies? Fauzia knew that Jalila and Ali teased him about that, as they teased her as well, but she was still surprised that he came out with the question before she did.

Do you think about that? Babies? he said. I'm not in a hurry if you are not.

Of course I have been thinking about it, but I am not in a hurry either. I have been reading more about it, she said. The chance of passing it on to your child, you know, the falling sickness, is greater if the mother is the one afflicted. I haven't had a seizure since I was six, so it may be that I am no longer afflicted, but that is what I read.

They were in their sitting room. Badar was at work, and for Fauzia these rare moments of privacy had come to be precious. It was not that Badar was difficult or intrusive, just that the space was cramped with the three of them. It was a good thing Karim had done, bringing him here and away from the ugly accusations, but it was a small apartment. The best thing when they first married was to have time alone, hours on end, without hurry or subterfuge, in bed and out of bed. Now she was aware of Badar when he was in the apartment with them though she mostly did not mind, except when she felt a need for silence or privacy, when she wanted to spread herself without restraint, to speak her love aloud rather than whisper it.

As you say, you have not had a seizure since you were six, Karim said with a sigh. But you don't seem able to convince yourself that it *is* likely that you are over it. Why can't you move on from this? It is wearying. In one of those papers you gave me to read, it says that if children are given inhibitive treatment, they get over it anyway as they grow older.

Unless they don't, Fauzia said stubbornly.

And the medical treatment is now very effective, Karim continued, ignoring her quibble.

In places where they have good medical facilities, which is not here, Fauzia said.

Listen, I'm convinced you'll be all right, he said, a hint of impatience creeping into his voice.

It's not about conviction, she said, not ready to give up. It's whether I'll pass it on to the baby.

He sighed again. You are over it, he said sharply, then as if hearing the irritation in his voice, he smiled, and allowed his smile to grow into a grin. And there will be nothing bad to pass on, but there is no hurry anyway.

Fauzia smiled back. She had found that Karim had a domineering streak she had not noticed earlier in their relationship, and that it surfaced unexpectedly now and then, often over trivial matters and then he had to have his way. At times a retreat seemed wiser than pointless argument, although her fear of passing on the sickness was far from trivial. Nonetheless, she did not pursue the topic. They sat in silence for a while, Fauzia pensive with her concerns and Karim a little preoccupied.

He had several things on his mind, as it happened, and he had been fidgeting restlessly while he tried to think of a way to change the subject. He had done something at work that bothered him. He had discovered inflated figures in the expense claim submitted by a junior member of his team. She was an older woman, and when he questioned her about the claim, she appealed to him to help her. Everything was so hard. It would be impossible for her and her family if she lost her job. He was a man with such a warm heart, he must surely understand that she was not thieving, just trying to live. And he had signed the papers and let the claim through. He told himself that it was a kindness, but as he sat there he wondered if it was the flattery that had won him over. He was doing very well at his job, making a difference, he thought. He did not want this mistake to become a blemish on his record.

Then there was Badar. Karim had rescued him from that vengeful old man, and he felt good about that. He would have ended up living on the streets as some kind of a criminal. He had been living with them for several months now, four months. Like a younger brother. Ali had done the same for him, although not quite at such close quarters. Badar was not his brother, and Karim was helping him out of generosity rather than obligation. Badar was grateful, he was discreet, ready to help whenever he was asked, or even without being asked. He helped Fauzia in the kitchen, and cooked some of the meals. One thing Karim had been right about him from the start was that he was attentive, a listener and a watcher. Karim no longer found it oppressive, how he listened so intently, how he watched, but he wondered if Fauzia found it as disconcerting as he had at first. She was not likely to complain, not yet, that was not her way, but he guessed she would prefer if he was to move on. That was another thing on his mind.

I think I've found a place for Badar to move to, he said into the silence. He had been keeping the news back because he did not want it to seem that he was making light of her anxiety about the sickness, although really he wished she would stop going on about it.

She made a tiny gasp of surprise at his news and her eyes briefly lit up. Where? she asked.

Not very far, near Darajani Street, toward Mbuyuni. Someone at work knows of a downstairs room for rent. I told him it was for our relative, and he promised to speak to the owner, he said.

How much? Can he afford it? The hotel does not pay him much, she said.

No it doesn't, but I think he is doing well so I'm sure his pay will increase soon. Also, he has not been paying us rent, so he will have a little money saved, I hope. I'll help him if need be, Karim said. I haven't told him yet, but I'll take him to see the room tomorrow.

Fauzia was smiling broadly. That will be good for him, she said. He can still come here for his meals or whatever.

Oh yes, he won't be very far, maybe fifteen minutes away, Karim said. I'm sure he would love to come here for his meals every now and then. He might even cook some for us. Now, mpenzi wangu, come over here and listen to me.

What now? Is there something else? she asked, frowning.

He laughed. No, nothing much. I just wanted to tell you that I think of nothing but you.

Don't exaggerate, she said as she moved over.

I'm not exaggerating, he said as he lunged for her.

The room that Karim found for Badar was in a house that at some earlier time had been occupied by a merchant and his extended family. The merchant had long since passed away and his family had scattered, who knows where, except for one son who worked in a furniture warehouse in Dar es Salaam and was keen to sell. The house now belonged to a man called Hakim who had been working for many years in Abu Dhabi, in a transport business delivering goods to shops and groceries all over the United Arab Emirates. His wife and children had remained behind in Zanzibar, living with his parents in a small flat in Miembeni. Hakim had come to visit them whenever he could. After some years, he was able to buy a small share in the transport business. There was already another part owner, a Somali man from Bukoba, whose name was Abdirahman, who like Hakim had also started out working in a humble position and by diligence and trustworthiness had acquired a share in the business. The main owner, the moneybags of the enterprise, was an Abu Dhabi man who concerned himself only from a distance but kept a close eye on the paperwork and knew how to reward his partners.

In Abu Dhabi, Hakim lived in a hostel along with other workers from his part of the world, and like them he saved every dirham that he could spare. In time he saved enough to buy the merchant's house. The merchant's son was not a good businessman and perhaps not very bright or was desperate for the money, and Hakim was able to get a good price off him. He cleaned up the house, decorated and furnished the upper floors, and moved his mother and father to the second floor, retaining the top floor for his wife and children.

On the ground floor was a room with its own front door that most likely had been the merchant's office at one time. Hakim rented it out as a modest grocery, selling tins of powdered milk and sardines and margarine, and packets of tea and flour and razor blades. The front door to the main house opened into two other ground-floor rooms. One was at the back of the house, beyond the staircase that led upstairs. The other was just by the entrance hallway. A shared bathroom was also at the back, and had a shower and a toilet. The bathroom was poorly lit from slits high in the wall, its concrete floor rough and pocked where the shower had eaten away at it. Hakim did what he could with the two downstairs rooms and rented them out unfurnished. After settling his family in their new accommodation, he returned to his business and his hostel in Abu Dhabi. He still came to visit whenever he could.

Karim knew all this from Idris, a colleague who was the tenant in the back room and had told him that the front room had become available. That room was large with a high ceiling, from the middle of which hung a dim naked bulb on a long wire. There was only one window, which faced the front. It was barred and had solid shutters that were stiff from misuse. Its emptiness seemed stark and gloomy to Badar, the concrete floor and white walls, that dangling bulb. It smelled of cement and lime, a result of the repairs and repainting that Hakim must have had done, but beneath that was something else, whatever had been stored in the room in the past. He thought he could smell cloves. There was nothing on the walls, not even a nail to hang a shirt on. Old cobwebs hung from the ceiling and everything needed a clean, but Badar did not hesitate. Yes, this is excellent, he said. He did not have much to bring, his few clothes, his novels, and a mat to sleep on. The room's bleakness reminded him of when he first went to work for the Mistress five years before, only now he was not frightened anymore.

He was eager to leave Fauzia and Karim's flat, not because he found their company difficult but quite the opposite. He loved them both. In some way that he could not resist, he watched them together and listened to them when they were in their room. He could not hear what they said but there were times he thought he could tell that they were making love. He tried not to watch them, tried not to listen to the movements in their room, tried not to feel neglected and envious, but he could not prevent himself. It was a surreptitious desire to share something of their happiness, but he knew it was not right. He knew they would be upset if they suspected anything, would think him dirty or even malicious. So he was eager to leave when the opportunity arose because he felt he was in their way, his presence a drag on their happiness together, and he would be relieved of the anguish of his guilty watching and listening.

Come and eat with us, Fauzia had said as he stood on the threshold of their flat, about to descend the stairs. Come and visit us whenever you want. Come often.

I will, he had said.

And he did, every other day to begin with. He missed them so much. At first he thought it was them as a couple, but he came to understand that it was Fauzia's company he missed the most, her face, her voice, her smile, the way she looked at him, steady and attentive. How stupid he was, how absurd, what a child! It was horrible that he should think that way about Karim's beloved, when Karim had done so much for him. Badar had loved the Mistress and was sad to be forced to leave her, but everything would have ended intolerably if Karim had not been there at that moment to steer him to safety. And here he was showing his gratitude by fantasizing about his wife. After that Badar made his visits once a week and then even less frequently but often enough to keep in touch with them and to maintain their affection.

From the market he bought himself a foam mattress, a plastic chair and table, and a light bulb with a higher wattage. He borrowed a sheet and a towel from the hotel laundry room, and a bar of luxury soap from the toilet supplies. Gradually other objects found their way into his room, books left behind by guests at the hotel, a lampshade, a calendar with photographs of Korean gardens, which arrived at the hotel as a promotion for tourists. He bought a small secondhand radio and had it on for a while every evening, listening to music and talk programs on different stations: Kenya Broadcasting Corporation, Deutsche Welle, BBC World Service, South African Broadcasting Corporation when he could get it, as well as their own Radio Taifa. When he tired of the radio, he read for a while or he just lay in bed waiting for sleep while his thoughts roamed over his days and years.

In the meantime, Fauzia came off the Pill and the two of them launched their campaign to make babies. Fauzia consulted the literature and read about optimum days for ovulation and fertilization and what to do afterward (put a pillow under your back to tip your womb upward and prevent the eager spermatozoa from trickling out). Karim did not think they should confine their attempts to optimum days. He suggested that they should have a go at every possible opportunity, optimum or otherwise. What harm could it do? They debated these matters and resolved them in conciliatory and at times hilarious ways, having fun and making love and fearing nothing. After supper every evening Fauzia made her preparations for the next day's class while Karim read a newspaper or one of his books or one of Fauzia's. He had given up going out to a baraza with friends, realizing now that he had been doing that to get away from the crowded flat. When Fauzia was finished with her school preparations, they went to bed and got down to work. They agreed that they had never been so happy.

She was twenty-one and he was twenty-five, everything in working order, what could go wrong? Worries about the falling sickness were banished into the murk in the midst of these ecstasies. Within five months of this delightful operation, Fauzia reported early signs of success. No period. Other signs appeared to confirm this first one, including distressing bouts of nausea and exhaustion. While Karim was overjoyed at the approaching outcome, Musa smiled silently, Khadija was tearfully enraptured and full of advice and self-admonishing, all at the same time (anything could still happen, God forbid), and Fauzia gritted her teeth and struggled through the early miseries.

Her mother told her, These early discomforts will pass and then you'll feel better than you have ever felt in your life. It's what a woman is built to do, don't worry, celebrate what has befallen you. Don't eat bitter food, no lemons or chilies or matumbo. It will sour your blood and make you retch. May God keep you safe. I could only do it once, when I so much wanted to give you a brother or sister.

Karim looked on with delighted grins when the pregnancy was confirmed. I did this, he told Fauzia, and she thought but did not say, What an ego my lover has. He bought her improbable little presents to cheer her up, a garish miniature music box that tinkled something that sounded familiar but that she could not pin down, a makeup set that included a bloodred lipstick when she did not wear lipstick, a DVD of Lebanese music when they did not have a DVD player.

What's happened to you? she asked, laughing, made happy after all. What's the point of this? We don't have anything to play it on.

We will soon, he said, undaunted. My salary has just gone up. He was waiting for her to start demanding unexpected things to eat at strange hours, the legendary cravings that pregnant women were supposed to have, but mention of food often made her ill, at least in the early months.

The only person who was not blasé about her torment was Hawa, who looked on aghast at what her friend had done to herself. I wasn't sure how wise this idea was, she said. Now I know. This is a life sentence, you know that. You'll vomit and struggle for months, and you'll then have that slave master in your belly there running the rest of your life.

Thank you, Hawa, you are a big help, Fauzia said, but really she knew what Hawa meant. It will pass, she told herself.

And it did. After the fifth month, her body calmed down and was serene. She began to feel the presence of something moving inside her. She saw Dr. Khalid regularly and met the midwife who worked with him and who visited her at home in the last days. She was there in the flat when her waters broke, and she took her and Karim to the clinic in her car. The contractions grew increasingly strong and extended, and the agony seemed endless and unendurable, but she persisted through the night. Her mother had offered to be with her but she asked Karim to stay at her side. He was with her until the morning, when the baby eventually slid out. They called her Nasra.

They came home after three days, Fauzia and Nasra, back to the top-floor flat where Karim was waiting excitedly for them. The clinic had rung late morning to say that they were ready to be collected and he said he would call a taxi and pick them up, but the nurse told him that Khadija was already at the clinic, had been there since dawn. She will bring them home, she said, there was no need for him to trouble. When they arrived at the flat, Khadija shooed Fauzia to bed to rest after the hectic few days she had endured, and put Nasra in the tiny cradle Fauzia and Karim had thought so lovely when they saw it in the shop. Then Khadija looked in the cupboard, in the fridge, in the freezer compartment to determine what meal she should prepare. They had the baby's supplies ready, and Khadija checked through those as well.

Karim went into the bedroom and saw that the baby was sleeping, but Fauzia was awake and held out her hand for him to come nearer. He sat on the bed and took her hand. She's in charge in there, he said, and they shared a smile.

Khadija stayed until it was dark and then left to return home. Musa was bedridden after another bad spell. Tell Ba I'll bring the baby round in a couple of days, Fauzia said.

No, don't tire yourself, her mother said. He can wait. I'll be back tomorrow.

They brought the cradle out into the sitting room after she left, and Karim sat watching with dumbfounded awe as the baby fed at Fauzia's breasts, snapping and slapping to keep hold of the nipple. He winced involuntarily as she promptly squirted something out of the other end, and then she howled—with what he assumed was self-disgust. It seemed such a comedy.

Khadija arrived early the following morning and went straight into the bedroom. He could hear her talking and bustling around in there, and after a moment she shut the door. She came out after a while with a handful of the baby's bed linen and seemed surprised to find Karim sitting in a chair with a cup of tea.

Ala, you are here, she said. Shall I get you some breakfast?

Oh no, I've had breakfast, he said, holding up his mug of tea.

That's good, I'll make something for Fauzia after I deal with this, she said, holding up the bundle of soiled linen. Aren't you going to work today?

I have the day off, in case anything is needed at home, he said. The work can wait.

No, no, nothing's needed here. I'll be here all day, Baba. I'll look after them. You go to work, she said.

He left reluctantly. In the nearly three years he had been married to Fauzia, he had not managed to get close to her mama. Perhaps he had not really tried. Fauzia visited her parents on her own usually, and they hardly ever came to the flat. The stairs are no good for Musa, Khadija said. Karim felt that just now she had spoken to him a little impatiently, as if he was being a nuisance, when she was actually taking over his space and his family. He did not like the way she was taking over. Best not to make a fuss for a day or two, he told himself, she was sure to be a comfort and a help to Fauzia, then afterward he would get his wife and baby back. It's natural. She's her daughter and you wouldn't know the first thing about what's needed at such a time. That was what he told himself as he walked to the office, at the same time preparing an explanation for his manager, who had generously told him to take a day off to welcome the baby.

Fauzia's mama continued to come to the flat every day, arriving before he left for work, and waving him off without delay. To hell with you, he thought as he slouched off to work. He tried to resign himself to her fussy presence because he knew that Fauzia did not find her intrusive in the way he did. On the contrary, she told him when he asked her, I find it comforting to have her here with Nasra and me. She is helpful, she tells me things, some of which I listen to and some I don't. She helps me with the baby, she's my mama and she loves the baby. It will only be for a few days. It would have been a lot harder for me on my own.

You're not on your own. I'm here, he protested.

I know, of course you're here, and you help me like no one else can, she said. I meant during the day, when you're at work. She takes so much off my hands.

So then he became reconciled to her presence in the flat every day, because it made Fauzia more comfortable. Khadija was her mother, as she said, it was natural she would, and it would not last forever. In the end it lasted three weeks because Musa had another bad spell and Khadija had to stay with him.

On the first day of her absence, he came home to lunch as usual to find Fauzia struggling with Nasra and with her chores. There's some leftover fish in the fridge, she said. I'm sorry.

I love leftover fish, he said. I'll go and buy some bread.

In the days that followed, he saw unmistakably how Mama had helped them. He came home to find Fauzia looking tired and ragged, and Nasra wailing. Sometimes Fauzia burst into tears as soon as he walked in. Nasra cried a lot more than she used to, wailing for hours at night, and neither of them seemed able to stop her for long. Instead of going home for lunch, he took to eating at a café, and it came to be that at the end of the day he found himself heading home after work with reluctance. Nasra's screaming was becoming unbearable. Night after night he was able to get only three or four hours sleep, listening for the little catch in Nasra's breathing that was the beginning of a yell. He dreaded that little catch so much that sometimes he heard it when she was sleeping and not about to cry at all. They tried to let her cry herself to sleep as they were advised in the book they consulted, but they could not do it. They could not bear her agonized howls.

It seemed at times that the slightest thing set her off, an accidental clang in the kitchen, a cough, his voice, or even just his arrival home from work. It seemed to him that it was he who set her off. He came home from work one afternoon and slowly eased himself into the flat, careful not to provoke the tyrant. He saw Badar sitting on the sofa with the baby on his lap and she was not crying, not even when he spoke loudly, cheerfully greeting Karim and then saying to Nasra, Hey, here's Baba, give him a wave, and the baby obediently waved her legs in the air.

Badar looked so comfortable holding the baby that Karim had to struggle to suppress his resentment. That's my baby you are holding there, he thought. Badar had been to see the baby before but had kept away while Fauzia's mother was in charge. This was his first visit since she stopped coming. Look how much she's grown, he said. Look at the little fatty. How many weeks is she?

Five, Fauzia said, looking on and smiling. You should come more often. See how quiet she is with you.

She cries a lot, Karim said, and thought he noticed a tremor pass through her little legs as he spoke, but it was a false alarm.

Badar held out the baby toward Karim, who shook his head. No, no, you carry on, you're doing a good job. She likes you, you hang on to her. I'll go wash my hands.

After Badar's departure, Nasra was back in business, crying at the slightest provocation or for no discernible reason. Each night they tried to encourage each other to let her cry herself to sleep, and to put her to sleep face down as the book advised, and at last it seemed to work, for a while. Sooner or later, though, she would shake off all restraint and begin howling. One night she cried with such abandon that she got into a frenzy, and whenever Fauzia made to go to her, Karim said, You must leave her.

She is having a seizure, Fauzia said in a panic.

No she is not, Karim shouted at her. She is just yelling. You must leave her.

Just when it seemed that Fauzia could not take any more and was about to rush to the cot, Nasra fell suddenly silent. Fauzia waited for the snuffles that usually signaled that she was winding down and drifting off to sleep, but there were no snuffles. She rushed to the cot, pressing the light switch just above it and found Nasra tangled in the sheets, turning dark.

She's suffocating, Fauzia cried, picking her up.

Karim ran to her and they stood together, looking aghast as their baby struggled to breathe. Then Fauzia pinched Nasra's nose and blew gently into her mouth, and after a moment she let out a soft gasp that was followed by a whimper and then a desperate gulping and sucking that signaled that she needed nourishment.

Fauzia feared it was the first sign of the falling sickness. Even though it was the early hours, she insisted they call Dr. Khalid, who came within minutes. He examined the baby and gave her a spoonful of something to calm her. She was now her normal color. He told them the tangled sheets were to blame and they should put her to sleep on her back. He also left them a prescription for something to calm her if she became frantic. We'll do a full examination tomorrow at the clinic, he said.

Later the next day, Badar went round to visit, knowing nothing of what had happened. He sensed something sullen in the air as he climbed up the narrow stairs to their apartment. It was evening and they were all there, Karim, Fauzia with the baby dozing in her arms, and Fauzia's friend Hawa, and all three looked unusually unhappy. Karim was frowning, eyes downcast. Fauzia seemed detached, as if half-asleep or perhaps exhausted. Hawa turned toward him with the briefest of scowls, as if his presence was a complication. He paused in the doorway and wondered if he had walked in in the middle of an argument.

Hamjambo? he greeted them. Are you all well?

There was an accident, Hawa said sharply, signaling that this was not a moment for happy greetings.

It was my fault, Karim said, his voice soft with sorrow, his eyes glistening. I said let her cry and she nearly choked to death.

No, no, Hawa said. It wasn't your fault, it was an accident. It happens with very young babies.

A sound like a sob escaped Fauzia. Yes, you said to let her cry, and she almost died. I should've known it was not over, she said.

Yes, it is over. This is not to do with the falling sickness, Karim shouted, a hint of desperation or annoyance in his voice. You heard what the doctor said! Stop going on about that!

The baby made a surprised noise and almost immediately afterward began to cry. Karim groaned, Hawa shut her eyes in despair, Badar went forward and held out his arms to take the baby. Fauzia hesitated, then after a long moment handed Nasra over. He took the baby and walked slowly away with her, out to the landing, away from the tensions in the room. He did not close the door, and made sure that he was always within Fauzia's sight. When Nasra quieted down, he went back inside and handed her to her mother.

Then they told him what had happened the previous night, Karim distraught, Hawa protesting as she had done before, Fauzia silent for a while, and then, as if to prevent further discussion of the event, she said with a smile, I don't know how you do that, take her in your arms and just like that she stops crying.

Badar visited them again the following evening and the one after that, and saw their unhappiness increase. He knew that Karim had been struggling since the baby's arrival and that his struggle was now worse after the accident. Fauzia was not convinced by Dr. Khalid's assurances that the seizure was not the beginning of the falling sickness, nor was Khadija. Badar could see that Fauzia was struggling with all the chores required of her, work he was used to—but she would not let him help her. She did what she could, feeding the baby, washing and cleaning, cooking, but she did it all reluctantly, clumsily, resentfully. Her resentment sometimes included Karim, who became withdrawn and defensive and did not seem able to suppress his irritation with her. In the midst of this lovelessness was Nasra, who continued howling and making her demands, deep in her own struggles with a life she had not chosen.

Khadija, too, saw what had happened and divided her time between Musa and Fauzia. Musa was no longer bedridden, and in his stoic way insisted he could cope quite well without help. In addition, they had a young man who came to help in the house and do their grocery shopping and accompany Musa for a short walk every day. In case I forget the way home, he joked. So there was nothing to prevent Khadija from leaving to be with Fauzia and the baby each day. Khadija prepared lunch for Musa and their young man, and brought some of it with her to Fauzia and Karim, although often he did not come home for lunch. He said they were too busy with a new project, and sometimes he had to drive out to the country to check on progress. Usually Khadija stayed for the afternoon.

Badar saw what was going on and was sad about their unhappiness. It will pass, he told himself. It must be what living with someone is like, learning to cope with what you did not know about each other. He kept his eyes open and his mouth shut, as old Juma had advised him years ago.

# 18.

The booking for Maria Caffrey was made on the phone by a travel agency in Dar es Salaam, which instructed that all charges be made to its account, so she was either a businesswoman or a VIP from an organization. She was on her own. It was pouring rain when she arrived. The deluge had begun in the middle of the night and was still in spasmodic spate in the early afternoon when she turned up at the hotel door sodden and disheveled, carrying a large backpack. She stood in the doorway laughing as she shrugged off the backpack and peeled off the thin plastic rain jacket, which had done nothing to prevent her from getting soaked. She squeezed the water out of her short bedraggled hair and tilted her head from side to side, draining the water out of her ears. Badar fetched some towels from the linen cupboard and waited while she vigorously mopped herself down.

I walked from the ferry terminal, she said, heaving a little after the excitement and the rubdown. It should have been five minutes . . . according to the map. It had stopped raining and then suddenly . . .

what a downpour. I'm soaked all the way through. Maria Caffrey, I have a reservation.

She was still laughing as she checked in: British, thirty-two years old, dressed in jeans and an olive green T-shirt that was now wet and clinging, well-built, a seasoned traveler from the stamps in her passport. Badar reached for her backpack as he prepared to show her upstairs but she made a restraining noise. It's all right, she said abruptly, unsmiling, the laughter suddenly gone. It was a large rucksack and she picked it up without any obvious effort. Badar wondered if there was something valuable inside it or if her brusque rebuff of his assistance was a habit of self-reliance, or maybe just impatience.

Of course, he said, retreating.

She was dripping as they headed upstairs, her trainers squelching with every step. She appraised the room coolly as he delivered his welcome routine on the hotel amenities. After he finished she said thank you, in an even, flat voice and then regarded him fully for a long moment. He looked away instantly, familiar with that condescending gaze. He saw then that her eyes were charcoal dark and that something alert and watchful lay behind their lazy appearance.

He did not see her again until breakfast the following morning, smartly dressed in green linen trousers and a loose pale blouse. Her hair had a curly bounce that was not evident when she was drenched. She nodded in return to his greeting and walked past him toward a man who was already waiting for her in the lobby.

Maria Caffrey, she said, offering her hand. You must be Sefu. Thank you for coming to meet me.

Yes, Director, you are welcome. I hope you had a pleasant evening last night, the man said with a tiny bow.

Oh yes, I managed fine, she said with a chuckle, and then set off ahead of the man who had come to meet her.

It seemed that Maria Caffrey had come to take up a post as director of something—Director, you are welcome—and was booked to stay at the Tamarind for an indefinite period of time. She was busy, coming and going briskly, preoccupied with papers during breakfast and paying little attention to the staff serving her. The moment she was done with breakfast she was off upstairs and on her way out soon after. One morning she paused by the office as she was walking past and gave Badar the same appraising look she had given him on the afternoon she arrived, as if something about him puzzled her. It was chilling. He did not think she saw him exactly. He could not work out the meaning of her gaze. Apart from that encounter, he did not see much of her during her stay, only briefly in the mornings as she hurried out and again when she checked out. She had stayed for a week while her permanent accommodation was being prepared. Maria Caffrey herself volunteered this information as she checked out. My apartment is now ready, so I'll be checking out tomorrow morning. Is there anything on the bill for me to pay? My agency will take care of the accommodation costs.

It was the most words she had spoken to Badar during her stay at the hotel. He guessed she was one of those guests, experienced travelers in this part of the world, who assumed that the people she dealt with were incompetent or worse. He did not ask her any questions about her new accommodation although he was curious to know what she was here to do. Something to do with aid or an

NGO, whatever that was exactly. He would look it up later. She was not a tourist. She was not a diplomat or a member of the UN staff. She would have been staying in one of the posh beachside hotels if she was, not in the boutique Tamarind in the tangled alleyways of the old town.

Maria Caffrey herself helped Badar satisfy his curiosity. She gave him her business card on the afternoon she left: *Maria Caffrey, Director, Relief Exchange International, Volunteer Recruitment.* The card had her office address, her email, and her mobile phone number. She slid the card toward him as he was closing her account on the computer and he looked up in surprise to find her dark, sleepy eyes fully on him, measuring him up again, before gliding away.

What are all these looks about? he wondered. He had assumed they indicated a condescending curiosity but perhaps they showed another kind of interest. He reprimanded himself for his vanity. He saw her twice in the town after she left the hotel but she gave no sign of recognition. The second time he saw her she was striding into a bank, and he wondered what work she would have done if she was around during the good old times of the empire. It was a thought that occurred to him with some of the guests, or some tourists he saw in town, prompted by something imperious and detached in their manner even when they smiled. He sensed that just below the surface of those smiles lay a sense of self-assurance and self-absorption, an unacknowledged feeling of superiority. Who could blame them, when they saw the paltriness all around them? Maria Caffrey did not even smile, not at Badar anyway.

Some months after that stay, Maria Caffrey emailed about a new booking. It was not for her but for a Geraldine Bruno, who could be a volunteer or a replacement director or a visitor. Maria Caffrey did not say. She wrote: *Tamarind Hotel Reservations, Requesting a room for one guest for a week from 16 March, with the possibility of an extension. The guest's name is Geraldine Bruno. Please acknowledge and confirm reservation. Regards, Maria Caffrey, Director Relief Exchange.* Badar acknowledged and confirmed.

It was Badar's third year at the Tamarind, still working under Assistant Manager Issa. He was experienced and assured in his work, and found a kind of ease if not contentment in his fate. He was still at other people's beck and call, but at least it was not such blatant servitude as it had been before. The people he served said please and thank you to him, and the hotel paid him a salary, which gave him a feeling of independence and self-respect. If it did not sound much like fulfillment to others, it did to him, it felt like a rest, a breather after so much uncertainty. He was still renting the room in Hakim's house, which over the years he had furnished and decorated in a haphazard way as whim or opportunity presented itself. He picked up items that caught his attention as he strolled the streets, a rug, a mirror with a silver frame, a curtain for his one window, a small fridge that he bought from a shop that repaired broken-down electrical objects. Idris was still there in the other downstairs room, now joined by his new wife, Maryam. They persuaded Hakim to refurbish the downstairs bathroom, or rather it was Maryam who made the difference. She made friends with Hakim's wife, who talked Hakim into improving the facilities for his tenants.

Badar liked working with Assistant Manager Issa although he would not be doing so for very much longer. Bwana Sharif Makame was refurbishing another building nearby in Shangani, turning it into a restaurant and hotel. The building had belonged to an Indian family, just like the Tamarind once had, but this other space was a mansion with many rooms, a large reception hall that was to become the restaurant, wide verandas across the two top floors, and a walled garden with an imposing metal gate. Badar did not know the family because they were already gone by the time he came to the town. All he knew about them was what Issa told him, that the big man of the family was a lawyer and his wife was a doctor and the family was called Adamji. They were renowned for their philanthropy, as so many of the Indian lords were. The government had confiscated the building from them, as they did every other building its barons coveted. Soon after that the family departed for Canada or Sweden or somewhere else where their skills were welcomed.

For a while the building was used as temporary accommodation for visiting foreign staff, at first the Soviets and Chinese and other fraternal experts, and more recently, after those relationships soured, experts from rich countries who came to give advice to the government. Their countries paid for them and their big cars, and perhaps their advice was heeded or perhaps it was not, but their governments could brag of their generosity while they extracted what advantage they could from the relationship and also provided work for their compatriots. The building was unoccupied a lot of the time, Assistant Manager Issa said, because the facilities were out-of-date or in disrepair, so now a consortium made up of foreign money and businessmen here at home, which included politicians and Bwana Sharif Makame, had acquired it and were renovating it into an international hotel with a world-class restaurant, which meant the food rich people eat. It was to be called Masri Hotel. Badar wondered if perhaps the foreign money came from Masri, Egypt, or from Gulf Arabs who loved Egypt. Or maybe hotel names need not have sensible explanations, just words to tickle a fantasy, or a brand name that signaled the glamour and prosperity of the rich world.

The creative supervisors of the refurbishing were the restaurant's chef-to-be and his wife, who was to be the manager of the hotel. Issa would remain an assistant manager, but now in a much grander establishment. Badar expected the same rules would apply there nonetheless. (Don't make jokes and don't laugh out loud. Don't touch them!)

The chef and his wife were Europeans although they did not come from Europe. He was from South Africa and she was from Mauritius. What he knew about them came from Issa, who sometimes talked about them, although Badar himself had also caught sight of them in town. He was a big heavy-looking man with short graying dark hair and a round face that seemed fixed in a benign half smile. She was as tall as him, slim and sharp-featured, her face more somber as if she were preoccupied with concerns. Issa said they knew their business. They certainly think they know how to deal with people like us, he said. The mister was a gentle giant but the madam was quick to give orders and was fierce with everyone, especially the decorators. It seemed that she was not sure they knew what they were doing. Issa had not worked under a mzungu boss before but he would learn, so long as they were not insolent with him. He had his suspicions, but he would not have insolence, he said, not for anybody's money. When the Masri Hotel was ready to open its doors and Issa had moved to his new post, Badar was to become assistant manager of the Tamarind.

Bwana Sharif himself told him after one of his day bookings in

room 5. Badar was long past the excitement of the first day booking, when he could hardly contain himself before telling Karim
about the event. Now he deliberately took no notice of the comings
and goings of the owner's liaisons, discreetly looked away, and
made up the room only if it was booked for a late-arriving guest.
Otherwise he left it for the cleaners to deal with in the morning. It
happened no more than once a month or so, at times when the room
was available. The boss's liaisons always happened in room 5, for
no discernible reason other than that was how the boss wanted it.

Bwana Sharif kept up the routine that gave his mistress the cover
to slip out without embarrassment. When Bwana Sharif's business
was done in room 5, he came down first, entered the office, and
closed the door behind him. Then he hovered at the door for a moment or two, looking refreshed and replete as he always did in the
aftermath of his day bookings, and made brief conversation before
opening the door once again. This care was quite unnecessary by
this point, since Badar knew that his mistress was the wife of a junior minister. The affair had been going on for a long time, maybe
four or five years. Bwana Sharif did the concealment business to
save the woman from humiliation, to respect her, but in the end he
probably did not care who knew. She was not his only mistress, just
the one he brought to this hotel. Issa told Badar all this.

After one particular day booking, when the works at the Masri
Hotel were well under way, Bwana Sharif said to Badar, You are
doing very well here. Very efficient, very discreet. Not at all restless. Have I told you that before?

Yes, boss, Badar said. Issa called him boss, and when Badar saw
that he liked it, he did the same.

Yes, very discreet. It must run in the family. Your uncle will be proud of you. When the Masri is ready, I will put you in charge here, he said, his face deadpan but his eyes glinting with mischief. Then he opened the office door and glanced over his shoulder to make sure his mistress was out of sight. Do you think you'll be able to cope? he asked.

Yes, boss.

Not too young?

No, boss, Badar said. Not at all.

Bwana Sharif laughed with the mixture of pleasure and mockery that was habitual to him, the big man's cackle, and then he raised an arm in farewell. He often mentioned Badar's uncle, by which he meant Haji. Karim had told him some while ago that Haji and Bwana Sharif had been college students together and still did business now and then, discreet business involving transfers of money out of sight of interfering authorities. Badar guessed that when Bwana Sharif praised him for his discretion, he was referring to his liaisons in room 5, and mentioning Haji in the next breath was to implicate both Haji and Badar in his devious networks. He hoped that Haji was not doing anything illegal, although it was nothing to do with him. All Badar was doing was keeping his mouth shut while the big man went about his pleasures.

In practice his duties were already no different from Assistant Manager Issa's. More often than not it was Badar who greeted the guests at breakfast, offered advice about car rentals and destinations, booked outings or tables at restaurants, ordered supplies for the kitchen, and dealt with more or less all online bookings. The only task that still remained Issa's responsibility was going to the bank to deposit any cash and to collect their wages. Guest payments were made by bank cards.

When the email arrived with the booking for Geraldine Bruno, Badar realized he had not given much further thought to Maria Caffrey since her stay. He remembered how she had arrived at the hotel laughing, her hair drenched, her thin plastic jacket useless against the downpour, her clothes soaked. The laughter must have been a moment of self-forgetfulness prompted by discomfort more than anything. He remembered that at the time of her arrival he did not know the name of the volunteer agency she directed, and only found out from her business card as she was leaving. It was the same agency that was to be charged for Geraldine Bruno's reservation. He wondered what made people like Maria Caffrey come all this way to do their good deeds, when it seemed to him that she did it with such ill humor. He wondered if Geraldine Bruno would turn out to be as stern as her.

It was raining sporadically on the afternoon Geraldine Bruno was expected to arrive, gentle showers between sunny spells before the full arrival of the long rainy season in April. Out of curiosity Badar checked through the computer for the dates of Maria Caffrey's stay at the hotel and discovered that it was in December, when the short rainy season was in full spate.

Earlier on the afternoon of Geraldine Bruno's arrival, Issa had left to check something on the works at the Masri, or so he said, though Badar suspected he went to see to some business of his own. His family often seemed to need his help. Issa never talked about them or about his life, or he did so in an outburst when he had to deal with something especially trying. Badar had been there long enough to hear something of Issa's family, that he had been married briefly but divorced and never bothered to marry again, that he lived with his sister and her husband and children. Issa waited until after lunch before leaving because when Bwana Sharif called on them, it was usually in the morning, unless he had a day booking. They were not very busy that day, only two rooms occupied and Geraldine Bruno expected. It was mid-March, a slack time for visitors, so Badar would not be overworked without Issa.

At around four thirty in the afternoon, that mellow hour when the sun begins to soften and people are again drawn out of their houses, Badar heard a taxi pull up outside the hotel and a moment or two later Maria Caffrey appeared in the doorway. She was dressed in jeans and a T-shirt, as she was when she first arrived, and she stood there for a moment and then walked toward the office where Badar had gotten to his feet. Behind her entered a slim young woman of glowing beauty—that was Badar's first thought—who broke into a smile as soon as she caught sight of him. Badar waited a moment for Geraldine Bruno to appear but only the taxi driver came in with a suitcase, and he then realized it was she standing in front of him. Badar looked at the beautiful young woman and laughed, a short, surprised, panting laughter. He had expected someone much older, another Maria Caffrey or else someone agonized by her conscience, which he guessed was the other variety among the volunteers. Maria Caffrey frowned at him and said, Geraldine Bruno, you have a reservation for her.

He made a copy of her passport as he checked her in: Geraldine Bruno, British, twenty-one years old. She wrote her address on the check-in form, *Gemstone Street, London NW3.* You have room 3 on the first floor, he said as he handed her the key. Breakfast is served over there across the terrace. I'll bring your luggage up for you.

There is no need, I can handle it, Geraldine Bruno said with a flashing smile, reaching for her case. It looked heavy but he did not argue with her.

I'll come back for you in a couple of hours, and we can go out to dinner, Maria Caffrey said. Unless you are too tired after the flight.

Hey no, not at all tired. That will be very nice, Geraldine Bruno said, smiling brightly, eager to please.

They left a fragrance of sweat and soap in the office, and something stale, which Badar recognized as the aroma of a newly arrived airline traveler. He ran his mind over Geraldine Bruno and sighed with pained admiration. She had fair hair, he did not know the name of the shade of fair but he remembered from the Mistress's magazines that there were multitudes of shades. She had bright light-colored eyes, gray or blue, he could not be sure, and was slim and tall, probably taller than him. She was dressed in blue cotton trousers and a white shirt. A long pale-colored scarf of very thin material was wound around her neck. Yes, a glowing beauty, he thought, and then returned to the newspaper he had been reading before they arrived.

A short while before the night clerk, Ramadhani, came to relieve him at six he heard the sound of a flute coming from upstairs, or at least he thought it was a flute. It had a deep tone although its sound was bright and throaty, so it could be another instrument he was unfamiliar with. It was a slow, thoughtful tune, perhaps pleading or yearning. He knew that the guests in room 1 had gone out a while before, and the ones in room 2 were on a day trip to the Crystal Bay

Hotel, in which Bwana Sharif's stake allowed Tamarind guests to use their beach facilities. So the flute player could only be Geraldine Bruno, a beauty with a flute. He went out into the courtyard and confirmed that the music was unmistakably from room 3. He resisted the temptation to go up to the first floor on some pretext so he could hear more clearly and went back to the office to wait for Ramadhani.

He was not there when Maria Caffrey came to collect Geraldine Bruno for dinner, but he was when she came for her the following morning. Badar was busy with the delivery of clean laundry and did not catch sight of Geraldine Bruno until she appeared in the lobby to wait for Maria Caffrey. She was dressed in dark trousers and a baggy shirt with two breast pockets and no sheer scarf, a more businesslike appearance. The strap of her shoulder bag ran across her chest, briefly drawing Badar's eyes to her breasts before he turned back to the laundry man. Issa was at his desk and took no notice of the beautiful young woman standing in the lobby.

Good morning, Geraldine Bruno said in an undertone, addressing him alone, and when Badar looked up at her he saw something in her eyes he had not expected, as if she was recognizing him or regarding him in detail, curious rather than taking him to be part of the landscape. Perhaps he had shown something of himself to her and she was trying to understand it. He needed to maintain his distance with guests, he reminded himself, even when they were as beautiful as this one.

Good morning, he said brightly, perhaps too brightly because Issa looked up from his desk with a small frown. He preferred to be cool and correct with the guests, to avoid any possibility of misunderstanding, as he put it. You be just as you wish, Mr. Assistant Manager sir, Badar thought to himself. You can be as indifferent to glowing beauty as you like, but I don't mind if I relish it.

I heard you playing the flute yesterday afternoon, Badar said to Geraldine Bruno.

It's a clarinet. I hope it was not irritating, she said with a sudden smile of pleasure.

No, no, it was very good, he said.

Wow, that's kind of you, she said, still smiling, just as Maria Caffrey walked into the lobby.

Maria Caffrey paused for a moment, taking in the scene, perhaps noticing the smile still lingering on Geraldine Bruno's lips and maybe hearing the echo of her words. Badar hoped so, anyway.

Good morning, are you ready? she asked Geraldine Bruno, and then turned round to leave without waiting for a reply.

Friendly, isn't she? Badar said to Issa as he walked back to the office.

Issa looked up, preoccupied, but did not say anything in reply. He went back to the computer screen and continued reading what was there. Badar went round and looked over his shoulder. There was a new review on the hotel website, awarding them one star. It read: *Overpriced. It calls itself a boutique hotel but really it is just a rip-off. Convenient for the sites and restaurants in the center but there are bugs in the room, TV is tiny, the AC doesn't cool the room, the water smells, and the bathroom could be cleaner and more modern. The break-fast is poor, greasy rubbish. The staff are slow and cranky. I am giving it one star because I can't give it a zero. Stay somewhere else!*

The name the reviewer gave was Jazzy. Who's this bastard? Issa asked, and spent the next hour going over recent guests to try to work out who it might be. He did so in a silent rage, unable to tear himself away from the screen. Badar left him to it and went to see how the breakfast service was going. The guests in rooms 1 and 2 were still lingering over their food, an elderly Danish couple in 1 and a much younger British couple in 2. The Danes liked to stroll the streets with their guidebooks and maps, looking at houses and museums and searching out cafés tucked away in the maze of alleyways. He was a retired marine biologist and she was a former teacher. She told Badar about a Danish spice dealer who had lived in the town for a decade in the nineteenth century. She had read an article about him before they came. One of their quests was to find the house he lived in, using clues he left in his letters, as detailed in the article. Did he, Badar, want to read the article? The author of the article was not sure that his subject had really dealt in spices and suggested that there might be a mystery about him. Had he, Badar, heard of this man? Did he have any idea where he might have lived? When Badar said he had not heard of a Danish dealer in spices and had no idea where he might have lived, the man said in a disappointed voice, Well, boy, it's a pity you have no interest in your own history.

The British couple—he was a journalist but she did not say what she did—preferred boat trips and the beach, and sought advice about restaurants for dinner, which Badar gave by rote since he had never eaten in any of the expensive places they would consider visiting. They had spent the previous day at the Crystal Bay Hotel, and this morning they wanted to tell Badar about the magnificent buffet served for lunch and the lovely garden by the beach where they had stretched out while waiting for the tide to come in. Oh you should've seen the Italians in the next-door hotel, stretched out on the beach on their sun beds, baking in the heat, dozens of them. It was not a pretty sight. Row after row of sun beds, with those bodies burning on them. Still, nothing to do with us. For us the only down-side was that the tide was so far out in the morning and did not come in until after lunch, but after that it was great.

Back in the office Issa was still at the computer, his thin mus-tache bristling, trying to find the guest who might have written the review. It's all lies, he said. I think I've found him. It's that French-man with flowery shirts and a straw hat, the one with the long shorts. He was here for some music event, jazz or something, you remember him? Here he is, Bernard Georges. That's the bastard. Look at the date. That's him. Jazzy.

Badar went over and looked at the date, which was the day be-fore the review. He nodded but did not say anything. There was no reason why the reviewer should have written his piece on the day after checking out. It could have been a week or more later. Badar had been working it out for himself. He read through the review again and noticed the spelling of *center* and *bugs in the room*, and guessed it was an American. An American woman had stayed on her own for two nights some two weeks previously. Badar remem-bered her very well. She was in her late forties, dark hair, sleeveless plunging blouse when she arrived on the early afternoon flight. Ba-dar checked her in and took up a bucket of ice as she requested, which he left outside her door after knocking. He did not catch sight of her until the following morning at breakfast and afterward when she came to the office to ask for directions to a gallery where she had arranged to meet a friend. Issa provided the directions and a map, but her eyes kept coming back to Badar and finally settled on him for a good look. Tina Derrick, her name came back to him. She took the map and left. Issa was in the office at the time, and when Badar glanced toward him he raised his eyebrows briefly, a gesture that Badar took as a remark on something odd in the guest's behavior. Or was it to do with how she was dressed, another sleeveless plunging blouse? Or had Issa noticed the long look she gave Badar before she took the map and left?

Badar was in the office alone when she returned late in the afternoon, and she called out a cheerful hello as she walked past. She looked as if she had had a good lunch. Some while later, maybe half an hour or so, she telephoned the office to ask for ice again. He locked the office as was the procedure when there was only one of them on-site and fetched ice from the kitchen. When he reached her room, he saw that the door was ajar. He knocked on the door, intending to leave the ice bucket on the threshold as he had done the previous day but she called out, Bring it inside.

She was lying on the bed, on top of the covers, wearing a dressing gown. Her legs were crossed and the gown had fallen open to reveal her legs up to her midthighs. He headed toward the table on the side of the room with the bucket of ice, keeping his eyes away from her.

What's your name? she asked softly.

Badar, he said, avoiding eye contact.

Badar, can you close the door, please? she said.

He hesitated, knowing that he should not, that their practice at the hotel was never to be in a room with a guest with the door closed. After a moment he closed the door and leaned against it. He understood what was happening and he was alarmed. Her face, he now saw, was flushed, and her mouth was slack. She had spoken in a soft voice but he saw a hard glitter in her eyes.

So handsome, come over here, Badar, she said firmly, holding out her left arm and making the dressing gown fall open even more. It was such a theatrical gesture that Badar laughed, and that released him from the grip of his surprise and paralysis. He reached for the door handle behind him and fled downstairs. He wondered if she would follow him down and berate him for fleeing. Badar had not yet lain with a woman, although he did have a girlfriend for a few months earlier in the year. Her name was Zakia. She was his first girlfriend, and they carried out their romance secretively, meeting in the evenings in secluded places and exchanging caresses. She refused to come to his room and they had nowhere else where they could be private, and the secretiveness wore Zakia down as she feared exposure and her father's anger, so they stopped meeting.

A short while after his escape from Tina Derrick, Badar was relieved by Ramadhani, the night clerk. He found out the next morning that she had checked herself out the previous evening. She'd told Ramadhani that something had come up and she had to go. Ramadhani said she seemed drunk, and when he went up to her room, it reeked of cannabis. He said all this to Issa, who always started work earlier than Badar to relieve him. When Issa told Badar about her sudden departure, he made a gesture that meant something like What do you make of it? Badar shrugged and did not say anything. His guess was that it was Tina Derrick who was Jazzy but he did not want to tell Issa that he had refused her invitation. He could not completely get over the feeling that he had been cowardly to do so, and he had to remind himself of her slack mouth and the hungry glitter in her eyes to reassure himself that he had been wise to escape.

The phone rang as Issa was fuming at the computer and he reached distractedly at it. Tamarind Hotel, can I help you? he said. He listened for a few seconds and then said, Haya, haya, okay. Inshallah. Utaniarifu baadaye.

You'll let me know later. He put the phone down carefully and at last turned away from the computer screen. Another aggravation had appeared on his horizon. Ramadhani, he said to Badar, a sneer of disgust on his face. I knew this was coming. He is unwell, again. He is becoming unreliable, that man. He is unwell, or a relative has passed away or something, always something. I know he's unwell, he drinks too much, that's his problem. I think he also works for someone else as well as us but doesn't want to give up this job.

Works for who? Badar asked skeptically.

I don't know, Issa said fiercely. How do you expect me to know? Perhaps he does deliveries for one of the beach hotels or is doing contraband for someone. What I can tell you is he is not coming to work tonight and maybe won't tomorrow night either. You'll have to stay on as night clerk in his place.

Badar nodded. He knew that Ramadhani was related to Issa by marriage in some way that had to do with his sister's husband, which was perhaps the reason he was not dismissed. It had happened on three previous occasions that Ramadhani called to say he could not come to work and Badar had to do his turn for him. Badar knew that Ramadhani went on drinking binges with his friends, and sometimes the moonshine they drank laid him low for a day or two. Ramadhani himself ruefully admitted afterward that that was the reason for calling in sick. Chupa kali, he had said more than once. The bottle is fierce. He is a sad case, Issa said, and it was true. It said so in his face and his scrawny frame. Most likely it was not just hunger that was responsible for that body but childhood illness or a life of unhappiness. Despite appearances he was meticulously obliging to the guests and completely reliable, except when he was not.

There was a fold-up bed that they kept in the staff store, and which Ramadhani used when he was on night duty. There was enough room in the office to open it, and after midnight, which was the hotel lock-up time, he stretched himself out on it for a few hours' sleep. Later that evening Badar fetched the bed from the store, then sat in the office alternating between reading a book and listening to the radio. In the middle of stifling yet another yawn, he heard the sound of a clarinet and knew that Geraldine Bruno was back in her room. He had not seen her come in. He went out to the courtyard to listen and stood under the veranda overhang to keep out of the rain. He thought the music sad, and wondered if she was feeling lonely in a strange country and if the music made her think of her home, or if she was tired after her first day at whatever she had come to do, or if the clarinet was an instrument that produced sad music. It was still early and perhaps the director would shortly be coming round to take Geraldine Bruno out to dinner again. He went back to the office and returned to the book he was struggling with. It was going to be a long night.

Some while later, he suddenly became aware of Geraldine Bruno at the door of the office. He had not heard her approach.

Hello, she said, her smile both tentative and casual, as if what she was about to say was not anything important. She had changed out of the sober clothes of the morning and was wearing jeans and a loose-fitting white shirt.

Hello, Miss Bruno, how can I help you? he said, beaming professionally.

I'm sorry to bother you. Is it possible to have a snack, maybe a sandwich or just a piece of bread? she asked, smiling with her lips and her eyes, her head angled ruefully.

No, I'm afraid there are no snacks. Our bread is delivered in the morning, he said, trying his best to look pained and apologetic. We only serve breakfast.

I know, she said with a sigh.

There are several eating places just a few minutes away, he said, standing up, ready to direct her.

I don't feel like going out right now, she said, making a face. It's raining out there. I'll explore tomorrow.

He took in the sight for a moment before replying. Really, he should just say no, not a chance, but this was a glowing beauty addressing him on a dreary evening and he felt himself relenting. There is probably some fruit in the kitchen, or maybe some salad or juice. I'll go and have a look. Please take a seat, Miss Bruno, he said.

He came back with a tangerine, a banana, a tomato, and a glass of milk. He put the tray down on the desk he normally occupied when Issa was also in the office. She had picked up the book he was reading and was inspecting the back cover. He gestured toward the tray, and she rose toward it, taking the book with her. He expected her to take the tray and head back to her room but she sat in the chair behind the desk and picked up the glass of milk. Fantastic, she said, and took a large sip.

Shall I boil you an egg? he asked. He could see she was not intending to move.

No, this is perfect, she said. She peeled the banana and took a bite. She did not say another word until all the fruit and the tomato and milk were gone, then as if she had become aware of herself she laughed briefly. I was starving, she said, and that was just cool. Thank you.

You are welcome, Badar said, and took the tray to the kitchen. When he came back, expecting Geraldine Bruno to surely be gone now, he found her still sitting at the desk with the book open in her hands. It was a book about young doctors in a New York hospital and their goings-on. He was contemplating abandoning it.

You can borrow it if you want, he said.

No, no, I was just curious, she said lightly, her voice a little less eager, perhaps tired after a long day.

Guests often leave books behind, he said, indicating a bookshelf against the far wall, right next to the Charter Airlines calendar. Holiday reading, I suppose, which they don't want to take back with them. Help yourself, any time.

She glanced at the shelf and then stood up to have a look. She browsed the shelf for a moment and then asked, Have you read these? He gathered from her tone and the slight twitch of a smile that accompanied her words that she was not impressed.

Yes, some of them, he said, and was aware of something defensive in his voice.

They seem either crime or romance, typical holiday junk. Are you enjoying this one? she asked, returning to the desk and picking up the book again.

He shrugged, it was turning into a proper interrogation, but he did not mind, it was nice to have company. It's not very interesting. I think it's supposed to be funny, but maybe I don't understand the details, the medical words and emergencies, or I don't see the joke. Or maybe it's funny in a way I don't grasp, you know, because I don't understand what is being made fun of and why this person is foolish and that one is clever.

She put the book down on the desk. I might borrow it sometime, she said with a tired smile. I'll report back to you.

May I ask what you are doing with the relief agency? he asked, breaking another of Issa's rules, asking guests personal questions.

Yes, I'm joining a project to digitalize government records, she said, perking up. Nothing sensitive, we're starting with health records because that's where the EU funding is coming from. I am a professional in software development but the agency has other projects. Other volunteers are teachers or economists or actors or whatever. Everyone is trying to do their bit, to help out. I'm doing twelve weeks, other people do less or more depending on their circumstances. I could only get twelve weeks off from my firm.

She was silent for a while, eyes cast down, thoughtful. He sensed that her mouth was full of words and that she would say more, tell him about her software or about London NW3. He would have liked to hear more but it was as if she had interrupted herself. Suddenly, she yawned.

Anyway, she said, rising, thanks for the snack. I'll be off now.

She was out of the office before he could think to say anything that would detain her. He saw that she had not taken the book and he did not blame her. He picked it up and read: *Amy hurried away from the emergency theater and headed for the changing rooms, unbuttoning her white tunic on the way. She hoped Dean would still be at the party when she got there. There was no time for a shower so she changed out of her theater whites and made for the exit. The party was in the residential block, and as she made her way there her body was already tingling with anticipation.*

Badar put the book down, knowing a soft-porn episode was on the way. He thought he would leave that for later in case he could not sleep. A few nights ago he had listened to a program on the radio about the Persian poet Ḥāfez, and some lines of a poem stayed with him.

> *Last night, as half asleep I dreaming lay,*
> *Half naked came she in her little shift,*
> *With tilted glass, and verses on her lips*

He clicked on images of Shiraz and looked for the tomb of Ḥāfez. He saw the crowds there as they strolled on pathways lined with bushes and flowers toward the steps of the mausoleum, men and women and children, some in long coats, some in shirtsleeves, in headscarves, and jackets. Up the steps toward the tomb round which mingled hundreds of people, some sitting on the steps exhausted, or reading from a brochure, some taking selfies, some praying, and other gazing silently at the pools and the cypress groves. They sat there in peace in the midafternoon shadows. A low yellow sun shone through the trees and on the dozens of flow-erpots that overflowed purples and white and reds. Other images showed pools and flagged cloisters that opened up to a large park. He logged off the computer and sprayed the office to keep the mos-quitoes at bay and closed the door. He went out into the street for a few minutes to let the poison work. The rain had stopped but the air was full of the smell of water. It was the time of year when mosquitoes were in their pomp and almost nothing could restrain them, and the only safe place to be after dark was under a net. After midnight he locked the hotel doors, went back to the office, and stretched out on the fold-up bed. He lay awake for a long time.

His thoughts rambled and then snagged on Fauzia and Karim. How subdued she had become since the sudden scare with their baby. He remembered Mama Khadija telling him that even as a child Fauzia had a grown-up smile. Now there was something hes-itant or uncertain behind it, as if she was no longer sure that all was well. Karim, too, was changed, disappointed by how things had turned out perhaps. Badar could not help noticing that he had be-come increasingly short with him, and he could not think what he had done to provoke this irritation. Over the years he had had to cope with bouts of condescension from Karim, usually to do with his rescue from Uncle Othman, or because he seemed content to work in a hotel, but this testiness was more intense and Badar was not sure why. Perhaps it was not to do with him exactly but with Karim himself, with his increasing ambitions at work, or with Fau-zia and the baby. He did not seem able to recover from his wounded withdrawal after the accusation Badar had witnessed. You said let her cry and she almost died. That had been weeks ago now, and love should have healed some of those abrasions but did not seem to have done so. He had not been to see them for many days. Fauzia was about to start back at school when he last called. He would go and see them the next day, on his way to the hotel. Unless Ramadhani recovered, in which case Issa might call him in for the afternoon. One way or another he would call round in late afternoon when Fauzia was sure to be back from school.

Ramadhani did not recover, so Badar knew he was on night duty again. He called round on his way to the hotel and found Fauzia in. She had just picked up Nasra from her mother's house, where she had spent the day. She was rushed and maybe a little distressed by all she had to do, return to school, take care of the baby, who was grizzling, as well as organize some food. Despite that, she seemed pleased to see him and handed the baby to him without further ado. Karim was not in. He'll be sorry to have missed you, she said.

I can't stay long, he said. I have to relieve Issa in about ten minutes.

Nasra was squirming and whimpering, but a few seconds in his magic arms appeared to soothe her, and so he rocked her and whispered to her while Fauzia prepared her food. He said his goodbye amid Nasra's joyful slurping of the pulped mess her mother had prepared for her. She's hungry, he said as he was leaving, as if he knew what a grumpy baby really needed.

Later that evening when he was once again covering Ramadhani's shift, Geraldine Bruno came into the office wearing a fitted sleeveless lime-green blouse and tight cream jeans. She was on her way out. She stood in front of him for a moment, elegant, her right foot a little ahead of her left, striking a pose, lightheartedly showing off. He joined in the display, applauding her silently.

You must've thought me very silly last night, coming to ask for a snack when there is delicious street food just a few minutes away, she said. I hadn't quite got my bearings.

Not silly at all, Miss Bruno. It was a pleasure to provide you with the fruit, Badar said, standing up as well. She seemed so relaxed, so friendly. He could not work it out. Their guests were not usually this easy. Maybe it was because she was young and the other guests were usually older.

I think I was still tired from the flight, and perhaps a little nervous about out there, she said, gesturing toward the street.

And it was raining. You're in a strange country, he said sympathetically.

To his surprise, she came around the desk she had sat behind the previous evening and took a seat. I love it here already though, she said, bright-eyed and smiling. It's beautiful even in the rain.

It's very nice to hear that, he said. Do you come from London?

She nodded.

Is London very beautiful? he asked.

She laughed. Well, maybe it depends on what part of London. I was born in Bermondsey, even the name is ugly. London is so big, like a country in itself. It's impossible to know it all, which is great because there is always somewhere beautiful that takes you by surprise.

So some parts of London are very beautiful, he said.

Oh yes, definitely, and some parts are ugly and scary, she said, laughing. I grew up in Clapham and I suppose that's beautiful in its way. There's the Common and the cafés and all the grand houses, but there's also all the traffic and noise and crowds.

Oh I know Clapham, he said.

Have you been there? she asked in surprise.

No, no, pictures on the computer. I was walking round there on the pavement a few days ago, he said, hoping to sound funny, but she looked a little dismayed.

Pictures, she said, almost pityingly.

They sat in silence for a while. What had she found pitiful about looking at pictures on a computer? He traveled to all parts of the world like that. Maybe one day he would get to travel for real. He wondered what she was doing there in the office, if she was waiting for her director or some new friend to come and collect her. She did not seem anxious or hurried. I don't live in Clapham anymore, she said. Gemstone Street NW3, he said to himself. Then she started to describe the street in which she lived, the main road at the top and her favorite café just round the corner.

Hey, I don't even know your name, she said, interrupting herself.

Badar, he said. Her hand was small and light as they shook, cool to the touch.

You know my name, she said, smiling.

My pleasure, Miss Bruno, he said, smiling too. Are you heading out to dinner?

Jerry, please call me Jerry. I will go out for some food soon, when I've plucked up the courage, she said. I wish I had company.

It's quite safe, just walk along the waterfront for a few minutes and you are there, he said, involuntarily glancing at her thin sleeveless blouse and tight jeans. There are crowds of people and you'll be fine.

She nodded and he wondered if he should tell her that someone was bound to approach a woman on her own and offer her company, especially someone so beautiful and dressed as she was. Should he warn her about the young men who hovered on the edges of the street food stalls, alert to any pickings? She seemed so easy and relaxed. Would she know how to deal with all that? She was sure to have been schooled by Maria Caffrey, so he did not say anything.

Are you still reading that book about doctors in New York? she asked.

He shook his head. Too demanding, he said, which made her laugh.

She stood up suddenly, decisively. All right, I'm off, she said, and left.

He returned to the computer and looked up Clapham again and spent a few minutes browsing the Common and the long leafy streets, the wine bars, and the cafés. He opened a map of London and marveled at the hugeness of the city. Something cringed in him, repelled by it.

He checked emails and acknowledged a new booking for a fortnight hence. He should call on Karim and Fauzia again, at a better time. They were the two people he loved most in the world. What did it mean to say something like that? He did not know enough people in the world for words like that to mean anything, but he knew he loved those two. Karim because he had looked after him when he was in need, and because he was clever and handsome and glamorous, or he was most of the time when he was not being bossy and domineering. Fauzia because she was tender and thoughtful and beautiful, even if now she was in distress. It made him happy to be with them, or at least it used to, and would do so again inshallah.

Jerry Bruno was back within the hour, the edges of a greasy paper bag between thumb and forefinger. She held the bag out toward Badar.

Badar asked, Did you enjoy your food? What's that?

I think it's octopus, she said with a distressed look on her face. I didn't know what it was and he just kept piling it into the bag.

He came round, took the bag from her, and handed her a paper towel. Did you get something to eat?

Thank you. I had some chips and a fish cutlet, she said. And I would love a tangerine.

He laughed. All right, I'll see if there is one in the kitchen. I am guessing you don't want to see these again, he said, holding up the greasy bag.

He put the bag in the kitchen fridge although he knew Issa hated that. When he returned with two tangerines and a glass of water, she was seated in the chair she had occupied earlier in the evening, though now looking a little more disheveled than she had before. She drank the water and peeled and ate the tangerines thoughtfully, one after the other.

I think I panicked, she said. It was so dark and there were so many stalls. I couldn't understand what the man was saying and there were so many people. I don't like crowds. No, I don't like crowds in strange places. No, that came out wrong, I don't like crowds when I'm a stranger in a place.

You don't have to eat street food. You can go to a café or restaurant where you can sit down and take your time. There are some nearby, he said.

Will you come with me tomorrow? she asked.

He pondered this staggering invitation for a moment and considered its implications. This glowing beauty who was almost a software genius was inviting him, an ex-houseboy turned flunky in a small hotel, to go out to dinner with her. Did she know what she was doing? How had she learned to be so assured? In any case, he did not go to the restaurants he would have directed her to, could not afford the prices, and did not even know the dishes the names on the menus referred to: fricassee, au gratin, thermidor, liver parfait, crispy belly, blah blah. He had read the menus on their websites. His usual fare was rice, fish, spinach, goat stew, and a variety of breads, all available from any café. Perhaps he could take her to one of those posh restaurants and leave her there, for surely she wanted company only while she was learning the ropes, someone to talk her out of her nervousness.

It depends on whether Ramadhani is back tomorrow. He is unwell and I'm covering for him, you know, the night clerk, Badar said. But sure, if he is back, I will come with you tomorrow.

That's great, Badar. You are so cool, she said with a broad smile.

When Issa arrived to relieve him the following morning, he told him that he had called at Ramadhani's house the previous evening and was told by his son that Ramadhani had been admitted to the hospital.

They think it's his liver, Issa said. His legs are swollen and his eyes are yellowing and his skin is turning pale. Apparently the doctor said it's jaundice. That was what the son told me. I don't know what jaundice does but the name is evil enough. Anyway they've taken him in for observations and tests. It could be a couple of days or a couple of weeks. I'll call Bwana Sharif and see if we can get someone to come in during the day and help me out, but you'll have to continue as you are. We can't just bring in someone we don't know. I need someone I can trust to look after things during the night. Is that all right?

Badar shrugged. What can I do? he said crossly. It's all right, but we'll have to think about how we do the shifts. He caught sight of himself in the mirror as he said that, and thought what a sulky, huffy young man he looked, and he smiled. Issa misunderstood his smile and smiled back with a little nod of relief and then slapped Badar lightly on the shoulder. Ahsante sana, he said.

He stopped at a café for breakfast on the way home. The TV was on, showing a replay of a football match with the sound turned down, Bayern Munich against another team he could not be bothered to identify. He had a bun and a large mug of tea and headed to his room. He lay on the bed for a while, debating whether he should have a shower now or try to get some sleep first. It had been a long and difficult night, his thoughts tangled with memories of childhood, of the Mistress, of discontent and unappeased longings. He had thought of Fauzia and how subdued she had become, when before she had been a figure of tranquility and happiness. It now seemed at times that an ominous shadow moved alongside her. He was tired of patiently enduring, of being at the mercy of accidents and chance, of being treated as if he was naive and ignorant, of being always at the beck and call of other people's needs, of seeing the world through the computer. He wanted to travel properly, have adventures in unexpected places and return with the gracious airs of the fortunate, his pockets bulging, his face plump, his potency visible to all, to be able to say what he wished. Instead he was to spend another night on a fold-up bed in a stuffy office, covered up with a sheet to keep off the mosquitoes.

He would not have to take Jerry Bruno out to a posh restaurant, after all, alhamdulillah. That was the next thought that came to mind. His room was home now, comfortable and peaceful, a table under the window, pictures on the walls, including one of the Blue Mosque in Istanbul. He had found it in the religious bookstore in Darajani, already framed. He had two comfortable armchairs, although really he needed only one as his only guests were Hakim's children, who roamed the house at will and sometimes banged on his door to be allowed in for their own pleasures, asking questions, picking up his things, turning on his radio, and hardly ever sitting in an armchair.

He tried to sleep but he was too tired for sleep. He showered and sat down to read one of his crime novels. He no longer found as much pleasure in them as he used to, and after a while he gave that up and sat quietly contemplating what he should do with himself, hands folded in his lap, waiting for the hours to pass. It was not intolerable. On his way to the hotel that evening, with the Masika rains pouring a deluge, he bought himself a loaf of bread, a portion of fried changu, and a dish of coconut chutney for his midnight feast. If this was to go on for a few days, he had better get himself organized.

# 19.

It was not a pleasure coming home anymore, not something he looked forward to as he once did. He took his time leaving work, where in any case he knew he was invaluable to the smooth operation of the business of the office. He was now the manager of the health-assessment team of the new town project proposed in the north of the island. The work was demanding and exciting, and it was no effort to stay on at the office. He tried to delay that climb up the stairs to their flat. He hated that last part. He knew he would find Fauzia surly and frowning, busy in the kitchen, or with Nasra or with her schoolwork, busy at something to keep him at arm's length. She did not shout or explode, just this silent misery. He could not work it out although he had his ideas. He had his explanations. She blamed him for the accident that nearly killed the child. He had said let her cry and she had almost strangled herself with the sheets. He had said he was sorry for that. That was months ago, and after all the child had survived without any further mishap. But Fauzia also had not given up the fear that it was the falling sickness, that she had passed it on to the child. He was so weary of this talk. For weeks after the incident she had slept on the sofa with the child's cradle beside her. He had offered tenderness to lure her back to their bed and in the end she had come, but she had refused intimacy at first, saying she had not yet returned to the Pill. That was such an unexpected rejection that he had been reluctant to make an approach again, and their nights were cold and separate.

He did not know how to talk to her. In any case, she did not seem interested in hearing from him. He wanted to be kind, and he knew from what he had read that sometimes mothers suffered from depression after birth, and that it could last for a long time. So it was likely that was what she was going through, but it was tough on him too. He hated, yes hated, the way she used the baby to shield herself from him, to push him away, to make an excuse for her sullenness, that she was always tired, inexplicably on the brink of an outburst that never came. He felt captured, thoroughly weary of this life with her. He knew that when he walked into the flat, she would frown at his arrival.

She smiled when he walked in. You're late. Is it busy again at work? she asked.

Just finishing a couple of things off, he said. Nobody seems to get anything done unless I'm there.

She nodded and glanced toward Nasra, who crawled toward her mother and then held her arms out to be picked up. I'll just feed her and then we'll have supper, she said, taking the baby to the bedroom.

He checked the pan on the stove. Tomato sauce, again. She never had time to cook properly anymore.

I forgot to tell you, she said when she came back with the baby in her arms. Badar came yesterday evening while you were out. He is on night duty at the hotel.

I told you I had a meeting at the ministry last night, he said because he thought he heard a note of grievance in her voice. I couldn't get out of that.

Yes I remembered, she said, and just that moment Nasra's face turned dark as she released a rattling sound from her other end. Oops, supper will be late. Fauzia laughed as Karim made a face of disgust that he quickly adjusted into a smile to join her laughter.

He was going to tell her that the minister was at the meeting and had followed up this morning with a text congratulating him on his contribution and inviting him to call his personal assistant to arrange a chat with him. It was thrilling to have the recognition, and he knew he deserved it. There was no point being modest when it was his due, he told himself. He called as instructed and was fixed to meet the minister on Monday morning. Whatever it was about was bound to be good for him.

Afterward, when Nasra had gone to sleep and they had eaten their supper of rice and tomato sauce, and Fauzia had settled down to her preparation for the next day's school, and the rain had stopped, he said he would take a walk and maybe call at the Tamarind in case Badar was on nights again. He would tell her about the appointment with the minister later, enjoy it on his own for a while.

He saw her in the mirror as he stood in the lobby of the Tamarind. She was sitting at the huge desk with the green leather top, facing the mirror, looking comfortable. He also saw Badar at the other desk, his head turned toward her. In the mirror he saw a beautiful face with intense eyes and dazzling golden hair. Badar must have sensed his presence in the lobby even though he was out of his sight line, because he saw him turn away from the woman and look toward the door. Karim moved forward and Badar rose to his feet in delight. Karibu, karibu, he said, waving him into the office and then leaning forward to shake hands.

At closer quarters and in the flesh she was even more striking, and he felt a brief jolt in his body, like a charge or a momentary surge of nerves. She regarded him with sullen interest, he thought, and he wondered if he had interrupted something. I see you have new staff, he said to Badar, although he knew she could only be a guest at the hotel.

This is Jerry, Badar said, and the woman raised an arm in greeting.

Karim saw that her eyes were a deep dark blue and her face was etched in fine proportion, her brow, her chin, her nose, all in harmony. She broke into a smile, and he felt as if she could read his thoughts.

She is staying with us, Badar continued, after Karim had taken a seat. I was supposed to be taking her to a restaurant tonight, but Ramadhani is in hospital and I have to stay on nights. She is not very happy with me, as you can see.

Jerry laughed lightly, then resumed her sullen face that Karim now understood to be a theatrical demonstration of her disappointment. He wondered if the woman and Badar were lovers. There was something flirtatious about their exchange, he thought with a stab of envy. He had come a long way, young Badar.

She had a bad experience with street food last night, Badar said, teasing. Someone sold her a bagful of pweza, which her delicate palate found revolting. Issa would have agreed with her. You should hear him talking about guests who bring their kebabs and what he calls the other filthy stuff they buy from street vendors into the rooms. Anyway, I agreed to take her to a restaurant but now I can't. I did buy some bread and fish with some coconut chutney that she is welcome to share, but she is not happy with that.

Thank you, you are too good. I was so looking forward to going out for a meal, she said, making a sad face. I've been thinking about it all day. Never mind, I'll go out and choose more sensibly.

It'll probably start raining again soon, Karim said carefully. You won't have much luck with street food in this weather. I can take you to the restaurant, if you wish. Where were you planning to go?

Those dark blue eyes sparked briefly, he was sure of that, and she looked at him levelly and with interest, calculating. She turned toward Badar, perhaps to seek reassurance, or perhaps to refer the question of where they were planning to go to him. Badar shrugged, noncommittal, and she said to Karim, Cool, wherever you think. I'm ready.

Karim glanced at Badar and saw a smile on his face but he could not be sure if it was jealousy or envy or amusement or something else going on in his mind. They left almost immediately.

Karim could not help a feeling of pride that she was with him, and that they attracted second looks as they walked. He took her to a restaurant on the edge of the waterfront promenade, a place of low lights and sea air. It was busy and they mingled inconspicuously. They made polite conversation at first. He asked her about her work, and as she talked he also told her about his, and they found they had a lot to share. We could do with that kind of service in our department too, he said. The evening passed pleasantly in conversation and food. She had a glass of wine, he abstained. On the way back to the hotel it rained, and as they hurried along under the umbrella he had borrowed from the restaurant, he smelled her perfume and had to restrain the temptation to stroke her hair.

Fauzia was in bed when he got in and he slipped in silently beside her. He waited to see if she would stir but she did not. It must have been a long day for her, and she was still only just getting used to being back at work again. He had not done anything wrong. He went to a restaurant with the English woman because she needed someone to accompany her. Perhaps she was already involved with Badar. He had lost touch with Badar's comings and goings, and for all he knew he was a charmer with the guests. He had done nothing wrong, all he did was talk with her while they ate. He had even told her about his wife and daughter, and she had said she would love to meet them.

She sighed in her sleep but she did not wake, and after a moment he relaxed. His thoughts drifted to the forthcoming meeting with the minister on Monday. He expected it was a project he wanted to discuss with him, perhaps it would also mean a promotion, if not immediately then sometime soon. Or perhaps it would be nothing, just a little pat on the back, well done. His mind wandered back to Jerry Bruno and the delicacy of her face, her eyes, her hair. Even her voice had something thrilling in it, an energy, self-assurance. Yes, that was it, a confidence that must come with beauty. He sighed and turned over and woke up only once in the early hours when Fauzia got up to soothe the baby back to sleep.

He kept away from the Tamarind for the next two nights, deliberately distancing himself from what his body was signaling to him. It was a passing excitement, something he needed to suppress, an impossible fantasy. He was too busy for such dramas. On Friday night they went to Ali and Jalila's for the evening. They talked and watched television while the children played, a happy domestic scene that allowed him to feel an ease from the tension of their own home. The following day was the usual Saturday chores, for him going to the market or to hunt down some household replacement from the hardware shop, for her doing the washing or cooking, visiting her parents or Hawa, and if Nasra allowed, spending an hour or so reading. He told her about the forthcoming meeting with the minister.

I don't know what it's about, he said. It will probably be more work and we're busy enough as we are. Anyway, you can't say no to the minister.

I expect there'll be some new program that he wants to bring you in on, she said. He must know how good you are at your work. Let's hope it's something exciting. Well, I'm sure it will be.

On Sunday they watched a film by a Malian director on the Daesh in Africa, then Badar called in the late afternoon.

How's your girlfriend? Karim asked, even though he had told himself not to mention her.

My girlfriend? You mean Jerry Bruno, he said, laughing. What are you talking about? She's not my girlfriend. What could've put that into your head?

Who's that? Fauzia asked, laughing with them while Nasra slipped easily from her mother's lap and crawled silently to her favorite uncle.

When I went to the Tamarind the other night, I found him sitting in the office with a woman, one of the guests at the hotel, Karim said. There they were, all on their own. They had planned to go to a restaurant that evening, but Ramadhani spoiled things because he was taken to the hospital, so our boy here had to take his shift. What else could I think except that you were taking her out? You should have seen them, disappointed and miserable, especially her.

Karim looked at Badar, to see if he would take up the story from him, if he would find a way to describe what had happened next that would make it seem blameless—he did not do anything wrong—but he was bending down to pick Nasra up and was not looking at him. Karim sensed that Fauzia was waiting for him to continue.

I accompanied her to the restaurant so she could get something to eat, he said. If you can believe it, Badar was offering her cold fish and stale bread for her supper.

Oh, you went to a restaurant, she said. So that's why you were so late back.

Was I? We were talking a lot. So, he said, turning to Badar, how is it going with her?

She is leaving the hotel today, moving to a flat with another of Maria Caffrey's volunteers. She was asking after you, Badar said, struggling to speak clearly while Nasra was tugging at his lower lip.

Karim felt a tiny leap of surprise but he did not speak.

She said you promised to introduce her to this naughty little girl, Badar said, and then leaned into Nasra's podgy neck and blew a loud fart into it, to the little one's ecstatic delight.

I told her about you, Karim said, turning to Fauzia. She said she would like to meet you, and that one there. I meant to tell you.

Sawa, she said. She is welcome.

When she rose to go into the bedroom to change the baby, Badar said goodbye and made ready to go. Out on the landing, as if as an afterthought, he reached into his shirt pocket and pulled out a slip of paper. He handed it over to Karim. She said to give you this, you can reach her on this number, he said softly and then turned away.

The minister's office was in a new complex on the road to Mtoni. Karim arrived as instructed at 10:00 a.m. and presented himself to the official in the outer reception office, who asked him to take a seat while he called the minister's assistant. There was no clock in the reception area and he was not wearing a watch, but it seemed to him that he was there for a long time before the minister's assistant came out of an inner door to meet him. He was a plump man of about his age, smartly dressed office style, white shirt, dark trousers, brilliantly polished shoes, respectful smile. He shook hands and introduced himself as Wakili Hassan and then led the way to the minister's office. It was a surprisingly small office, and felt even smaller as a result of the huge desk behind which the minister sat. He was a short man with a diffident smile. He made as if to rise in welcome but it was just a gesture and he remained seated. Wakili Hassan held out an open hand toward one of the chairs facing the desk and Karim sat. Wakili Hassan stepped backward and took another chair farther back from the desk. Polite words of welcome followed from the minister, who then explained that the government was recruiting a team for a sustainable green development plan. The EU had promised several millions to advance the plan, which had been approved by both parties, so the way ahead was clear. The team would be made up of staff recruited by the EU and by the government. The ministry was now in the process of identifying suitable candidates and he, Karim Bakari Abbas, had come to the attention of the minister's advisers as a suitable candidate.

Congratulations, the minister said softly, smiling shyly, as if he suspected that what he was offering was nothing very much. I assume you will agree to this move from your current position, which I understand you are filling with distinction. I should say that in order to join the team you will have to undertake further training in Denmark, where they have considerable experience and expertise in green development projects. Of course you will be on a very different pay scale once you are a member of the team. May I take it that you would be willing to join us?

I will be very happy to join the team, Karim said, struggling not to grin with delight.

Thank you very much, my brother. We appreciate your cooperation, the minister said, rising at last and shaking hands with Karim. Our brother Wakili Hassan will take you through the details.

So that's the deal, he told her when he got home. I'll be employed in this green development project and paid a salary determined by the EU, which is going to be a great deal more than my current salary. I will be going to Copenhagen for ten weeks of further training. It will be quite soon, once they've got the paperwork sorted out.

She was sitting in front of him, listening with a half smile on her face, and he was not sure if she was taking it all in, if she was quite grasping what a brilliant piece of news he was telling her. Aren't you excited? he asked her. It will open doors, it will make new career pathways possible. Sustainable green development, I mean how much more up-to-date can you get than that?

I am excited, she said, and very pleased for you. You deserve it. Hey, Nasra, see what a clever baba you have. Give him a kiss to congratulate him.

Karim was relieved to see that she was smiling and laughing as she handed the baby over, joining in his delight at last. He had not yet told her that Wakili Hassan had told him that he would be going to Copenhagen on his own to minimize expenses. In any case, she had her job, and living in Europe with a baby for several weeks would not have been easy. It would be time for him to recharge, to be on his own for a while, to escape the everyday grumbles that were clouding their lives. Later he rang his mother in Dar es Salaam with the news, and spoke to Haji too, who said he had always known that the young hooligan was going to do well.

He was still in this euphoric mood when he went to the Tamarind a couple of days later to look up Badar. He needed to tell people about his good fortune. He went there on his way home from work but he was not sure what shift Badar would be on. He found him in the office on his own, and Badar was enthusiastic and excited by the news. Brilliant, brilliant, he said. You'll get to see the world. It lifted Karim's spirits wonderfully to see his joy.

You want to do something for yourself too, Karim said. You can't stay in this shitty job all your life.

Yes, Badar said diffidently, accustomed to this particular harangue.

Anyway, how's our friend? Karim asked. I was going to ask you if she was okay at her new accommodation. He had been thinking about her, wanting to tell her his news, wanting to see her, but he had held back, fearing that his excitement would sound foolish to someone like her, from the great world.

Jerry Bruno? She rang this morning. Actually she asked after you, Badar said. She asked if I had given you her number. She asked why you hadn't called her.

What did you tell her? Karim asked.

That I had no idea, Badar said. But I said I would mention her call next time I saw you.

I'll call her when I get home, Karim said.

They arranged that he would meet her at the same restaurant where they had dinner on Saturday afternoon and he would walk with her to his flat. He had not yet returned the umbrella they'd borrowed that night, and this would be an opportunity to do so. She was waiting outside the restaurant when he arrived, dressed in a loose mauve shirt and blue jeans, and she was so beautiful that he felt a brief ache in his sternum.

At last, I thought you'd forgotten about me, she said, smiling and looking at him appreciatively. That's a nice shirt. Hey, you know, I'm really looking forward to meeting your baby and your wife. Badar was telling me about them.

How is your flat? he asked, as they set on their way.

It's okay, I share with another volunteer. She's also okay. The water goes off sometimes, something to do with the pump, and we have to call the landlord. Maria is on it, she'll get him to fix it. The street is noisy in the daytime, cars, people shouting. It's near shops, you see. Nothing as elegant as the Tamarind or even the offices where I work are. But like I said, it's okay.

She said this as if it was all a bit of a joke. He told her his news and she grabbed his arm briefly and said cool several times. Oh that's really cool, you must be so pleased. When they reached the flat, she exclaimed about its spaciousness, went on her knees to greet Nasra, smiled, and said lovely to meet you as she shook hands with Fauzia, and Karim thought how generous and unreserved she was, how willing to express her pleasure.

So many books, she said later, as they were drinking tea.

Mostly his, Fauzia said, his university books and crime novels. He consumes those novels.

No, no, many of the books are hers, Karim protested without rancor. She reads serious books, not the frivolous mysteries I consume.

Jerry Bruno browsed the bookshelf for a while and at times called out a title in surprise or recognition. Dante, *The Divine Comedy*, *Hamlet*, Plato's *Republic*. Are these yours? Do you understand them? she asked, turning to Fauzia.

Oh, she is quite the intellectual, Karim said genially. Fauzia did not speak but smiled politely, acknowledging the question and the description, ignoring the condescension from both of them.

This is serious stuff, Jerry said, and continued browsing. She read the blurb of another book and said, Wow, this looks interesting. Can I borrow it?

Fauzia nodded, not very enthusiastically, Karim thought. She did not like to lend out her books. Because they never come back, she had said several times. It was a copy of Zárate's *The Discovery and Conquest of Peru* that he had bought for her on one of his trips to Dar es Salaam. The spine was intact, as if the book was unread, but he knew it had been, very likely more than once. That was how

Fauzia read books, as if they were fragile objects that required careful handling. She frowned at him when he put a book face down or forced one open to loosen the spine. He had bought her the book because of her abiding interest in South America and in that historical period in particular. She had not been able to forget about it since she learned about the Spanish conquest at school. She told him that when they first came to know each other, and since then she had read anything she could find on that subject, horrified by the brutality of each new episode she came across. If Jerry had looked more carefully, she would have found other books on the subject, including De Las Casas's *A Short Account*. Perhaps she chose Zárate because the title made it sound like an adventure.

She called him the next day to thank him for taking her to meet his family, and called him again a day later to suggest that they meet on the waterfront later that evening if the rain stayed away. She could make another attempt at street food, he suggested. But it rained heavily so he called to postpone until the next evening. No, she said, she was going to an event at the Music Academy, and why didn't he come? He could now no longer mistake her interest in him, and he knew how he thought of her and wanted to be with her. He was not unaware of what he was stepping into, even if a part of him still thought it incredible.

He had never been to the Music Academy although he knew it was in the old Customs House. It was a workshop performance by the resident ensemble of the academy attended by a very small number of people. He felt virtuous being there, paying homage to culture, and thrilled to be with her, and a little guilty because he had lied to Fauzia. He had told her that he was meeting some people in Forodhani and might have something to eat with them. After the workshop performance they did go to Forodhani and bought bread and kebabs and sambusa and then found a secluded table at the waterfront café. He walked her to her flat, because it was late and he was not ready to part from her.

That was lovely, we must do it again, she said, and touched him on the arm before turning away.

He could not stop thinking about her, and he knew now that matters had reached a dangerous point. He could pull back and suppress his interest, no, his arousal. He could make it clear that he was there as an occasional companion but not always available. That he could not risk the chaos that loomed. But he could not stop thinking about her, and several times a day he had to suppress the urge to call her.

Then on Friday morning she called him and his resolution collapsed. Hey, it's been a hell of a week. All kind of fuckups with the system. It's Friday, what are you doing with yourself this evening? Maria tells me there is a good restaurant near my end of town. We could go there, unless you have a better idea.

I don't have a better idea, he said, his heart pounding in his chest. He had not expected to feel so frightened.

Cool, why don't you come by my place and we'll go from there? she said.

He lied again to Fauzia, telling her that he was meeting with some people from work and they were going to a barbecue in Mbweni. It was a bonding exercise. Hawa was coming round that evening, so she would not be on her own, but by then it hardly mattered to him how she would be. The meal with Jerry passed in a blur. He thought the restaurant dingy and the atmosphere stifling. She talked freely, at ease, whereas he felt tense. He listened to her voice but did not take in all her words. He wondered if he was getting it wrong, if she was comfortable with companionship when he was imagining something more intense. Or if she knew what she wanted to happen and was leading him to it.

He walked her home from the restaurant, and when they reached her building she said, as he hoped she would, You haven't seen my flat, come in.

It was a small flat, two bedrooms and a shared area with a wooden-framed settee, an armchair, and a Formica-topped table with two dining chairs. There was a sink in one corner with a four-ring gas hob next to it. She gestured toward the armchair, inviting him to sit. What do you think of our emporium of luxury? she asked, sitting on the settee. That's my bedroom there, and that is Edna's. She's away on a weekend break to Nairobi with some friends.

Just at that moment her phone pinged. That's probably her, telling me what a crazy time she's having. Look at this, she said, laughing, they must be having a crazy time. Come, have a look.

He sat beside her while she scrolled through the pictures. Then she rested her head on his shoulder and he put his arm around her waist. She turned to face him, her beautiful eyes half-closed and her lips opening. He moved slowly toward her so that when they kissed, their lips swelled gently into each other. They did that repeatedly, slowly kissing without moving, without speaking. Then she stood up and headed toward her bedroom, and he followed.

Fauzia was already in bed when he got home but he knew she was not asleep. She sniffed softly, as if testing the air, and after a moment he smelled it too. He had had a shower afterward so he did not bring the musk of their lovemaking home with him, and as he lay in bed in the dark he could smell the perfume of Jerry's shower gel.

That must have been some barbecue, she said, her tone friendly, perhaps even with a hint of teasing.

It did go on a bit, he said.

He felt her turning over and seconds later her hand was on his chest. He flinched involuntarily.

Sorry, you must be tired, she said, and turned over on her other side.

Yes I am, he said, and did not remember anything else.

Jerry rang on Sunday morning, asking if she could come round to see them that afternoon. Fauzia was in the room at the time, sitting in the armchair, trying to read while Nasra was occupied with hitting her leg with a plastic rattle. She glanced up when the phone rang, and he mouthed Jerry.

Yes, of course, he said. You are welcome to come round.

He looked at Fauzia and she nodded and then shrugged. If you are happy with that, I'm fine. He was surprised that she wanted to come to their flat, the audacity of it. Instead of keeping guiltily away she was making a show of normality. It was exciting, taking such risks, being so brazen. When she arrived, she got on her knees as she had done before and played with Nasra for a few seconds, cooing at her and tickling her and calling her darling. She put the Zárate book on the table without a word and then suggested that they take Nasra out for a walk. They went out together, Karim pushing the stroller while Fauzia and Jerry walked on either side of him. It felt good. They were both women he had bedded. He wondered if this was how it felt to have two wives. He could not imagine what it would be like to have three or four. He wanted Jerry again, and the urgency of it was distracting. He let Fauzia walk ahead on the narrow pavement and then briefly put his hand on Jerry's waist. She gave him a quick secret smile and walked on to catch up with Fauzia.

I see you've brought the Zárate book back, he said when they were back at the flat. Did you read it?

Oh, thank you for lending it to me. Yes, I did read some of it, she said. It was a little too dry for me, I'm afraid.

They spoke to each other every day on the phone, and on Friday evening he went to see her. He did that the following Friday too and the one after that. Jerry spoke to Edna, who made herself scarce for a couple of hours, not that it mattered anymore. It seemed at times that they were invisible. It was all so new to him, the feeling of reckless love. At other times he felt a hot panic, and wondered if he should confide in Badar, ask him to arrange a hotel room for them if there was one available, but he decided not to. He was not sure he could trust Badar. He thought Badar was too devoted to Fauzia and might make him feel bad about what he was doing. He did not want to feel bad. When he went out in the night streets after he had been with Jerry, he knew he had done something irrevocable, something he did not wish to revoke.

Let's go away for a weekend, she said to him while they lay in bed after love.

I can't do that, he said. It would be too much for her.

You can't hold back now, she said. This is special. You don't get to feel like this every day.

Yes, he said, and they began making love again.

I'll book a weekend break in Dar, she said afterward, snuggling up to him. There's a nice cheap hotel Edna was telling me about. We'll go and spend a couple of nights there and have fun. It will be great. Don't be afraid. It will be all right. There is nothing to keep you here. You have to live your life and I don't think you'll find it here.

## 20.

Some things seem predictable after they have happened, when before they might have seemed unlikely. He was gone, and it was as if she had known he would be. He was gone, and when he came back, if he came back, she would not be there. She did not want to speak to anyone, not yet. She sat on the sofa, the sun streaming in through the window behind her, considering how to proceed, contemplating what she could retrieve from the wreckage of her life. In her own heart she had started to suspect that love was ailing some time ago, but she had not known that it would come to this so swiftly.

Nasra was preoccupied with her new game. She was now able to walk while hanging on to a chair or a table leg and occasionally letting go to totter uncertainly toward another piece of furniture. The room was cluttered so she had plenty to hang on to. It was coming up to her first birthday in a week. She had thought he would remember. She waited for him to remember, but he had not. His mind was on other matters. And why would it have made any difference if he had remembered? She was stunned by what he had done but somehow not surprised. How was that? Maybe she had always known, really, that sooner or later he would leave. He had been getting so angry with her, seething even when he did not always rage. She had not been able to be for him what he wanted.

It was Nasra's coming that had turned something in him, she was sure of that. Looking back, she could see his growing self-absorption. No, she had seen it all along but had not wanted to acknowledge it. She did not think he had ever really imagined himself a father, despite the talk of making babies. The sleepless nights and the constant attention the baby demanded must have worn him out. It had certainly worn her out, and she had felt so tired and so dejected, with so much in pain in her body and in her head. Dr. Khalid had said it was postpartum depression and it would pass. Look after yourself and your child, and try to make your husband happy if you can. Above all, look after yourself.

You are a poet, Dr. Khalid, Fauzia said.

Now you are teasing me, Dr. Khalid said, with that chuckling intake of breath so habitual to him.

She had tried to do as he advised, and that Latin name for what she was experiencing helped her to cope with her feebleness. It was postpartum depression that had made her feel so tired, so defeated. She was not just a person who was useless and without talent; she was experiencing what many other women experience after birth. Yes, she tried to make him happy but she could not. She did not have the strength, despite her desire to help him overcome his distress and impatience. She could not reach him in his self-regard. It was true, though, that after her seventh month she had begun to feel better, which was perhaps to do with returning to work, having company, getting out of the house. Then she saw him do something that wrenched her stomach and now as she sat there remembering, she wondered if that was one of the moments when love had begun to die. Because she knew there was not one event that had suddenly changed everything, but that was a moment she returned to repeatedly in her mind.

He had brought some papers home from work and was trying to understand the details and the figures. He needed to have this work done before the morning when he was expected to present at a meeting with the head of his department. Nasra in her cot in the bedroom was crying and had been crying for some minutes. The bedroom door was open so that Nasra could see them but that did not seem enough to calm her. Fauzia was at the stove, ignoring the crying so that she could finish off the dinner preparations. She had put Nasra in the cot to keep her out of the way for a while.

Can't you stop her? he said angrily. I can't concentrate on this stuff with all that racket.

I'll go and see to her in a minute, Fauzia said wearily. She's hungry. I'm just waiting for the rice to boil.

As if provoked by this exchange, Nasra became even more distraught, her crying reaching an almost hysterical pitch. With a sudden cry of rage, he rose to his feet and went into the bedroom, reached into the cot, and picked up Nasra by her head and lifted her up, his hands on either side of her temples while her body dangled free. The shock audibly forced the air out of her and choked off her cry. He let go of her and dropped her back into the cot, then turned away and stormed back to the chair where he had been sitting. Nasra let out a desperate cry of anguish and terror.

Fauzia had watched as if paralyzed. It had all happened so suddenly, so unexpectedly, but she had seen it all, seen the way he lifted her so that her neck took all the strain of her body. Did he not realize . . . ? She rushed to the child and picked her up, murmuring to her and rocking her, while he sat on the chair with his head in his hands. She shut the bedroom door and whispered and murmured to Nasra until gradually she subsided into an agitated snivel.

That was dangerous, he said when she went out into the sitting room, Nasra still in her arms, clinging to her. I'm sorry. It was just too much.

She did not speak; she could not speak. Instead she gave Nasra some water and then fed her. The vision of him holding the child by the head returned to her repeatedly, and each time it did so, she felt a nausea close to retching.

She did not want to speak to anyone, not yet.

He had told her that morning, a Saturday, that he was going to Dar for the weekend. He did not have breakfast, just a cup of tea, and then he told her. She had asked, On your own? He could have lied, or he could have shown astonishment at the question, but he did not. It was as if they both knew the answer. No, I am going with Jerry, he had said. Minutes later he picked up the small bag he had evidently prepared and was gone.

Now that it had happened, it seemed like something she could have known would happen. She had seen the way he had looked at her that first time she visited them. He seemed unable to take his eyes off her while she crawled on the floor with Nasra. Then that night he had come home late, having supposedly been at a barbecue with workmates. Instead of the stink of smoke and meat and perhaps tobacco and alcohol, he smelled of perfumed soap. She had not wanted to believe what she was now confronted with. At the time she had not allowed herself to admit to her suspicion. She had reached out to touch him and he had flinched and turned over. It had felt like a rejection, but now on reflection she wondered if perhaps it was disgust at her touch. Later she had seen an exchange of looks, when Jerry visited again and they were out for a walk. Yes, she had known but could not trust her knowledge, or had not known how to speak about it or to whom.

Badar had come to see them one evening a few days before. He was pleased with himself because he was off nights after a whole month. Ramadhani was on his feet again and able to resume his duties. Night duty is inhuman, Badar had said. Everything happens without you. Nasra had been in her cot and about to drop off when he arrived, calling out greetings. She must have recognized his voice because she was not interested in sleep after that, and had only become content once she was comfortably perched on Badar's lap. You are a spoiled little brat, Badar had said. You should be in bed. Where is your baba?

He's out, seeing some friends, Fauzia had said, and had seen a flicker in his eyes that told her he knew or understood something. She had not wanted to speak about what she feared, not then. Now she knew that she would call him, and she would call Hawa. It was Saturday morning and they would be at work, so that would have to wait. She would pack her things and Nasra's things and then call Badar to help her move to her parents' house.

Later that afternoon, she called Badar but did not say much on the phone, just Could you come and help me after you finish at the hotel?

I'll come now, he said. Issa is here.

He's gone, she said when he arrived. She was surrounded by bags, a suitcase, two boxes of books, and baby supplies. Nasra's cot was dismantled and leaning against the wall, her stroller was ready by the door.

Gone where? What do you mean?

To Dar. With her, she said.

No! he exclaimed in anguish. No!

She wondered that he did not ask who her was. Did you know about them? she asked.

He shook his head. No, not for certain, he said, and she nodded. What was he thinking of! he cried.

She is very beautiful, Fauzia said. I expect he could not resist. Can you help me move this stuff to my parents' house?

Fauzia called her mother while Badar went for a taxi. Khadija was waiting by the door when they arrived, her hand over her mouth in distress, her eyes red with tears. She hugged her daughter and granddaughter at the same time and pulled them inside, leaving Badar to unload the taxi. Her father tried to struggle to his feet but he could no longer do so without support and collapsed back in his chair. Fauzia went to him, smiling, and kissed him on the forehead. Well tried, old man, she said, and then turning to Nasra she said, Say hello to Babu.

Musa held out his arms for the child, who obligingly allowed herself to be held and kissed. She spent her weekdays with her grandparents so Musa was no stranger to her. After a moment Nasra slipped off her grandfather's lap and tottered off to attend to her own affairs. Musa looked at Fauzia and shook his head, Alhamdulillah, he said.

Later, after Fauzia was installed in her old room, Nasra had gone to sleep and Musa had dozed off in bed in the fitful sleep that was all he could manage these days, Khadija said to her daughter, He did not deserve you. He has gone away to do dirty things with a tourist woman, in front of everyone, without shame. I can't speak about him, he has no shame. This woman must have put a madness in him, whoever she is, some tourist vagabond with money but no honor. What do these people want with us? Why do they come here? They come here with their filth and their money and interfere with us and ruin our lives for their pleasure, and it seems that we cannot resist their wealth and their filthy ways. What do they want with us? Everywhere you go you see them, in the narrowest alley and street, there they are, looking into people's houses and down people's throats, and alongside them will be one of our shameless young men, grinning like a monkey while he does his blather. Don't they have seas and beaches in their own countries? They come here with their heedless ways to add to the troubles we've seen. There was something we knew about living that we no longer know now. We have become shameless of our own accord.

All ages beguile themselves like that, imagining that once they knew what was of value and now no longer do. Fauzia thought this but did not speak. She understood that her mother was speaking in outrage and she did not have any urge to interrupt her. They sat in a deflated silence for a few moments, then Fauzia said, She is not a tourist. She is a volunteer.

What's the difference? Khadija said sneeringly. Volunteer! You see them in their big new cars, bringing us their goodwill. They should stay in their own countries and do their goodwill there.

Anyway, a lot of people make a living out of tourists, Fauzia said. It seems ungrateful to complain.

Khadija sighed in resignation. You had better go to bed, she said. Will you be able to sleep? Shall I make you an herbal drink? Call me if you need help with Nasra.

It was later, when she was in her old bed in the dark, that the shock of it sank in. He was gone, and she was on her own with the child. She would never find happiness again. There was a pain sitting like a lump in her chest, a proper presence, and an anxious charge like a current through her limbs. Her ears hummed as she lay trembling in the dark, and for the first time in that long day her tears flowed. It felt as if love had fled from her forever.

It's no good blaming her. It's like blaming a scorpion for stinging, Hawa said, when she came to see her the next day. It's him, he should've known better. What will you do? Will you be able to go to work tomorrow? I can call in sick for you if you want.

I can't think clearly, but I'll go to work. Suddenly everything is confused, Fauzia said.

Of course it is, that's why you should take a day off, Hawa said.

And do what? Sit here at home and grieve?

You don't know how things will work out yet, Hawa said. He may come to his senses. Maybe it's just an infatuation, an affair, and right now he is already regretting what he has done.

No, it's gone. I know it has, Fauzia said.

Did you know about them? Hawa asked. You didn't say any-thing.

Maybe I did know, but didn't want to, Fauzia said.

He is an animal, Hawa said, at last allowing herself to say some-thing brutal about him.

She is very beautiful, Fauzia said.

Oh Fauzia wetu, you don't have to be nice about that bitch, Hawa said, laughing with stinging eyes. You are even more beauti-ful than her.

I don't feel that. I feel discarded, useless, without talent or pur-pose, she said.

We can't have that, Hawa said, coming close and embracing her friend. You are the most talented person I know. You could wipe the floor with that man. Is there anything I can do? Shall I go to the flat and bring some of your stuff over?

No, I've got all I want, Fauzia said. He can keep what's there.

Come on, let's not mope. Let's take that bundle of fun of yours for a walk and visit my mother. She hasn't seen her or you for weeks and she is complaining.

Did you know? Fauzia asked. About what he was doing?

Hawa looked troubled for a moment, thinking through what to say, then she said, My boss, Sultan, said he saw Karim at a restau-rant with a young English woman. He did not know who she was. He thought it was a tourist but I guessed it was her. That's all, it could have been nothing so I didn't mention it. I didn't want to cause trouble between you and him. And anyway, you said that she visited you in the flat more than once, you went for walks together and she borrowed your books, so I thought maybe you were all friends. No, that's not really true. Sultan said they were talking in a way that was unmistakable, but he has a dirty mind and sees sex everywhere. I didn't know whether to believe him, but it made me wonder. I couldn't tell you all that just like that, could I? But how could he have done this? Gone away with her as a way of announcing his . . . What shall we call it? Infatuation?

I told you—

But Hawa interrupted, I know, she is beautiful, but something about her must have overwhelmed him, seduced him. She probably thinks she is just having fun, but he should have known. He could have just cheated and had fun too and then got over it. That doesn't sound nice, does it? Well then, he could have talked to you and explained himself before just tailing off to his fuckfest. Oh let's go and visit my mother or I'll say something wrong. She will soon put everything in perspective.

# 21.

Badar had known, but only just that morning. He could not bear to tell her. She had looked as if the world had sunk under her feet.

Badar had seen how awestruck Karim was by Jerry that first time she sat with him in the office. He had seen that at once. It was unmistakable, and he thought Jerry had seen it too. When Karim had offered to accompany her to the restaurant because Badar could not, he had felt a foreboding. He had hoped that Karim would not do something foolish, would not embarrass himself by making crass advances. He could not say anything to Karim, they were not like that with each other. Karim lectured him and Badar listened and hardly ever corrected him or complained. It was how it had been between them from the beginning, but certainly after he came to his rescue, as Karim put it to him again and again. It would have been unlike Karim to make advances, but Jerry was at her glowing beauty best and he had been awestruck and might have lost his marbles as a result. When it came to guests or tourists—they amounted to the same thing—he always reminded himself of one of Issa's iron laws. Don't touch them!

He had sensed something was amiss when he visited them, Fauzia's unusual coolness as if she was too weary to make the effort, Karim's unconcealed irritation with the demands of the mother and the child. It grew worse because what was wrong between them then became more concealed, more withdrawn. He had sensed something hardening in Karim, not all at once but as if with each passing achievement at work he was growing more distant and preoccupied, he was growing into a proper man, he was finding something to despise in Badar. He had always known that Karim could be bossy and even overbearing, but he had loved him for all that and had been grateful for his affection even if at times it felt patronizing.

The love between Fauzia and Karim had seemed so secure, the transformation from kind lover to exasperated father strangely swift. Then Jerry came and he lost himself in the excitement of her. Perhaps she was a relief from the daily aggravation, from a sense of being sucked under by tedium and discomfort. Does beauty like hers make its own rules, disregarding responsibilities and duties? Or was it that coming to a place like theirs she felt entitled to please herself because in the end it was she that mattered?

Maria Caffrey had come to the hotel that Saturday just before noon, her eyes sleepy-looking and her face full of contempt. It was just after late breakfast and the hotel was buzzing, the guests getting ready to go out, the cleaning staff at their work, Assistant Manager Issa at the computer answering emails, and Badar sitting at the side desk checking the monthly invoice from the delivery service. She had walked into the office unhurriedly, wearing her usual jeans and T-shirt, carrying a canvas shoulder bag.

Good morning, she had said, and waited for Badar's full attention. Where is your friend? I don't have his address or phone, so I am forced to intrude on your establishment. I need to speak to him, to give him an opportunity to explain himself, otherwise I'll go to the police.

She paused, took a deep breath, and ran her hands lightly over her bosom. Badar sensed Issa looking up, and he turned briefly toward him and saw his eyes hardening and his frown deepening. I am sorry to be so dramatic, Maria Caffrey had said, not looking sorry at all. One of the volunteers, Edna, who shares a flat with Jerry Bruno, you may remember her, she was a guest here a few weeks ago, has reported a theft. Some of her money is missing. Your friend, I don't know his name, you know who I mean, has been visiting the flat and spending hours there, visiting Jerry Bruno and doing whatever. We warn volunteers about such liaisons, we go on at them ad infinitum. It's none of my business what people do in private but I do have to keep an eye on the volunteers to make sure they don't get into trouble. Anyway, this is a different matter. Edna reports that some of her money is missing and Jerry is not around, gone away somewhere. She called me for advice. So first of all I want to give your friend the opportunity to explain himself, and hand the money back if he was the culprit, otherwise I will report the matter to the police. It's no good giving me that diffident look, that hotelier visage. It doesn't fool me. Please be kind enough to get in touch with him and ask him to call me, otherwise I will take this matter to the police.

Assistant Manager Issa was on his feet. Badar raised his hand to stop him from issuing the blast of rage he sensed was coming. I don't believe Karim would have done that, Badar said. I don't believe the police will either, or care. So go ahead and report it.

Madam, this matter is nothing to do with us, Assistant Manager Issa pronounced gravely. Kindly leave the premises.

Maria Caffrey released a short bark of derision, turned on her heel, and walked languidly out of the office.

Is your friend messing around with that young woman? Issa asked.

Badar shrugged. I don't know, he said. I thought they were friends, all three of them, with his wife as well. I can't believe he would steal money from this Edna.

Just then the phone rang, and it was Fauzia, asking him to come round. And when she asked him if he knew, he said no, not for certain, but he had understood what Maria Caffrey was saying, that they were together somewhere.

He was in his room on Sunday morning, his day off. They took alternate Sundays off, he and Issa. He wondered if he should go round to her parents' house to see if he could be of any help. Fauzia looked stunned, and her mother had her hands full with her ailing husband, maybe they might appreciate a visit if only to raise morale. He did not want to intrude, or to seem like a lonely fusspot interesting himself in other people's tragedies. He would leave it for the moment and go later in the week, help with the shopping or something. In any case, Karim would be back by then and they might need time to work something sensible out of the mess he had made.

To his astonishment, it was Jerry who came to the hotel one afternoon in the middle of the week. It was raining again and her hair was wet, which made her look disheveled and attractive in a different way. He expected that she would look beautiful even after crawling through a pool of thick mud.

I'm leaving the day after tomorrow, I thought I'd come and say goodbye, she said, smiling cheerfully, almost coquettishly. You were the first friend I made when I arrived. I'm only sorry we never got to go to dinner together. Oh, I hear Maria Caffrey came to give you hassle about Edna's money. It was me. I borrowed it because I was short of cash for the trip and she wasn't around to ask. I've paid her back. It's all okay now.

He wondered if she would say something about the weekend, about Karim, about the misery that had befallen Fauzia, but she did not. First she glanced at her reflection in the mirror on the wall, made a face and ran her fingers through her wet hair, and then perched on the desk that he still thought of as the Mistress's dressing table.

I really thought we might get it together, you and I, she said, smiling teasingly. There's still time if you're free.

She did not stay long after that display of frivolity. That was the last time he saw her. For a long time after, her image would pass through his mind, and he would hear a phrase or two of her clarinet.

Three days later, when he thought she would have left the country, he went to Karim's flat early in the evening. He had not wanted to go before for fear he would find them together, and for some reason the idea of that made him feel queasy. Even though she had told him she would be gone two days hence, he still went to the flat with some uncertainty. She might have changed her mind and decided to stay an extra week to have even more of him. He did not know how he would find Karim. Grieving her departure? Guilty now that passion was spent? Sitting forlorn in the chaos he had created? Somehow he expected he would find him defiant and perhaps annoyed, just because in recent times he had often seemed on the point of impatience with him. Then also Badar had taken nearly a week to call on him after Fauzia's departure, which he might have taken to be an indication of which side he was on.

He found him watching a soap on television. Karim switched the set off and sat back, looking casual and untroubled, or trying to give that impression. He looked tired as he stretched. The flat seemed calmer, less crowded but otherwise not much different from before. Badar had somehow expected a ruin, a state of disorder. They had left it in a mess that afternoon when Fauzia moved herself out, but Karim must have tidied up.

How have you been? Karim asked, as if all was routine and nothing much had happened.

I'm fine, Badar said. And you?

Karim shrugged. Not bad. Plenty of work. Have you seen her? he asked.

For a moment Badar was not sure if he meant Fauzia or Jerry. He nodded to cover both possibilities but did not elaborate.

Well, she knows where I am, Karim said, so he had meant Fauzia but did not want to say her name. Badar could already sense some bristling under Karim's manner. He realized as they sat in silence for a few moments that he did not know how to move the conversation forward, that he did not know if he should urge a reconciliation, or inquire about his feelings, or just keep silent on the matter and act as if nothing had happened. He realized that it was always Karim who led the conversation and he who followed.

I've got some news, Karim said into the silence, taking charge. You know that project I was telling you about, the sustainability thing? It's all confirmed. Wonderful news. I'll be going to Copenhagen in four months' time, sometime in November. You know, I've never been to Europe. It will be winter in Denmark then, so that will be something to cope with, won't it? They want to transfer me to Dar for some preparatory training before then. I don't know when that will be, soon I expect. The headquarters staff are all based there, so the plan is when I finish in Copenhagen I will be based in Dar. It will be a big change.

That's wonderful, Badar said, smiling to show his pleasure because he thought that was what Karim expected of him. You have done so well in this job, and I'm sure you'll be brilliant in the new one.

Something in Badar's voice or his words made Karim straighten up slightly. Perhaps he expected something more admiring than Badar had managed and was made suspicious by what seemed to be coolness, or perhaps he sensed disapproval, or a hint of derision, or maybe hostility after all. Or maybe he was just ready to strike. He looked intently at Badar, working him out, and then his tone began to change.

What's your problem? he asked, his voice soft with suspicion.

No, no! Badar said quickly. I just meant it's good about the new job, a great opportunity.

Yes, yes, I know, but is there something else? You have something to say? Because if you do, you'd better spit it out, Karim said stiffly, glaring.

No, no, Badar repeated placatingly.

Karim glared in silence for a moment or two longer, stepping up his rage, and then he said, lips taut with suppressed feeling, It wasn't working anymore, not for me, not for her. You weren't there to see it all. She is too deep in her misery, too wrapped up in her worries, too much baby. Everything is about the baby. I can't live like that, grumbling all the time, tension all the time. I didn't want to hurt her. I'd just had enough of it. It wasn't just about . . .

He hesitated and then did not say Jerry's name either.

It wasn't just what you think, he said, and then as if stung by the memory of the one he had not mentioned, he leaned back in the chair, deflated. It was her, it was Jerry he was mourning.

Badar wanted to ask how it ended between them. Did they just kiss goodbye and part? Did they make plans? Were there heartbroken scenes and promises to meet in Copenhagen or London? Was she coming back or was it just a holiday fling?

After another long silence, during which Badar wondered if his presence was becoming intolerable, if Karim really wanted to be left alone with his TV and his memories and his future plans, Badar said, Well, I just came by to say hello and to see that all was well with you. If there is anything I can do . . .

Karim sat up suddenly. I don't need anything, he said, his voice hardening.

That's fine, just hello then, Badar said calmly, making as if to rise.

Karim held out his arm to detain him, a sharp peremptory movement. And by the way, I don't need any lectures from you, Karim said, his voice steadily rising. Do you understand? I don't care what you think about this. You know nothing about it. You can think what you like, just don't come here bothering me about it. I would've expected some gratitude from you, but no, you come here with your long face and your stupid what can I do to help you. You, help me! If it wasn't for me you would have been cast out by that horrible old man and would have become somebody's servant again. Or a criminal or a drug addict begging in the streets. I took you away from there, away from that. I let you live with me and fed you for months. I found you a job and looked after you. You are an ungrateful idiot.

Karim paused for a moment, looking away and breathing heavily. Badar was too surprised to speak, stunned by Karim's anger, his disdain.

That's right, an idiot, a weakling. It's in you, he said, glaring.

Badar made to rise and again Karim's arm shot out to detain him.

I haven't finished, he said, his rage now in full possession of him. There's something servile, something deferential in you, something groveling. You have become used to it. You have submitted yourself to it. You'll never amount to anything unless you change your attitude. You have no one in the world who cares for you but me. Look at you, skivvying in that derelict hotel for years, when you could've found something else, something more rewarding. I kept telling you to think for yourself, to have ambition, but you have no self-respect. There you are, living in that room on your own, masturbating your life away, and you think you can moralize on me.

Karim! Badar protested, surprise turning to shock at the cruelty of his words.

Karim made a chopping gesture with his hand to silence him. Shut up, I don't want to hear any of your whining, he said, spitting out the words and then looking away, his eyes molten and shimmering.

Thank you for what you did for me. I'll always be grateful, Badar said into the silence, speaking calmly despite the hurt he felt from Karim's scorn. He stood up to leave.

Sit down, Karim said angrily, and waited until Badar sat down. She wanted us to have a weekend away together, and so did I. That's all. What's wrong with that? It was great, to get away from all this moaning and grumbling. Night after night I could not sleep, did you know that? That baby crying all the time, and her sulking about who knows what. Did she have any time for what I was going through? That baby ruined our lives. I didn't even want her.

Badar remembered Karim's excitement when Fauzia was pregnant and when Nasra first arrived. He did not say anything but stood up again to leave.

Sit down, Karim yelled at him. I haven't finished yet. How dare you come here moralizing on me! I don't believe it, a little wretch like you. You have no idea! A little ignorant wretch like you coming to lecture me! What did you think, that you'd come here and find me remorseful or something like that? Do you know what I've learned from this? Not to be afraid. I have learned not to be afraid. I did not plan to cause anybody pain, but I have learned not to be afraid. I have learned to take my life in my own hands, to look to the future without fear.

Then after a lengthy, tense silence Karim said, What have you learned in your life, you useless wanker?

Badar stood up again and paused at the door of the flat for a moment as if he intended to speak but did not say anything. He left before Karim could rage at him again. Later he thought, I have learned to endure.

## 22.

It seemed a long time ago in some ways, only in other ways it didn't. It seemed just yesterday. Karim went to Dar es Salaam soon after all that misery and moved in with Haji and the Mistress during the period of training before going to Copenhagen. Badar knew that he had moved back to his old room in Dar for a while because Haji had rung the hotel in bewilderment soon after the breakup, asking him what had happened. Badar did not know what Karim would have told them and replied cautiously. Why don't you ask him?

He's here with us now, staying with us, Haji had said. He says it wasn't working. That's all he keeps saying. How is Fauzia? Does she need anything?

No, she's with her parents, Badar had said. She doesn't need anything. I'll tell her you called.

He probably did not stay with them for long, because he was due in Copenhagen in November. Afterward he would have been on an EU salary, inflated and probably in golden euros rather than their tin shillings, and he would have been wealthy enough to find a place of his own. He did not return to Zanzibar, except to visit his brother or on government business, or so Badar heard. Hawa had predicted that he would become a minister one day. Hawa herself had told Badar that, intending it as mockery of an ambitious upstart, and it seemed that she was going to be proved right. He was not a minister yet, but he was heading that way by all accounts. Yes, it did seem a long time ago.

It was four years since Karim left for Dar es Salaam, and now it was Nasra's fifth birthday and Badar had promised to collect the cake Fauzia had ordered from the bakery for her. He remembered that the weekend when Karim went with Jerry to Dar was a few days before the little one's first birthday. It was that memory that brought Karim to mind. It saddened him to think that Karim had left them so completely. He had often thought about that time when he went to see him and he had turned on him with such venom and contempt. He had felt his eyes smarting with hurt at his words, at the loss of his love, at the knowledge that he had found him pitiful from the start. Was that hatred in him all along? It did not seem like that most of the time. He must have just been a nearsighted idiot, as Karim called him, not to see that he despised him so. Or was it a new cruelty he had arrived at with the potency of a lover of a glowing beauty?

He had met him once since that time, at the funeral of Uncle Othman. Haji had rung him and told him that his father had passed away. Would Badar be able to come and pay his respects? It would be so generous of him, and it would erase any remaining bitterness in Badar's heart. Badar did not feel bitterness any longer but he did feel gratitude to Haji for his many kindnesses, and he went because

Haji had asked him to. He took the early-morning ferry and was there in time for the funeral service at ten, and was then home before nightfall. He saw Karim there at the funeral prayers at Msikiti Zambarau, in the front row beside Haji. It was a small congregation of mourners, mostly neighbors and some of Baba Othman's old café friends. Juma was there, looking frail now, but his eyes had still danced with laughter as he shook hands with Badar. Karim looked quite grand, in a kanzu and kofia and a silk jacket. Haji had wanted Badar to join him in the front row facing the bier but he had shaken his head and had held back. There were too few of them not to know who was present, and a moment arrived when Karim and Badar made eye contact. Badar raised his arm in greeting and Karim nodded, then he raised his arm in reply and touched his chest with his palm, a gracious greeting from a grandee. They did not speak.

After the funeral prayers Badar sought out Haji and excused himself from the cortege of cars that was heading for the cemetery. He could be away for only the day and the cemetery was a long drive, and he would most likely miss the ferry if he went to the burial. Yes of course, it was good you were able to come, Haji had said. You have done more than your duty. I'll speak to you later.

Before leaving, he called on the Mistress. Out of respect for the departed, her head was covered but he could see wisps of gray where her kanga had slipped. She was still beautiful, despite the wrinkles under her eyes when she smiled. Ah, Badar! she said in exaggerated surprise. It's been so long. He made the late-afternoon ferry and was home after nightfall.

He was still at the Tamarind, now the assistant manager, but not for very much longer. Issa was moving to the Crystal Bay where he would be required to wear a jacket and tie, and Badar was to move to the Masri Hotel, Bwana Sharif Makame moving his pieces on the board. The Tamarind was to be sold to another consortium that planned to turn it into a restaurant. On the afternoon of Nasra's fifth birthday, Badar was in the hotel office with little to do. It was the dead time of the day when all the staff had left and the guests were either out or in their rooms. It was too hot and too bright to read, so he thought he would browse the internet, and because he had been thinking about Karim and Jerry, he searched the map for Gemstone Street NW3.

There it was, her street. Four years after she left, there he was, at the junction of the street with the main road, gazing down at what looked only a little like what she had described that evening, although she had not described the street at length. She had not said that it was so long that he would not be able to see the end of it, or that his vision would be confused and obscured by the trees that lined the pavement and shrank the horizon. He did not remember her mentioning any trees. Perhaps the trees had grown since then. They looked young, maybe recently planted, so had not been there when she told him about the street. They had taken well, already bushy and plump. He did not know their names, but he was instructing himself to notice such things.

It was a long street, without doubt, even with the distraction of the trees, with houses that stood shoulder to shoulder in their self-assurance and determination, somehow. He did not know how else to describe their robust sturdiness. He had taught himself a great deal, he liked to think, but had not yet had the chance to educate himself on residential architecture in London streets, or to study anything at all about architecture really. He was just a dabbler in bits and pieces, that was how he would describe himself. But he did not think he needed to know what style or what architectural wisdom the houses in that street obeyed. To look at them was to know there was one. They looked the same, in some way, but also they did not. The front doors were different colors, for example. The one nearest to where he stood was varnished the color of milky cocoa, the kind that could not be bought anymore but that legend told of old Habib who used to sell it from his kiosk in Forodhani. There are certain tastes and colors that linger on the mind even when the tongue and palate can no longer recover them.

The door to the house next to the milky cocoa was painted white. Farther down he saw a green door, then some more lightly varnished doors, one gray, and in the distance a gold-painted one, which he guessed was the home of an extrovert, perhaps an artist. The windows were all in an identical style, maybe that was a regulation.

She had told him about her street, she had described it. This is where I live, and one day maybe you'll come and visit, that was what she had said. People say that but do not mean it. She had said Gemstone Street NW3, and then laughed. She was on holiday, or a kind of holiday, a volunteer for the good of humanity, and he knew that people said things at those moments that were a result of the mellow companionship they had found in unexpected encounters, and had no expectation that their generosity or invitations, a spur-of-the-moment gesture, would require fulfillment. She had not told him the number of the house she lived in. It was not that kind of conversation.

He noticed that on the left side of the screen was a man with a long stride. He could see that the man was one of his people, perhaps a native of that street or perhaps a stranger.

Badar saw that a door was ajar further down and a man was about to step out. It was too far for him to have a clear look at the man's face but he saw a tall dark-haired man in a white shirt and blue jeans with a clean-shaven face. Did he know Jerry? Was he Jerry's brother, perhaps, or even her husband or boyfriend? Was he the one she came back for? If this was the man Jerry came home to, you could only see the rightness of it. Yes, even in a brief blurred glance, you could imagine he was a man worth coming home to. But perhaps it was not him, and he was nothing to do with Jerry.

He wondered if she was looking out of one of the windows and noticing that man striding on the pavement, and considering if he was a menace or if he was lost. He wondered if she might look care-worn, humbled by life, or if she was still that woman who could do as she pleased. He wondered how she would look back at that chaos she caused. Perhaps in her eyes she had just had a fling with an attractive man while she was away from home, a brief and joyful adventure. There had been no need for her to consider repercussions. When her time was up, she had returned home and continued her life. That was probably how it turned out for her. He wondered how Karim looked back on that time. Badar remembered that last conversation with him. I have learned not to be afraid, he had said. So perhaps his reflections would not be remorseful but grateful for a kind of release from something he no longer wanted.

He switched the map off and checked emails. There was one

from Fauzia: *Don't worry about the cake. Hawa will collect me from school and we'll pick it up on the way home. Love F xx.*

He had known for a long time how much he wanted Fauzia, how beautiful she was, how much he loved her serenity, but it felt disrespectful while she was married to Karim, disrespectful to both of them. Then after Karim's betrayal and departure, that feeling developed and matured, and he was resolved to be patient and wait to see if she could feel something like that for him. He had hesitated for a long time and could not make himself believe that it was possible that she would love him. Yes, he had said that word, *love*, when for so long he had been too fearful to use it to describe how she might feel about him. He had not wanted to lose her regard by being importunate. He had known she relied on him in those early days after Karim left. Not for emotional support—she had her parents for that—but they had enough on their hands and he could help with practical, sweaty matters. He had been happy to be relied on.

As the months passed and she regained her composure, he began to feel that she treated him with greater affection, in her tone of voice, in her smiles and in the way she expected him to be attentive to her and her needs. He always felt welcome in their house, and did not mind running errands for them. To himself he said ruefully, Once a servant always a servant, but it did not feel like that. He began to feel that in some small way he belonged with them. It began to seem clear to him that the way they were together had changed. It seemed to him that she called his name unnecessarily, as if she liked saying it, and sometimes when they made eye contact, they smiled to each other without speaking. He was not in a hurry, he told himself, but really he was just not sure what to do.

Then in the end it was quite easy. Hawa had borrowed the travel agency car, which she did regularly, and had taken them for a drive to Mangapwani Beach. She was playing with Nasra on the water's edge while Fauzia and Badar strolled along the beach. Then without saying a word, she took his hand, and they walked like that all the way to the copse of tidal palms that fringed the sea. They stopped there and embraced and then walked back toward Hawa and Nasra.

When Hawa saw how things were, she lifted her eyebrows to heaven and smiled. I thought you would never get round to it.